WHEN I HAD YOU

New York Times Bestselling Author

S.L. SCOTT

ISBN: 978-1-962626-17-0

*Visit my website for warnings. Please note this page contains spoilers.

FOLLOW ME

To keep up to date with her writing and more, visit S.L. Scott's website: **www.slscottauthor.com**

To receive the newsletter about all of her publishing adventures, free books, giveaways, steals and more:

https://geni.us/intheknow

Follow me on TikTok: https://geni.us/SLTikTok
Follow on IG: https://geni.us/IGSLS
Follow on Bookbub: https://geni.us/SLScottBB

ALSO BY S.L. SCOTT

To keep up to date with her writing and more, visit her website: www.slscottauthor.com

To receive the scoop about all of her publishing adventures, free books, giveaways, steals and more:

Visit www.slscottauthor.com

Join S.L.'s Facebook group here: S.L. Scott Books

Read the Bestselling Book that's been called **"The Most Romantic Book Ever"** by readers and have them raving. We Were Once is now available and FREE in Kindle Unlimited.

We Were Once

You do not want to miss the international sensation, **Best I Ever Had**. This book has won readers over with its emotion and soul deep love. **Best I Ever Had** is now available in ebook, audio, and paperback, and is Free in Kindle Unlimited.

Best I Ever Had

Audiobooks on Audible - CLICK HERE

The Westcott Series (Stand-alones)

Swear on My Life

Never Saw You Coming

Forgot to Say Goodbye

When I Had You

Poppy Stanfield's Book

The Everest Brothers (Stand-Alones)

Everest - Ethan Everest

Bad Reputation - Hutton Everest

Force of Nature - Bennett Everest

The Everest Brothers Box Set

Hard to Resist Series (Stand-Alones)

The Resistance

The Reckoning

The Redemption

The Revolution

The Rebellion

The Crow Brothers (Stand-Alones)

Spark

Tulsa

Rivers

Ridge

The Crow Brothers Box Set

DARE - A Rock Star Hero (Stand-Alone)

New York Love Stories (Stand-Alones)

Never Got Over You

The One I Want

Crazy in Love

Head Over Feels

It Started with a Kiss

The Kingwood Series

SAVAGE

SAVIOR

SACRED

FINDING SOLACE

The Kingwood Series Box Set

Playboy in Paradise Series

Falling for the Playboy

Redeeming the Playboy

Loving the Playboy

Playboy in Paradise Box Set

Stand-Alone Books

Best I Ever Had

We Were Once

Along Came Charlie

Missing Grace

Finding Solace

Until I Met You

Drunk on Love

Lost in Translation

Sleeping with Mr. Sexy

Morning Glory

WHEN I HAD YOU

SPECIAL EDITION

S.L. SCOTT

S.L. SCOTT

1

Cash Ryatt

I'M great at two things—*winning and fucking.*

Depends on the day, but I always take my skill set seriously when it comes to women and my career. I go big, especially when screwing up my life.

"Good job, Cash." Hansen's voice breaks through my thoughts. Good is relative, I suppose, but Westcott Racing's race engineer isn't bad for my ego.

To be the best again, I need to get my head off how I just fucked up. And per the last team meeting, I need to sport a "sunny disposition" when I come off the track for the owners' benefit. Apparently, my bad moods aren't good for business.

Sunny and losing aren't synonymous, and getting overtaken on the last corner pushed me into seventh position on the grid tomorrow. "Fucking hell."

"Bring her around, Cash," Hansen instructs over the radio. As my race engineer with Westcott Racing, I give him the respect he deserves. "You did well today."

I flex my fingers around the steering wheel as anger surges through my veins. How can he say that when I've made it twice as hard to top the podium tomorrow? "Good job, my ass," I snap back over the radio. I don't have a cool enough head to go into the issues of the tires spinning out instead of sticking. I take a deep breath and slowly release it, easing my anger the best I can. *For now.*

Hansen doesn't say anything else. He's smart enough to let me get my frustration out of my system on the cooldown lap.

As soon as I pull into the pit, the crew surrounds me, and I release myself from the confines of the cockpit. "Sunny disposition" slips through my thoughts, and I try for a smile behind my helmet. Yeah, not happening. I leave my helmet on, saving my harsher reaction for the privacy of the dressing room, out of sight of the press, team, owners, and spectators.

Why does everything in this sport have to be so goddamn public all the time anyway?

Money.

I'm not naive enough to be deluded by what makes the world and this sport go round. Not anymore anyway. Principle One racing is a rich man's sport. There aren't just millions on the line. There are billions to be made. Despite the warnings I've been given, With my visor down, protecting my face and hiding my mood, I head toward the paddock to get weighed so I can bolt to my driver's room right after.

I don't get five feet before the team's manager glues himself to my side and matches my pace. Not everyone is as good as Hansen when it comes to timing . . . "We're happy with seventh, Cash." My back is patted, causing me to look left. My helmet may be limiting my field of vision, but I already know who it is from the gruff voice. Three years tobacco-free can't fight against the forty he had a cigarette hanging from the corner of his mouth. Darren Ellis has been in the racing game almost as long as I've been alive, so I trust his wisdom. He adds, "If this were the race, we'd have points on the board. I'm not upset by this result, and neither are the sponsors."

More importantly, his opinion matters and carries weight. That he sounds happy is the calm I need in the middle of this turmoil. We keep walking, and he says, "I get it, Ryatt. You want pole position, but we're a new team. That we're in the top ten in our first year of racing means we're doing everything right."

"The crossover on—"

"The last turn. Yes, we're looking at the footage. The wheels spun twice, which gave Leandro time to pass."

"The spin makes me think it's the track, not the tires," I grumble, knowing damn well we have no control over the track. "There's no rubber left at this—"

"Don't worry." He stops walking. When I turn back, he says, "We'll have it figured out before the race tomorrow."

"It's *my* job to worry about it."

"No, it's your job to drive that car as fast as you can tomorrow. It's our job to fix the issues." His gaze travels over my shoulder. "Anyway, you have other things to worry about."

"Like?"

When I glance over my shoulder, he replies, "Play nice. The owners brought their family."

"Oh yay," I mutter, remembering the memo I got yesterday, and start walking. The faster I go, the quicker I'll be done.

The crowd of Westcott purple parts for me as I head for

the paddock. I touch a few hands as I pass, my gloves blocking any real connection, which is how I prefer to keep my life these days. It's a lot easier this way. Looking ahead, I have maybe thirty feet to cover until I'm away from the onlookers and can leave this unofficial meet and greet in my rearview mirror.

Announcements blare overhead, but I'm focused ahead and specifically on the left.

White shirt against tanned skin.

Brown hair mixed with some blond, which reflects in the sun.

My attention is set on the woman ahead . . . the woman who is too busy to look up from her phone to notice me. I pause, waiting for her to see me. This is a meet and greet, after all. Everyone is only here to greet *or* to meet me. *Except her.*

Her eyes stay trained on the phone in her hand. As if I didn't just prove that this team is a real contender. As if I'm not the star of this show. As if I don't even exist.

What the fuck?

People pay thousands of dollars for this opportunity, to have this proximity to greatness, and she's going to stand there and look at her phone? *Fuck that.*

I swerve left, the device slipping from her hand just as I pass. *Oops.*

"What the hell?" Her voice is just a distant memory as I walk away, grinning like the bastard I am.

Wanting to relish the fact she's now paying attention like she should have been, I slow my pace and glance back. I'm met with blazing blues, lips pursed, hands fisted at the sides of her wound-up little body I wouldn't mind unraveling. The anger flushing her cheeks gives a hint of innocence that's tempting to destroy with a good fucking. Though when she cocks her eyebrow and narrows her eyes at me, I know the fire she exudes will burn.

Two layers of a racing kit won't hide my body's reaction that she pulls to the surface. The tinted visor doesn't protect my eyes from her piercing glare either. I keep walking, turning my back to her.

I have a bad habit of finding trouble when I should be steering clear, and that sexy vixen is not only a distraction but a problem I don't need.

Entering the shop, I pull off my helmet. I barely get it tucked under my arm when I'm shoved from behind. Although it's too weak to send me forward, it's the point that someone has the balls to push me at all. "What the—?"

Whipping around, I'm ready to lay into whoever has the nerve to touch me but am stopped when our eyes latch together. I should have known it would be the firecracker with the phone. One hand is clasped around the curve of her waist and the other holding that phone like it's a lifeline. I smirk. She's hot. I'll give her that. She's also amusing.

Images of sinking into her, feeling the tips of her nails digging into my shoulders, those pink lips begging me to let her take me deeper. Fuck, and I bet those tits would look great pressed against a bathroom mirror. "You want my attention, babe. I'm all yours."

Holding the phone up to my face, she says, "You owe me a phone."

I step back, my gaze darting to the shattered screen and then to her. She's prettier up close, even if the devil has taken over the details of her expression. "Accidents happen."

"It wasn't an accident."

I turn to leave. "Bill the team."

"The team didn't do it, asshole." Her voice stops me, and I shoot her a look over my shoulder. She adds, "You did. On purpose. I saw you." *Of course, she did.* She hasn't taken her eyes off me since. I grin. "So *you* owe me a new phone."

Taking my time, I take her in, my gaze hanging on her perky tits just long enough for it to be noted. *By her, of course.* I know how to push a button or two myself.

"Eyes up here." She crosses her arms over her chest with such authority as if the simple act has solved the world's problems.

Closing the gap again, I leave a small space between us, close enough to get a hint of her floral perfume but far enough just in case she comes out swinging physically like she has verbally. "I don't take orders from anyone except those who sign my paycheck. So run along and find another driver to harass. I have no patience for an intolerable fangirl."

I've never found fury as fascinating as when it consumes her, shifting her body into a tension that I'm fairly certain is not doctor-recommended. "Fangirl?" Her mouth falls open as her eyes widen farther. "Me harass you?" The fire returns, an inferno burning her up as a storm brews in her eyes, darkening her blue skies. "You have some nerve, ass—"

"Marina?" The voice is firm but calm, the exact opposite of this little spitfire in front of me.

Good. Noah Westcott enters the paddock, rushing toward us. As an owner and the marketing director, he'll be able to handle her better than I will. Then I see Loch and Harbor as well, flanking him. *Fuck, let's just make it an owner's party, shall we?*

They're all good guys. Noah is as close to a friend as I'll ever let anyone. But having all three of them at the track isn't typical operating procedure and puts me on edge.

I wait, giving a small nod to signal toward the woman who appears justified in her stance as she grins in their direction. Her confidence is impressive, considering she's about to be escorted off the property and probably banned for life from Principle One Racing as soon as security arrives.

"Marina," Noah starts again. "I see you've met one of our drivers."

Did they call her Marina? *As in the youngest of the West-cott siblings, Marina?*

As in, the little sister gifted a share of the team last year for her birthday? The same sister who's an actress?

Shit . . .

"Cash," Noah says, "I see you've met my sister Marina."

"I sure did." I glare ahead, refusing to give her the pleasure of my eyes on her again. One fucking shot and I'm about to blow it because the owners' little sister decided to go on a rampage. "Fuck me," I mutter under my breath.

Curiosity killed the cat, so like a fool, I glance over to see her struggling to restrain the left side of her mouth from pulling into a full smile. I say, "But we hadn't quite gotten around to the introductions."

Holding out her hand, she says, "I'm Marina Westcott." I barely recognize the woman before me now. From the brightness of her eyes to the soft smile, even her tone is coated in pure sugary sweetness. "It's nice to meet you, *Misterrr . . .?*"

She's quite the actress. *Uh-huh.* Like she didn't just see me climb out of a fifteen-million-dollar Team Westcott race car. Rolling my eyes, I scoff. *She's got to be kidding, right?*

Oh, that's right. She was too busy staring at her phone to notice. "I'm the fucking driver—" I bite my tongue before I get fired for what I really want to say. *Play nice . . .* "Cash Ryatt." Sunny disposition.

I smirk.

She says, "Oh, you're one of the drivers? Cash Ryan, you say?"

"Ryatt. Cash. *Ryatt*."

"It must be so fun to drive around on the track, like go-karts at the Park 'n' Pizza place. Putt-putt was always my favorite. Ohh, the bumper boats. Loved those."

What the fuck is she going on about? Did she just compare— "No, it's nothing like go-karts at the fucking Park 'n' Pizza place."

"I had my tenth birthday party there."

Snickering draws my gaze to Noah. He shakes his head. "Here we go . . ." As the marketing director, he could handle this better by having her removed or doing the job himself. As her older brother . . . he could do the same. *Some friend and teammate he is.*

My gaze pivots away from him—since he clearly has no intention of showing his sister the door—to her again as she bats her eyelashes. Her feigned innocence is lost on me.

"I had my tenth birthday on a track, winning regionals instead of spending it at the local go-kart place."

"But did you have fun?"

The question hits left, making me ready to take off my suit to relieve some of the body heat it's trapping. "I always have fun winning." If I didn't want to get on with my day and have a good sulk in solitude over my performance today, maybe I could appreciate her smug smile and force myself to lighten up. Through gritted teeth, I add, "I'm sure we all have things we need to do. I know I—"

The crew's celebration fills the paddock as they file in ahead of the other driver. A member takes my helmet, and I'm handed a bottle of water with the signature safety straw standing tall beyond the lid. I don't get a sip down before she says, "Nice sippy cup."

Her brothers are distracted, leaving her to fuck with me again. "It has a purpose."

"It's cute how you—"

"Report to the office." I'm not upset the announcements cut her off. But I don't appreciate the brothers bailing on me either.

At least Noah has the decency to wish me luck before he walks out.

"What the hell do I need luck for?"

Looking back, he laughs and nods toward the viper he's left behind to attack me.

Luck is the last thing I need when it comes to her. It's not like I'm afraid of her.

"Guess it's just you and me," she says when they're out of earshot.

"There's no you and me, babe."

She passes, landing a condescending pat on my chest. "Yet you remain here like you have nothing better to do. And don't call me babe again."

"I have plenty to do."

"Oh really?" A weaker man couldn't handle the striking blue of her eyes, and most would miss the glint of pure sin hiding inside them.

She may act innocent in front of her brothers, but she holds her own just fine behind their backs. *So why am I letting her get to me?*

"Get to the scale, Cash," Hansen commands from behind me, snapping me back to reality.

Running my fingers through my sweat-soaked hair, I don't know why I haven't already walked away. "It's been . . . interesting, but I, yeah . . ." I thumb over my shoulder.

"Yes, you should run along." With her eyes set on mine,

a winning grin graces her face. Just as I turn, she adds, "It was good to finally meet the great Cash Ryan."

Is she for real?

"Fucking Ryan," I grumble, tired of this game, and walk away.

"Cash?"

I make the mistake of giving her my attention once more. She eats it up, serving me some of my own medicine in the form of a wink. "And you still owe me a phone. *Babe.*"

"Cute. Real cute." Can't say I didn't try to stay sunny, but when push comes to her literal shove . . . "Considering those red-soled shoes and the designer bag wrapped around your body, I'd be willing to wager that a phone is the last thing you're worried about when your last name is Westcott. So I'll take this interaction for what it really is—*foreplay.*"

She bursts out laughing. "You think highly of yourself, but foreplay, or anything else of that nature, is the *last* thing I'd ever want to do with you."

"All I can hope is that you're as good in bed as you are with banter."

"Better," she says, leveling me with a glare. "But you'll never know."

She walks away and I let her, but I swear to God those hips shimmy for me. Little Miss Westcott has Oscar-worthy acting skills where her brothers are concerned. But I see right through her.

"Ryatt. Scale. Now," Hansen shouts again.

"Yeah. Yeah. Coming." I head toward the other side of the paddock, where he and Darren wait for me to record my post-qualifying numbers but stop to glance back. Though I know she's already gone, I'm still left grinning in the aftermath of our collision.

2

Marina Westcott

WHAT AN ASSHOLE...

My hands are still fisted as I bump the door open with my hip and step outside into the sunshine. The burn of rubber still lingers in the air, and the sound of engines and announcements has followed me out back. Despite my efforts, it's race weekend, so there's no escaping the crowds at the track.

"Hey, Marina?"

Noah's voice reaches me before the exit door closes. I brace the door and wait for my brother to catch up. "What's up?"

Grabbing the door, he lets it fall closed while we walk out together. "Are you taking off?"

"To the hotel, but I don't leave Miami until early in the morning. I was told to be back tomorrow afternoon just in case we need rehearsals."

"You'll be at dinner, then? I'd like to hear about life in Vancouver and how you're doing."

Despite a reputation that he honed like a knife of being a player, Noah has always had a heart of solid gold. He never cared what others thought about him unless they mattered to him. Like his wife. Liv has never taken his love for granted. And he loves her to the end of the earth and back again.

A girl can only be that lucky to find the guy of her dreams willing to fight for her. They sure don't exist in Hollywood.

I didn't realize how tense I was, probably from the encounter I just had with that jerk of a driver, until my shoulders eased. "You don't need to worry about me. I'm fine."

He grins, looking up at the cloudless Miami sky. "*Okay.*" His tone tells me he's not falling for my cliché response. He always could see right through any act I tried to put on, whether it was for my parents, who always had too much faith in me to make wise decisions, or my oldest brothers, who tried their best to connect with me despite our age gap. Eight years between me, the youngest, and Loch, the oldest of the siblings.

Maybe it's because we're closest in age and spent the most time together, but Noah knows the real me. He was there for me through my teenage heartbreak and taught me not to take anyone's crap, especially from a guy. When my Broadway show closed just two weeks into its performance run, and I wanted to hide from the world, he helped me hold my head high. He's always been there for me . . . when I've let him.

I haven't let him for a few months because I don't want to discuss the turmoil of my life. And because if he finds out about Corbin cheating on me, he'll kill him, and if he doesn't do the job, Harbor will, and then Loch will make sure there's no evidence to convict. Maybe it's not such a bad idea after all.

I find myself grinning, not about murder, but is it so wrong to want to see Corbin scared out of his mind? Probably ... I still smile.

He looks at me out of the corner of his eye, studying me. "What's on your mind?"

Murder is probably not the appropriate answer here. "Nothing. Just enjoying the warm weather."

"If you don't want to discuss it, that's okay." Coming around, he hugs me to him. "I love you, little sis."

I rest my head against him and give in, wrapping my arms around his middle. I haven't noticed how closed off I'd become or how disconnected I am from everyone I care about until now. "I love you, too, big bro."

We step back from each other, and he smiles at me. "So I'll see you at dinner tonight?"

"Yep." I grin and start backward to where the car waits. "I'll be fashionably late, so start without me."

"We've learned our lesson."

I'm quick to add, "Congrats on the qualifying race."

"Thanks." He swings the door back open and chuckles. "Hey, and maybe don't give our drivers such a hard time when you see them. They're prickly at best."

"Assholes at worst." I laugh. "My mistake for thinking we were in the big leagues. If they can't handle little ole me—"

"Not many men can, Marina." His chuckle rocks his shoulders. I still don't think I'm fully accustomed to all of us being adults, but here Noah is looking the part with his lanyard and embroidered name on his shirt. Khakis. He's all in on the work these days, and into dad mode dressing. It suits him because happiness is the most obvious thing about him.

Teasing, I fluff my hair on one side. "You say that as if it's a bad thing."

"Never a bad thing when it comes to my sister." Nodding, he adds, "Stay away from race car drivers, though. They're nothing but bad news." The warning doesn't hit as hard when he says it so passively, but I get his drift. Harbor and Loch may not have picked up on anything more than a conversation I was having with that driver in the paddock, but Noah's tone echoed in caution when he walked in.

I took it as a pat on the back that he was worried more for the driver than me.

I duck into the back of the Town Car. Leaning against the vinyl, I release a deep breath as the car pulls away from the track.

"Traffic is bad," I say, peering up at the driver in the rearview mirror.

"It's always rush hour in Miami."

I check the time on my watch, realizing I should have left earlier. "How long do you think it will take?"

His eyes glance down and then into the mirror again. "Forty-five minutes to an hour."

"Really?" I tug on my lower lip and glance out the window. "I have a video call. Do you mind me taking it in the car?"

"I'll raise the privacy glass for you."

"Thank you."

I open the email my agent sent and read through the questions, trying to come up with answers that don't make me sound so pathetic. I'm struggling since I still can't wrap my head around what happened myself.

A text vibrates my phone, and I look down.

Lauren: *Can you talk?*

I take a breath before facing my fears—my agent—and replying.

Me: *Yes.*

She's a badass, and no one fucks with her in Hollywood. She does the fucking . . . *Ummm* . . . I giggle, which feels good after the heaviness of the past few days.

Lauren is fiercely protective of her clients. She's the perfect one to have my back in the middle of this mess.

I barely have time to send the text before the phone rings. The privacy glass slides up, and I answer. My agent is usually impeccably put together, but I can't help but notice the dark circles under her eyes and strands of hair that have fallen in front of her face. She swipes them back and then leans forward on her desk. "How are you, Marina?"

"That feels like a loaded question."

"You're looking good. I think Miami was the right decision. It's a quick trip but got you out of the fire of the situation." She taps the top of her glass desk. "It also gave me some time to get ahead of this before the press has a field day with it."

"It's not like we're A-list celebrities, Lauren. No one will care about me or Cor, Co . . ." My tongue stutters around his name, causing me to avoid saying it altogether. "Or him."

"You're in a movie, and your star *is* on the rise. That makes you newsworthy and gossip-column fodder." A heavy sigh fills the audio as it leaves her chest. "Listen, Marina, I'm sorry you're going through this. Men suck. Your boyfriend sucks."

"*Ex*-boyfriend."

"Indeed. Although he's the one who cheated, this is now a make-or-break moment for you. I was awake half the night trying to think of every possible angle to spin this. The reality is that men can cheat on their wives of fifty years with their son's twenty-year-old girlfriend. Everything bounces off them like Teflon, and they become the most in demand they've ever been. Ask me how I know."

Sitting back in her chair, she continues, "Women are the ones who fight the labels, and those labels will trail you like cans tied to the bumper of a wedding car as you maneuver through your career."

"That's quite the visual."

She nods. "I've seen it happen time and time again in Hollywood. It's utter bullshit, but you being the one cheated on can leave an unsavory taste in some studio execs' mouths, as if you're now undesirable. Careers are ruined before they've had a chance to bloom, so I'll be honest with you. We need to play this just right."

"I agree. What do you suggest?"

"We crush him. We take Corbin Darian down first."

As much as I love a great revenge plot, my heart aches at the sound of his name. "I don't know, La—"

"I spent the last two days on calls with his team. I've convinced them it's in his best interest to keep the new girl under wraps while you two finish the second movie and attend the premiere in a few weeks. That gets you out of all public engagements, through the press tour for the first movie, and moving on with your lives in separate directions."

"Nothing feels right. This doesn't feel natural."

"You're in disbelief and hurting." Her tone softens from the hard-ass who called me and has probably been up all night dealing with my mess. "Understandably, but this tale is as old as time. You were blindsided by someone you trusted." Clearing her throat, she adds, "By someone you loved." The word loved doesn't sit quite right with me. She continues, "I've been there. Things move fast in this town, so if we don't control the narrative first, we'll never get another chance. This is why I'm here, to contain the damage before it spreads."

I take a deep breath as tears begin to form in the corners of my eyes as shame seeps in. I refuse to let them fall. Not over him. I raise my chin. "Okay. What do we do?"

"You need to be seen in public like you were this weekend, but look . . . how do I say it? Happier than ever. Free from the burdens of that bastard. Look the best you ever have, but don't say one word to anyone about it, especially the paparazzi. Just show them he fucked up."

"By looking good?"

"By looking drop-dead gorgeous." She smiles. "You already do, but I'm having a killer wardrobe sent to you in Miami.

"You don't need to. I have the perfect dress in mind. It's going to make quite the impact."

"Don't hide when you get back to Vancouver either. Go out. Have fun. Live your best life. Be seen. Show off the hard work you do at the gym. Dress to kill Corbin with every photo that's posted."

"Won't that clue them in that I'm going out without him?"

"We want clues. We don't want a story to drop." She tells someone standing off camera that she'll take another call in five minutes.

Massaging my temple to tamp down the impending headache, I'm confused by the plan. Is it a plan or a revenge tactic? "Am I trying to make him jealous?"

"That wouldn't be so bad, would it?"

I stare at her for a moment, letting my head wrap around this idea. "What if he speaks to the press?"

"He won't. His team knows this looks bad for him. We're

not letting him off easily. It makes him look worse if he bad-mouths you. So he'll be trying to sell his side of the story the best he can, and we'll let him as long as we get through our agreed-upon events first. When we're ready, you will sit down with the right person, an interviewer, a woman who knows how it feels to be cheated on, and tell your side for a large fee."

"I never wanted to become famous, especially not for a scandal."

"This is the hand you've been dealt, Marina." She picks up her phone and brings it closer, lowering her voice. "I'm not asking you to do anything except exist and look great in public. When the time is right—"

"What if I never want to talk about the breakup? I have money. I don't need to sell my personal life for a paycheck."

"Then you never talk about your personal life, and hopefully, you're already onto your next projects."

I breathe a sigh of relief. "I like that."

"I need to go, but let me know if you need anything, okay?"

"Thank you, Lauren."

"Bye." She hangs up, leaving me staring at my cracked screen. At least it still works. *For now.*

I look out the window at crowded beaches, shops, and blue skies. Everything is sunshine down here, which lies in stark comparison to the cloudy days of my life up north right now.

The destruction of my life isn't out for public consumption yet, but there are plenty of people behind the scenes who are already well aware of what's going on with me, *him*, and the wardrobe girl he had sex with. This story is a ticking time bomb waiting to explode, my life and career being hit the hardest. *It's not fair.*

It's not fair to be the one left to pick up the pieces after the mess he created because he couldn't keep his dick in his pants. Instead of admitting that we're not a match made in heaven, which I would have agreed, he had sex with someone located only two trailers down from me.

I didn't know someone could be so cruel. *Now I do.*

And Lauren is right. Happiness is the best way to retaliate, even if I need to force myself to fake it. I can do what I need to. I'm a professional. I just hope I packed a revenge dress in my suitcase.

I'll make him swallow his pride, and he'll beg to take me back when he sees me. It will be too late, but fun like that tenth birthday party and the go-karts.

Cash comes to mind. *The grump.*

I have no idea why it was so fun annoying him, but I enjoyed it more than I probably should have.

As soon as the car pulls up to the hotel, I head to my room on a mission.

Before talking to Lauren, I planned to attend the family dinner and then have a quiet night in, bingeing movies where the hero dies. But maybe, just in case I'm in the mood, I'll go out instead.

A night out is beginning to sound a lot more appealing. Might as well have a little fun like Corbin did. I text a few friends to see who's in town for a good time since I can't think of a better place to let loose than in Miami.

3

Marina

THIS DRESS WILL KNOCK men dead. *I just wish one of them was my ex...*

Running my hand over the bare skin of my sides and lower over my hips covered in beads of the short dress, I take one last look in the mirror before sucking in a breath and grabbing my purse on my way out.

My dad and brothers won't be as impressed, but hopefully, I'll garner support from my mom and sisters-in-law. They usually have my back when it comes to how I dress or at least soften the blow for those who tend to still see me as the baby in the family.

Which I suppose I am, although I'm twenty-six and fully grown.

Cheated on, my dream job pulled out from under me, pivoted in my career, and I remain the only Westcott still flying solo. It seems I've earned almost all the stripes of adulthood in the past two years alone.

I don't know why I'm nervous. Dressing for dinner with

my family like I'm going dancing might be causing me to feel anxious, though I know the thought of the breakup being splashed across the web at any time is most likely the culprit.

The paparazzi could be hanging around South Beach as we speak. It's PI race weekend. The place is crawling with internationally known celebrities, and I could end up being caught in the crossfire of photos.

I love the dress and feel sexy in it. And since I saw the text from Lauren that Corbin is partying with buddies in Vancouver looking a lot like he doesn't have a care in the world, I can do the same. It's all going to work out how it's meant to. I take a breath and punch the elevator button.

Her text might have been why I changed from a black dress with ruffle sleeves to this pale blue little number with the ice beads that catch the light and every flash within twenty feet of me. That it only reaches the middle of my thighs is what has me wondering if I should have waited until after dinner to change into it.

I'm admiring my sexy silver shoes in the reflection of the elevator when the doors open. I feel lighter for the first time in days, maybe even months, empowered by my newfound freedom.

Until I'm met with green eyes locked on mine and a rogue smile that would make me weak in the knees if the man sporting it didn't grate on my nerves. I restrain an eye roll as I step inside the elevator with him. I'm quick to turn my back and rapid-fire punch the lobby button several times as if that will get us to the lobby any faster.

"*Ms.* Westcott." He says my name like a dirty word . . . one he'd say in bed if he were trying to seduce me. He's not, and that deep voice that probably drives the girls wild won't work on me.

"Mr. Ryan," I grit through my teeth. The little teasing is just enough to make me peek up to see if that smirk remains settled on his face.

It's gone, but unfortunately, he looks better with a little anger fired in his eyes. I tear my gaze away, refusing to give him the satisfaction of my attention. But I steal one last glimpse at him before returning to stare at my feet because I failed to notice just how attractive this man is despite the time we spent together earlier.

When he took his helmet off the first time I saw him, my breath choked in my throat. His hair was not as dark as I expected. His features were stronger. His eyes are lighter but not so pale that it's creepy when held in his arms under the moonlight. A shiver runs up my spine thinking about that scene I filmed with Corbin by the lake. I couldn't see his pupils, and it freaked me out. Maybe that was the turning point.

As for *this* jerk, why does he have to be so attractive? Ugh. Jerks usually are. *Remember that, Marina.*

At least I know how to handle him. I look at him again, really look, noticing the slight lines that make him seem more rugged, a little wilder, as if age has anything to do with it.

"Do you always blush around men you detest?"

His cadence isn't clipped like this afternoon, but I'm not interested in making nice, much less sharing small talk with him. My hand still flies to my cheek as if to check for the lie he's telling.

My heated skin defends him like the traitor it is. And then my manners get the best of me. Clutching my small bag in front of me, I keep my eyes trained on my shoes, careful not to meet his eyes again, or I will be more flushed than I am already. "I'm not blushing."

My gaze darts to the reflection in front of me only to have any semblance of a clever comeback denied. *Dammit.* There is absolutely no reason to blush around this man when he does nothing but irritate me. "It's just hot in here," I add, though who doth protest is so guilty of blushing.

"Is it?" he muses. "I'm quite comfortable."

"I bet you are." *What am I doing?* I clamp down on my tongue to keep from continuing this ridiculous conversation.

"I'm not sure what I did—"

"You broke my phone." I turn around, looking him dead in the eyes. "Are you buying me a new one?"

A half-hearted laugh escapes before his wry grin stretches across his face. "No. I was going to say I'm not sure what I did to make you hate me. Accidents happen, so I'm confused by the dramatics."

My jaw slacks open. "You have got to be kidding me. Dramatics?" Whipping a finger in the air in front of his smug face, I say, "First of all—"

Ding.

The elevator doors slide open. Naturally, the universe rescues him. "Saved by the bell."

"I don't need saving." He walks past me without so much as a courtesy glance. "I can handle anything you dish out, sweetheart."

I'm stuck trailing him, so I quick step to catch up. "That's funny. You couldn't handle sharing the limelight with a cell phone. Is that why you knocked it out of my hand? We all suffer from insecurity, but you can only tackle it when you admit the problem."

He stops, but my heels are so high that I stumble forward and slam into a hard wall of muscle, a.k.a. his back. With my cheek pressed to his suit like I'm now a part of the design, I run my hand over the fabric because I can appreciate a well-made suit on a man. It's one of my weaknesses, that and the opposite, a man in a great pair of casual jeans and a T-shirt. I can be complicated at times and a bit indecisive.

I push off in horror because it's still Cash Ryatt, jerk extraordinaire, wearing said fine suit. The safety of an arm wraps around me, a large hand covering the bare skin of my lower back. "Steady there, princess."

He turns around too fast for me to escape, holding me close as if we're on a date. I know better than to fall for a bad boy, but I don't take his warmth for granted. Instead, I savor it and dive deep into the Mediterranean waters of his green eyes, my body easing under the deliriously enchanting scent of trees after a heavy rain, the ocean under the cover of a dense fog, and something musky that makes me weak in the knees.

I hate myself just a little for being so easy to please. A tailored suit, great cologne, and strong hands are all it takes for me to destroy my stance against him.

I look up again, only to be met by the intensity of his gaze and a heavy breath releasing from his chest. My own breath is caught in my throat as I find myself still in his arms, savoring the feeling of being engulfed by him and his enrapturing scent.

But it doesn't matter how good he smells. He's not someone I need to be entangled with. It doesn't matter how gorgeous he is, how broad his shoulders are, or how good it feels to have someone hold me like I'm precious to their survival. Or it shouldn't. *What the hell am I doing?*

I remove myself from his hold that frees me too easily, if I'm being honest, and take several steps away from him. I need to clear my mind from the clouds my head is stuck in when I'm too close to him. Dusting my hands over the front of my dress, I raise my chin. "I'm," I start, my head still spinning a bit from the Cash-induced euphoria. "I'm fine." I clear my throat, worried that my tone will give away a weakness of mine. "Perfectly fine."

He pauses in front of me, his gaze dipping down and soaking me in from head to toe. "We could share a car."

Snapped back to reality, I should be surprised that he's so forward, yet I'm not somehow. "I have plans that don't involve you."

He narrows his eyes, his brows pushing together. "Figured since we're both going—" He grins with a chuckle, scraping his fingers over a freshly shaven jawline. "Never mind."

"Never mind?" I hate that I feed my curiosity. *Why do I indulge his whims?* "You know what? I don't want to know." I wave him off and am already on my way through the hotel. "Have a good night," I call over my shoulder without so much as looking back. I won't tell him that I'm hightailing it away because he's so freaking attractive or that I can still smell his cologne lingering on my nostrils from face-planting into him. I definitely won't mention not looking back because my body still buzzes from my contact with him. I'm not mad about any of that—the trip I took into his back or his scent making me weak all over for him— because it feels good to feel this alive again, even with the sensory overload of that man.

If only available and less insufferable men could make me feel like this . . .

"Allow me."

I'm too familiar with the voice not to automatically tense. I look at Cash standing behind me in full bravado. The door of the Town Car is wide open, waiting for me. "I can get in a car by myself." I climb in the back and reach for the handle. Tugging it, I add, "Thanks."

But the door doesn't shut.

Especially since his hand and body are now blocking it. "What are you doing?" I ask. "Move it. I don't like to be late."

"You're already late, babe. Scoot."

"Nope. Not scooting for you. Find your own ride, hotshot." I tug on the door again, but he still stands in the way like a mountain blocking my view. "Do you mind?"

He holds the door firmly in his hand and grins while looking down. Glancing left and then right before his eyes return to mine, he kneels in front of me. "It's my car, Marina. I called it, but I'm happy to give you a ride wherever you'd like to go."

I look at the driver, who has climbed into the driver's seat. He nods, and a wave of embarrassment washes through me. I throw a foot out, but Cash stands, effectively blocking me from exiting the vehicle. "Please," he says, lowering his voice. "We can ride together."

"There is no *we* in this scenario. There's me going to dinner with my family and you going wherever someone like you goes at night."

"Someone like me?" He chuckles. "Why do you make me sound so seedy? I'm simply going to dinner. Just like you."

"Except somewhere else." I push against his bicep, which is unwavering against my best efforts. "Are you kidnapping me, or are you going to let me out?"

A grin splits his cheeks, and then he says, "Sorry to be the bearer of bad news—"

"Why do I get the distinct impression that you're not sorry to bear any bad news to me?"

"I'm not as horrible as you seem to think I am."

"I'm going to need references for that before I change my mind when it comes to you."

He's still smirking, basically looking devilishly hot, and I'm not referring to the Miami heat, though that's a thing that's making me sweat. Or him. My body is in a state of confusion around this man. Super frustrating. He says, "I'll let you talk to your brothers regarding my nature."

"The press sure does love you."

"By love, you mean hate, and that's fair to throw in my face. I've made mistakes, but I own them."

"As much fun as this is," I deadpan, although I'm snacking on every interesting tidbit he feeds me. I check the time on my phone. "I'm now late for dinner."

"We should go, then." He maneuvers down and starts sliding in.

I move or get sat on, so I slip across the seat to the other side. "Fine." I cross my arms over my chest in protest. "But you're dropping me off first."

As soon as he shuts the door, the car pulls away from the hotel. "You got it, babe."

I glance back through the back window, realizing the last of my sanity was left under the hotel carport. Turning my eyes to the cracked screen of my phone, I tap lightly, hoping it works until I can get back to Canada to buy a new one.

I sit back, watching the world pass by outside, and release a breath that had been weighing on my chest.

"Is it that bad?"

Angling my head to face him, I ask, "Is what that bad?"

"Sharing a car with me?"

I could stick it to him by saying something snarky, but I ease up, already tiring of the fight. "I have a lot going on."

"We all do."

Annoyance wrecks my composure, and I roll my eyes. "I get that, but you asked me specifically if sharing a car with you was bad." Waving my hand between us, I add, "I was simply saying it's not only about you. I have other stuff going on in my life, and you just are the cherry on top."

"Normally, I'd take it as a compliment." Leveling my gaze on him, I stare while he continues, "Since you don't seem to be having a good night, or day, week, maybe month, I'll let it slide."

"You're too kind."

"Do you want to talk about it?"

I balk. "To you?" Shaking my head before the words have time to escape, I reply, "Thanks, but I'd rather let it fester inside and eat me alive."

I'm left sitting here expecting a great comeback when he just turns away from me and directs his attention out the window. Slow blinking several times, I finally turn to look out my window as well.

When the car pulls up to the restaurant, Cash gets out and holds the door for me. He even offers a hand when I step onto the curb, which I don't take. "Well, thanks for the ride."

He shuts the door, but he's not inside the car. "You're welcome."

Crinkling my forehead, I say, "You can go now."

"Thanks for the permission." He walks past me and opens the door to the restaurant.

"You're eating here?"

"Guess you didn't get the memo or, more specifically, the text." He flashes a text thread in my direction. I barely catch Harbor's name at the top before the screen darkens, though.

"Wait, what memo was that?"

"The one that invited me to dinner with the owners *and family* tonight."

"Are you freaking kidding me right now?"

"No." Nodding toward the inside, he asks, "You coming?"

Begrudgingly, I walk toward him and hold my phone up as I go inside. "My phone is broken, remember."

"The screen is cracked, but I still saw you playing on it."

"I wasn't playing on my phone." Waving my hand around on my wrist, I reply, "Anyway, potato. *Potahto.*"

It's the first time I see somewhat of a genuine smile. Naturally, I find it maddening how flattering it is across his face. I'll give credit where it's due, though. God gifted this man with more than talent on the racetrack. He can be as attractive as he wants and ridiculously appealing, but he's still . . . *him*.

He chuckles, finding me so amusing. I don't feel the same about him. Cash Ryatt is a thorn in my side, and now I have the great misfortune of dining with the jerk himself. *Oh yay . . .*

"I'll go if you want me to," he says. "I don't want you to feel uncomfortable."

"Really?" Maybe a tiger can change its stripes.

"No, I was invited, and I can't wait to watch you squirm all night." He walks to the host stand, leaving me to my own devices, which are currently shooting imaginary daggers into his back.

He checks us in, and we're led through the restaurant toward an arched doorway at the back. The lights are dimmer in the room ahead, but candles light the way when we get closer. My mom's laughter reaches my ears before my eyes have adjusted to the low lighting. He stops, and as soon as I make eye contact, he whispers, "Isn't this romantic for our first date?"

I harden my gaze on my target. "Let me be very clear. This is not a date."

"If you say so."

"I most definitely say so."

He shrugs like he's not on board with my threat.

"Marina. Cash?" Harbor stands to greet us while his gaze darts between us. "You made it."

"We made it," I reply humorlessly, though I'd love to share how I really feel about this situation. I sit between my mom and Noah, and Cash settles between Loch and my dad. "Isn't this just so cozy?"

Cash winks at me . . . friggin' winks at me in front of my family like he's the guest of honor who does as he pleases. Adding salt to my already salty attitude, he sits across from me. Of all the places . . . That makes it a lot harder to block him out, and I foolishly make the first mistake of looking up.

"Hungry?" he asks with a smug-ass grin settled on his face. "Because I'm starved." Nothing about his tone sounds like he's referring to food. Oh, so now we're supposed to be flirting?

I don't think so, mister!

Although the innuendo is wholly inappropriate—considering we're surrounded by not only my family but also his bosses—Cash Ryatt's dulcet tones speak straight to my core. I take the wineglass as soon as it's filled, though, and gulp a solid fourth of it in response. Keeping the glass in hand, I look right at him this time and grin because two can play this game. "Let's eat."

4

Cash

FIRE AND ICE.

She's mouthy.

Her temper is easy to trigger.

And she's demanding like a spoiled princess as the baby of one of the wealthiest families on the East Coast.

And so fucking sexy because of that pouty pink mouth of hers, her fiery disposition, and confidence that boosts with every bat of her long lashes. It's a shame she's part of the family, thus making her off-limits, or I would have fucked her already to help her get me off her mind.

The woman is clearly obsessed with me. *I get it.* Most are.

I've met women like her before, though. Fury is foreplay. I'm the bad boy every good girl wants to take for a spin. I have money, looks, and don't have their parents' approval. I'm a wet dream for every Goody Two-shoes.

Yet it's my ears that perk up when I overhear Marina say, "Corbin and I are—"

"Would anyone like to order dessert? The crème brûlée comes with my highest approval," the server says, stopping behind her.

She replies, "Nothing for me. Thank you."

He continues distracting the others from what she was saying, except for me, as he rounds the table. I'm still hanging on to one specific part of that earlier phrase. "Who's Corbin?"

Her blue eyes leave the plate in front of her and shift to mine. I've caught her looking at me several times over dinner, but she looks away even quicker. This time, spinning the stem of the glass between her fingers, she replies, "My costar."

Costar is an interesting way to put what seems to be more if I'm reading the situation clearly. "And?"

"Boyfriend." She doesn't smile or put much of herself into the response. It's also fascinating she relegated him to nothing more than a coworker. That speaks volumes about their relationship.

I watch her from across the table, and the light and laughter from earlier conversations have faded from her eyes. Even the fire has disappeared into an expression of neutrality.

"How long have you been dating?"

Taking a sip of wine, she maintains her gaze on mine. When she sets the glass down, she leans in and whispers, "Is there nothing else more interesting to discuss?"

"This is pretty interesting."

Her lips twist to the side before the slightest of smiles shapes her mouth again. Maybe it's the wine or the intimacy of the conversation when surrounded by so much other chatter, but we exchange a silent understanding, laying our verbal weapons down. "It's not something I really want to talk about right now."

Dessert is served to those who ordered, and our connection is mired in the surrounding conversations.

The qualifier today and the race tomorrow.

Kids.

Travel.

And the usual chitchat among friends. Though I'm careful not to say too much or get too involved. I've learned from the past that it doesn't matter how close you are to your team. If they want to fire you, they will, and then eat next to you at a steak dinner like they did you a favor.

So I keep my personal life as private as I can. The usual judgments I hear don't do me any favors and stresses the peace I'm trying to maintain with my ex-girlfriend. And since Terpidy controls my access to Cullen when I'm traveling, I play nice and keep things light, so nothing posted online upsets her.

Even though it's only to satiate a curiosity I have about Marina, it's not my business, so I offer her the same option I've given myself.

Noah asks, "What's your routine the night before a race?"

He's been great to have my back in the justification tour he had to do when Westcott Racing hired me. He's also a good guy and easy to get along with. We've had an occasional beer together before the season and started to hang out a bit.

Looking down at my plate, where plain chicken and vegetables weren't nearly enough for my appetite tonight, I grab my glass of water to finish for the third time since sitting down. "No alcohol, though, until after the final race. Lean meats and vegetables. Nothing exciting, but I don't want anything heavy weighing me down. Sleep. I'll work out in the morning, probably run. You work out, right? Want to join me?"

"Yeah, text me the time, and I'll be there. I'm going to need it after that pasta."

I catch Marina hiding a small yawn behind her hand and turn to her. "I'm not the most exciting guy."

"Exciting means different things to different people. I love to binge a show or take a long bath. Not exciting."

There's no anger or sarcasm in her tone. A thin thread of a white flag waves in the air between us. Maybe we don't have to fight a battle every time we're around each other, which might be more this weekend since she's in town with her family.

The rest of the guests are restless, some shifting to other seats so there's no yelling across the table. Noah's gotten up, leaving a vacancy next to his sister, to move down by Harbor.

Her mom holds her attention for a few minutes before her parents start a round of goodbyes. I stand to shake hands and take a hug from Delta because she's a sweet woman, and she makes me feel like I'm a part of the family every time I see her.

When the end of our table is emptied and the others have shifted closer to the door, I reconnect with Marina, our eyes latching together. She holds up her glass, and then says, "I think this makes you an honorary Westcott."

I crack a smile and hold up my empty water glass. "I've been called worse."

She laughs. It's light, but I'll take it, wanting to hear more of the beautiful sound.

It's hard to take my eyes off her. Five-six, maybe seven on a good day and in sky-high heels. Brown hair that finds just

enough light to shine in the dimly lit restaurant. Eyes bright
with mischief. She's a stunning woman. But it's that dress . . .
that fucking dress hugging her body that has a chokehold
on me every time I look below the neck. I'm a cad, so that
happens more than I'd care to admit. I've never been jealous
of a garment before, but I wouldn't mind trading jobs for a
night.

Should I be having these thoughts about the bosses'
sister? Probably not, but I'm only human. I don't know
what's come over me. I haven't had anything more than
water tonight, but suddenly, mouthy and demanding doesn't
seem like such a negative when thinking about her. I can
respect her for not taking anyone's shit, especially what I
dish out, but it's the side of her that she's sharing now that
has fully captivated me.

She's being vulnerable under the guise of wine, but I
know she's not drunk, not enough to share her secrets with
me of all people.

She says, "My boyfriend isn't my boyfriend anymore."

"That's too bad. *For him.*"

She smiles wider, and her cheeks heat like they did in
the elevator before she tries to distract by tucking her hair
behind her ear and taking another sip of wine. I see through
the act she put on for her family tonight. I heard "It's good"
or "I'm fine" so many times but never saw the answers reach
her eyes.

With me, she dropped that confession like she needed to
get it off her chest. I look around the table, hear the chatter,
and realize she's learned to play the game. She doesn't
compete with others. She sits in her space, content to hide
the truth from them.

But I see her.

She's lovely, even if she comes with a big dose of kick-ass

snark. I want to hear everything she's willing to share with me. Taking advantage of the situation, I ask, "How are you really doing?"

"The relationship was dead a long time ago, but the repercussions of not being together will reverberate for the next year or more."

"Or until another scandal breaks?"

Her unexpectedly loud laughter frees her to let go of whatever she was so staunch about holding on to. I think it's whatever happened between her and the ex-boyfriend. "Exactly. Got one handy that we can drop to the press?"

"I've been there, but I'm currently fresh out of bomb-shell headlines."

"Lucky you," she says, still laughing enough to keep that smile shining on her pretty face. "Mine is about to hit."

"That's too bad. Anything I can do to help?"

"Stop the presses?" With her elbow anchored on the table, she rests her chin on her hand. I like how relaxed she is, ease running through her shoulders and bending them forward. Whether I'm responsible or the wine gets the credit doesn't matter. *I'll take it.*

"Are there still presses, or is everything breaking online?"

"Sounds more dramatic with press. Like someone's going to run in and wave their arms frantically to literally stop the presses." She sits up again and empties the last of the red wine before setting her glass down. "Sometimes I wish there was a lack of immediacy to give time to process or dig deeper and time to breathe and realize you're not where you're supposed to be. But life moves fast, and I haven't been willing to sacrifice to get off this merry-go-round."

"I live for fast. It's when I slow down that the problems creep in."

She sets her napkin on her plate and pushes off the table to stand. "Guess we're opposites that way."

"Opposites have been known to attract."

She hits me with a sideways glare. "You wish."

I stand. "I wish for a lot of things. Sex isn't something I have to wish for."

"Whoa," she says, jerking her head back. "That escalated quickly. We jumped from attraction straight to sex without a step between?"

"Isn't that how it usually is?"

I'm given a solid eye roll before she laughs without an ounce of humor. "You're not bad—"

"Thanks." I straighten the sleeves of my jacket.

"Until you open your mouth." She turns on her heel with her chin raised high and walks toward the door to join her parents.

I burst out laughing, but it's a good reminder that I'd be wise to steer clear of anything to do with Marina. Too many red flags are attached to her last name and association with the team. Nothing good would come of us fucking around for a night, and a lot could go wrong in my career if we did.

Her father pats me on the back. "Thanks for joining us for dinner, Cash."

"Thank you for the invitation and the meal."

"That's all Harbor," he says, his eyes tracking over to his middle son. He sees his daughter and pulls her into a hug. "How's my girl really doing?"

With her eyes finding me over his shoulder, she replies, "I'm good, Dad. I'm fine."

"That's good." Turning toward me, he asks, "We're

staying at a house on the water. Do you mind seeing my daughter back to the hotel, Cash?"

"I don't mind at all, sir." Though I'm sure she won't be happy about this arrangement, she doesn't say anything.

We say our goodbyes and make an exit. Marina's quiet, seeming to get caught in the moods of her thoughts, which I sense aren't favoring me kindly after we slide into the back of the Town Car. Though I do catch her gazing at me before she turns away quickly, not uttering a word.

"Are you okay?"

"Actually, I'm not."

And here I was, thinking she'd be pouting in silence over there. "Well," I start, checking the time on my watch. "We have about ten minutes if we don't hit much traffic. Since we're here, air out your grievances."

Her hand flips out. "I don't need anyone to see me home or the hotel or anywhere else for that matter. I'm a grown woman, but I'm still viewed as a child."

"I don't think that's what he meant—"

"I don't need you to justify it for him. I love my dad. He did nothing wrong in his mind." She sighs, dropping her hands to her lap and fidgeting with the seat belt.

"You didn't ask my opinion, but since we're here doing this dance, I don't think anyone at that table sees you as incapable. Quite the opposite. I think they are more worried about the people you encounter. Ouch!" I joke, rubbing my arm where she lands a solid wallop on my bicep. Chuckling, I say, "Tell me I'm wrong."

She tries to be serious but just can't seem to get there, so she laughs instead. "You're not wrong." With a fading smile and a heavy released breath, she looks away from me. "I'm not sure where I belong anymore."

I thought we'd be sitting in silence, letting her emotions

move in and out with the tides regarding my company. I like this better. She's not putting on a pretense or trying to appear happy for others. Next to me, she wears sadness like no other emotion fits. Though I can't say I'm glad she's sad around me. I wish it were the opposite. *With me, she's real.*

And I'll take real any damn day of the week. Sure beats the fake I'm usually served by people trying to infiltrate my inner circle for personal gain.

"I was wrong."

Her eyes widen in surprise. "The great Cash Ryan is admitting fault? Wait, let me get my phone to record this confession. Oh, wait . . . I can't film because my phone is broken." Her glare locks on mine under a demandingly arched brow.

"We need to cut the Ryan shit."

"What are we going to do, then, Mr. Big Shot?" The corners of her lips tilt upward. The vixen.

"As for the phone, are you really that upset? It was an accident."

"You're really not going to admit you did it on purpose?"

She makes everything tempting, like a siren calling her prey to drown in the darkest depths of the ocean. "I'm good."

"Interesting," she replies.

The hint of attitude I detect in her tone makes me grin. Her sadness may soften my harsher comments, but her confidence is fucking spectacular.

The car stops, and the hotel valet staff opens both back doors at the same time. "Welcome back, Mr. Ryatt."

"Thank you." I step out of the vehicle, button my jacket, and wait for Marina to come around to escort her inside. A promise is a promise, even if she doesn't believe I should keep it.

She walks straight past me as she heads toward the lobby. "Okay, then." Shoving my hands in my pockets, I drop my eyes to the ground in front of me, hoping no cameras are around to spy. When I enter the hotel, Marina waits by a huge vase of flowers in the center of the lobby. My heart beats. My heart . . . *beats*. I feel alive at the very sight of her—the same as when I'm behind the wheel.

I smile like the luckiest fucker in the world walking toward my girl. Marina Westcott is not mine to claim in title or otherwise, disappointingly.

My sleeve is tugged, causing me to stop and look behind me.

"Sign for me, Cash?" a kid asks, holding a room key card and a marker toward me. He can't be much older than Cullen, six or seven years old at most. Scanning the area, I try to find the kid's parents since he's too young to be alone.

Donning a Westcott Racing hat, the dad steps closer with caution. "Sorry, hope you don't mind," he says. "We're big fans and here for the race this weekend."

"Happy to sign for the kid. Thanks for coming." I take the Sharpie and sign the key card before waving it to let it dry. When I hand it back, I rub the kid's head, messing up his hair. Though I'm sure Cullen will get annoyed if I keep doing that to him when he's a teen, he still finds it funny for now. So does the kid who giggles, then shows his dad my signature.

He jumps up and down. "Thanks, Cash Ryatt."

Kneeling, I ask, "What's your name, and how old are you?"

"Ryan." I almost want to laugh since I'm a Ryan as well, according to a certain beautiful and frustrating woman I just met. "I'm six this weekend."

"Happy birthday, Ryan. My son is five, six at the end of

the season." It's been a week since I've seen him, and I can't wait to get back to New York City to hang with my little buddy again.

The kid asks, "Does he like cars?"

"Unfortunately, he does." I grin. "Fast ones, like his dad."

"My dad drives a minivan."

I glance up at his father and chuckle before turning back to Ryan. "Safest vehicles on the road. Shows you how much he cares about you." I stand. "I need to get going, but it was nice meeting you, Ryan." I shake his hand and then his dad's. We take a quick photo together. I hear the kid *oohing* and *aahing* when they walk away. Kids are the best, so pure in their joy. I miss that. *I miss my son even more.*

When I turn around, the vase of flowers is still there, but Marina's gone. I don't know why I stand there staring like she might reappear, but it takes me a few seconds to realize she's left.

That's too bad. I was quite enjoying getting to know her better.

Red flag, Ryatt.

Red fucking flag.

I reach the elevator and punch the button. Pulling my phone from my pocket, I tap the screen to see a photo of my son. We had fun that day at the park. He treated me like his hero instead of how the rest of the world views me. I can live with the bad reputation. That's a consequence of behaving badly, no matter if it's justified at that moment. History doesn't look kindly upon me.

I'm here now to change my legacy and to make my son proud of me. My chest tightens, knowing I won't get to see him for a few more weeks.

I travel up to my room and sit on the edge of the mattress. I don't care about the lights of Miami shining outside my windows. I miss my kid, so I send a hopeful text: *Can I call him?*

I don't have time to take a breath before his mother replies: *Cullen's sleeping.*

It's after ten, so I'm not surprised, but my day doesn't consist of a nine-to-five we can rely on. Since Terpidy didn't answer earlier when I called before dinner, that's three days in a row I haven't gotten to hear my son's voice. It puts me on edge when it's been too long.

I'm known for a short fuse. The internet is full of my tantrums. My temper was part of the reason I lost my seat on the track last time. I can't risk everything for a momentary lapse. *Not again.*

I strip down and get ready for bed, but I still haven't heard from her.

Breathe.

I type: *I can call at ten in the morning. I'd appreciate if he's available.*

There's a long pause that has my hope she'll come through for me fading. I need to hear his voice and laughter and make sure he knows how much I love him. I add: *I miss him, Terpidy.*

A text pops up: *Eight a.m. sharp. We have a playdate at the park at nine.*

I try to be considerate of Terpidy, as my son's mother, but it's never been an easy relationship. And although this isn't a negotiation since we share custody equally, I respect the plans they've made, especially when it comes to Cullen's schedule and his life.

I sent one more text before calling it a night: *I'll call him at eight a.m. sharp. Have a good night.*

Though I try to be cordial, she doesn't make the same

effort. That's standard, considering the relationship with Terpidy Byrne is the worst collision I've ever been in.

But those darkest days gave me light. *My son.*

I set my alarm for the morning so I don't miss this chance, and then I fall into bed.

I'm dead to the world in no time . . . until my phone wakes me at one thirty-nine in the morning. I jump from bed and scramble to find my phone on the nightstand. With fear of the worst happening to those I care about most, I press the phone to my ear. "What? Hello?"

"Cash?"

It's not the voice I expected.

It's not my son or my mom. It's not Terpidy.

Pulling the phone back, I check the screen to see if it's a number I recognize. It's not, and it's not from my personal black book of contacts I keep. As my mind muddles from sleep to reality, causing me to grip the phone tighter in my hand, I give up and ask, "Who is this?"

"It's Marina . . . *Marina Westcott.* I need you."

5

Cash

SHOULD I have asked a few questions?

Probably.

It felt like I had enough details to sort the situation out, and quickly.

My mistake.

As I stand outside at two in the morning taking photos with the bouncers, the hour justifies the means to get in, get out, and try to get some sleep while I still can. When the rope is finally lifted to let me into the South Beach nightclub, I think I should have gathered a few more facts before agreeing to rescue my bosses' little sister from the bathroom inside.

Blue and pink lights flash into every corner of the two-story dance venue, including under the edges of the sunglasses I hope help to hide my identity. I cut through a sea of sweaty bodies dancing to endless beats that are supposed to resemble music. Although no one wants to hear a race car driver analyzing music tracks, I do have an affinity for great music, and this isn't it.

I finally reach the hall and walk past what some might call lewd acts. I'm no saint to judge others. I've not always made the best decisions when a pretty woman offers the pleasure of her company, or mouth for that matter, on a drunken night out. It's been longer than I care to recall since that happened. Italy, maybe Brazil. Too long. But when I'm off the track, I don't get to be a priority. That's the sacrifice I've made to put my son first.

I find the hallway that leads to the bathrooms. Two women's bathrooms on the right and the exit to the alley farther up on the left. "Marina?" I call just outside the first bathroom. No answer. I repeat in front of the other door. When there's still no reply, I pull my phone from my pocket and text: *I'm here.*

Because I'm impatient as fuck—I'm a race car driver for a reason—I also knock on both doors and then stand back to see which one opens.

The door on the right opens enough for one narrowed and beautiful eye to see me before it widens. I come forward, but the door doesn't budge. "You going to let me in?" She looks me up and down one more time before cracking a smile and stepping away for me to enter.

I walk in and lock the door behind me. "Get your stuff, and let's go."

Surprise shapes her face before she anchors her hands on her hips. "Just get your stuff, and let's go? You're not going to ask me why I called you?"

"You're drunk and called the hottest guy you've ever met because you need to get laid?"

As tempting as her open and deliciously rounded mouth is, her eyes tell a different story. "Um, no." She flips her hair over her shoulders, then raises her chin in the air like the very thought of being with me is offensive. "No. Liam Hemsworth didn't answer."

Removing the dagger from my ego, I ask, "You've met Liam Hemsworth?"

"It was one date before he met his current girlfriend."

"He's in a relationship? What happened with Miley?"

She smirks. "Why? Are you interested in him?"

"That's a riot."

Laughing, she snorts. "Riot. *Ryatt*. Like you."

I side-eye her, not amused in the least. "I knew you knew my name." Okay, fine. She's sort of amusing and cute when she's tipsy. *Flirty.*

This still isn't my scene. Not anymore at least. I grab the doorknob, ready to bolt. "Can we please get the fuck out of here?"

"You're not having fun?"

For a nightclub that appears to be popular by the size of the crowd outside this door, the corner of the mirror's frame is rusting, the toilet roll is bare, and the lock is barely holding by how it rattles when someone checks to see if the bathroom is occupied. By how long she's been in here, it's a good thing other restrooms are available.

Spying her cracked phone on the edge of the sink, I slide it onto the counter to keep it secure. The screen lights up, so I guess it's not as broken as she claimed. "How'd you get my number anyway?"

"I have my ways."

"Mm-hmm." I've never seen a more mischievous grin on someone than the one she's sporting now. "Whatever, stalker."

She reaches for her bag and pulls a tube out as if we have all damn night to hang out in here. Leaning against the sink, she drags a wand across her lips, leaving them shiny and capturing my full attention. Maybe I'm not in such a hurry after all.

Her lips were already appealing, but the way they shine for me, combined with that killer body, makes them so damn tempting to kiss just to find out if they taste as good as they look. My thoughts get away from me, imagining her bent over that sink with me taking her from behind with our eyes locked together in the mirror.

Fuck.

Or maybe I've been reading her wrong all along, and she tricked me into her little lair to have her way with me.

I shift my dick.

She drags her gaze from my erection to my eyes and shrugs. "You make it so fun to push your buttons." Poking me in the chest, she adds, "Why are you wearing sunglasses in a nightclub anyway?" Taking them from my face, she puts them on and smiles like we're spending the weekend in this place.

She looks better than I do in them. "To keep from being recognized."

"I think you'll need more than sunglasses, Cash."

"That's big of you to admit." Guess she's ready to drop the act that she didn't know who the fuck I was at the track yesterday.

"What?" She feigns innocence, which I'm starting to think is her fallback. I'm also beginning to believe she gets away with a lot because she's so hot or because she's a West-cott. I don't imagine she hears no very often. "That you're a hotshot race car driver, according to you, who can't go into a dark club without getting recognized?" A quick huff leaves her mouth. "If you're going to draw all of this supposed attention, I shouldn't have called you."

I reach for the glasses, but she backs away and crosses her arms. *So fucking hot and cold.* "What exactly was your plan again? Why are you hiding out in a bathroom?"

"I called someone who promised my dad to take care of me." She rests back on the edge of the sink and stares at me like she's searching for answers.

"Bullshit. Why'd you call me, Marina?" Leaning against the door across from her, I say, "Look, this was fun, but it's late, and I'm not in the mood to play these games with you." I've fucked up by being here. I need to be in top condition, and I'm playing tit for tat with her at two a.m. "I'm tired, so we need to wrap this up." Squeezing the bridge of my nose, I try to restrain my rising temper from tipping to the boiling point. "I promised to get you back to the hotel safely after dinner. Not to be your bodyguard as you go dancing around Miami in the middle of the night."

"Morning."

"Exactly." I shift my disposition along with my feet, trying to devise a plan, but our only option is to walk out of this place. I look at my watch. *Fuck.* "I'm not sure if you're aware of this, but I have a race today with millions of dollars and my career on the line."

"I know. I'm sorry." She sounds surprisingly sincere. Coming close again, she places the glasses back on my face and carefully pushes them up the bridge of my nose. "I called you because I knew you'd help me get out of here, that you would understand."

I catch her wrist, gently holding it between us before lowering it. "Understand what, Marina?"

Our gazes are fixed. Despite the loud music on the other side of the door, I can hear her swallow before she whispers, "I shouldn't have gone out. My agent wanted me to be seen, so I went out."

"Alone in Miami?" The anger, the upset, the smart-ass comments and slick tongue are forgotten.

The virtue shines in her eyes as she exchanges her trust with a modest smile. "My friends hooked up and left me."

"You need better friends."

"I'm starting to think I need a whole new life."

Her honesty makes me feel . . . something. I rub my chest to break up the knot. "I'll get you out of here." I grab the doorknob again. "Stay close."

"We can't go out there, Cash." Panic rises in her tone. "The paparazzi will ask me about Corbin."

"That's what this is really about? Your ex-asshole of a boyfriend? Competing for headlines?"

She takes a shaky breath, a nerve left raw in her exposed expression. "I wasn't thinking." Looking down as shame washes through her pretty features, she pauses. As if to collect herself, she summons her eyes to look up at me again. "It wasn't my best idea, but at the time and after more wine in my room . . ."

I exhale a deep breath, wondering how she thought either of us would get out of here unscathed. "I've had the shittiest ideas over the years and made plenty of bad decisions, so I get it. Alcohol only fuels that fire." I rub the back of my neck, trying to think of anything that makes this makes sense. "You called someone the paparazzi loves to harass and has been following all over Miami to help sneak you out so you can avoid the paparazzi. There may not be a clear path out of here without being seen."

Her eyes stay on mine, but not a word escapes. As the silence lengthens between us, she finally replies, "You were my best option."

"I'm your only option since Liam Hemsworth wasn't available."

She cracks a smile, and the sight instantly lifts my mood.

"I'm going to get us out of here, but tell me why they're targeting you. I deserve that much."

She rolls her eyes, getting some of her spunk back. "Other than I'm in movies?"

"What's the story beyond you and your ex not being together anymore?"

Pushing off the sink, she appears ready to finally leave. Standing in front of me, she says, "He cheated on me."

I nod, unsure what to say. The fact it happens to almost everybody at some point won't make this situation or her feel better. But as I stare into her blue eyes, the words come easy. "He's a fool." Then I look down at my phone and text the driver: *We're leaving through the exit door in the alley. Meet us there.*

Taking her hand in mine, I say, "I don't know what we're about to face, but I'll shield you the best I can. Stay close to my side. Don't make eye contact with anybody or say a word, not even 'no comment.' Okay?"

"Okay." Her fingers tighten around mine just as we're about to leave. "Don't let go of me."

I turn back, stealing a second to take her in. She doesn't sit in sadness this time, but her vulnerability still comes through her pleading eyes. I give her hand a squeeze and reply, "Never."

I don't open the door until I receive the driver's text: *I'm here.*

"Let's go."

Two girls barge past us as soon as we move into the hall. Holding her hand, I shift Marina under my arm and lead her to the exit door. Pushing through, we don't get two feet outside before I hear both of our names being shouted. I look left to see photographers from the edge of the street running down the alley toward us.

We rush, but I don't see the car. Shit. "Where's the fucking car?" I look right and see the red taillights, quick to pivot with Marina at my side.

"I can't run in these shoes."

I'm so tempted to pick her up, but that will add blood in the water for the sharks to devour and splash across every site tomorrow. Though I might be kidding myself even now about the impact of us being seen together.

I don't know where the guys flashing their lights bright in our eyes came from, but I hold my hand up and duck to the side. "Five feet straight ahead," I say, wondering if she can even hear me over the shouting.

"New hot couple alert."

"How long have you been a couple?"

She's bumped, causing her to stumble. She's safe in my arms, but I glare at the fucker who had the nerve to get in her way. "Get the fuck away from her."

Questions still fly, hitting us from all sides.

"Are you dating or fucking Cash?"

"Where's Corbin Darian, Marina?"

"Gonna blow the race again, Ryatt?"

We reach the car, and I shift Marina in front of me to keep her out of the line of paparazzi fire. She ducks into the back seat, and I'm right behind her. As soon as the door closes, I lock it. She does the same on the other side.

Turning back to face each other, our hands are still clasped between us. Neither makes a move. We may be tucked safely in the back, but my ears still ring from the thunder of shouting on the other side of the glass.

The driver gets in and starts driving.

The flashes haven't stopped. We both look out the back

windshield to see the aftermath of the chaos we escaped. I drop my head down into my hand and massage my brow. "We're fucked." *How am I going to explain this tomorrow?*

Marina sits in silence, her hand slowly pulled free from mine and left alone on her lap.

I turn to the window, the streetlights not as bright as where we came from, and try not to think about the shitstorm ahead. I can't let my head get caught up in something I can't control. They will write what they want, and I'll have to defend myself. It's nothing new, but something I had hoped to avoid this season.

A soft touch draws my eyes to my leg as Marina's delicate fingers come to rest on my thigh. When I meet her gaze in the dark of the car, she whispers, "I don't hate you, Cash."

"You don't?"

"No. I just strongly dislike you." Her cheeks tug her lips into a smile she tries to restrain but can't. It's the sweetest of smiles she's given me yet, my favorite one on her so far.

I burst out laughing. Dropping my head back to the seat rest, I cover her hand with mine and tilt to face her. "That's good. Progress, right? That leaves the door open for the—"

"Not a chance." She laughs as she rests back as well, leaving her hand planted right under mine like we do this all the time. Rolling her neck, she looks at me, the laughter fading. "I'm sorry, Cash."

I exhale, releasing what tomorrow brings and focusing on the present with her. "It's okay. I can handle whatever comes my way. I'm not called the comeback kid for nothing."

"I thought you were the bad boy of racing?"

"It depends who you ask."

"I'm asking you." Her gaze stays locked on mine as if she's genuinely interested.

I wasn't expecting it. "I prefer to be judged by who I am today rather than my past."

The car pulls to the front of the hotel without a photographer in sight. It's one of the reasons I like to stay here when I'm in Miami. They protect their guests' privacy.

Marina doesn't leave like we're strangers when we get out of the car this time. She comes around and waits for me to get out of the vehicle, and we walk into the lobby together. Although it's a one-time thing and there may not be respect, there's trust between us. So there's no need to fill the air with empty niceties.

Our eyes stay ahead instead of each other until we step into the elevator. "So . . ." She rocks back on her heels. "Where ya going, Ryan?"

I grin, shaking my head. I think I'm more upset that I'm getting accustomed to hearing that name than her calling me that in jest. I don't mind, though. It feels too good with her to fuck it up with some snippy comment.

Not wanting to ruin this moment, I let the name go because it doesn't matter. Nothing does but the here and now. "Anywhere you are."

6

Marina

I UNDERESTIMATED the power of Cash Ryatt's charisma.

Now I understand why so many women crush on this man. At least he tells me they do. I'm taking him at his word until I have time to do my own investigative research when I return to Canada for filming.

What I do know is that it's easy to get lost in his green eyes, especially when they're locked on you like prey. I can't tell if he wants to eat me in the most delicious way or kill me, for real. I'm okay hanging around him a bit longer to find out because he's stupidly handsome.

A cross between a surfer with his sun-lightened brown hair, a *GQ* model, and well, a race car driver, he breaks the mold regarding expectations—physically and in personality.

That I find him so appealing is frustrating.

I shouldn't want a man like him—someone who can't resist challenging me at every corner, has no qualms about calling me out, and tips into banter that leans more toward finding me intolerable than desirable.

Does he find me desirable? Is that the problem he has with me, or is he just as unsure about me as I am about him?

Narrowing my eyes, I watch him standing at the sliding glass door, laser focused out the window. Tall, hair perfectly sexy in its mussy state, broad-shouldered, cut jaw, and a late-night shadowing of scruff that has me rubbing my legs together like a cricket while wondering how it would feel against my inner thighs. It's been too long since I've been with someone.

Someone who made me a priority.

Someone who treated me like I was the world to them.

Someone who touched me in ways that would make me blush again.

Cash keeps causing me to blush, but that's from anger, not from the heat of our proximity or because he's looking at me like I'm the only woman in a crowded room. No, it's not from this ludicrous attraction I have to that man. *At least, I don't think it is . . .*

He makes me feel out of control, but thoughts of seduction are the last thing I should be thinking about when it comes to him. *Yet here I am.* Thinking about him in ways I shouldn't be.

Biting my lip, I turn away to collect myself. I've had a lot to drink tonight and not enough to eat. That's all. But then my gaze finds him again, savoring every muscle that white shirt clings to, studying that incredible ass as if he's a reference for a marble statue. It's been a really long time since I've felt anything for someone.

I slip into a chair because this is a doozy of a dose of reality. When was the last time? When was the last time I even made myself come since Corbin wasn't doing the job?

More importantly, am I only eyeing up Cash like he's a late-night snack because he was kind to me?

Short answer: Yes.

I didn't know how sad and sexless my life had become until now.

Looking at him with his presence consuming the room and implanting dirty thoughts into my brain, I indulge before he opens his mouth again.

That's when we tend to get into trouble.

He loves to disagree with me. I kind of love that he does as well. He keeps me on my toes. Who needs another yes man hanging around like a groupie in your life anyway? *Not me.*

Cash Ryatt is the kind of guy who doesn't beat around the bush and tells the truth like his life depends on it. Basically, he doesn't take it easy on me, and I like that for some reason. He's refreshing in the most unassuming of ways and grumpy from a side that feels more like a bad mood than a personality trait.

None of that matters, though, now. I've never felt more protected or safe than when I'm in his care.

Cash is the opposite of Corbin and every other guy I've dated. They were pretty and predictable, from their upbringing to their schooling to the expensive haircuts and perfectly pressed jeans that their stylist picked out.

I never knew a troubled bad boy was my jam, but tonight, Cash Ryatt sure is.

My mind is fuzzy in the last rays of moonlight, and I'm tipsy in the early morning hour. Sucking in a breath, I slowly exhale, allowing my body to loosen the tension. "My dad always told me that nothing good happens after two a.m."

Cash's eyes find mine across the room when he turns around. "He's right."

Resting back against the leather, my bad decisions feel bigger in the back seat. "I shouldn't have gone out." Or maybe it's just his presence consuming the airspace and my attention.

"Probably not, but you should have left when your friends did." Crossing his arms over his chest, he studies me as if he's seeing art for the first time—intrigued, delving as deeply as he can without touching.

My breath picks up under his heavy gaze as I stare at him, counting the tics of his jaw before he speaks again.

One.

Two.

Three.

Four.

"I get that your agent told you to be seen, but what were you hoping to achieve?" he asks in a lowered tone, letting down his guard and defenses along with it.

"I wanted out of my head for a while. I wanted to be free without worries like I used to be."

"Is your life that awful, Marina?"

The absence of babe, sweetheart, and even princess is noticeable, making me wish I could hear them from him again. If for no other reason than to fire me up in some form of irritation instead of sinking into the deep end of my emotions again. "I like to dance. Have a cocktail and be with my friends. Not always having to think about everything. Just move to the beat and lose myself. That's all. No great mystery. It was fun until I turned around and discovered they were gone. I got a text. What am I going to tell them? No, you can't have sex with the guy you were just making out with on the dance floor. We're twenty-six."

"Twenty-six? That's your age?"

"Yeah."

I watch as he crosses the room, rubbing his forehead. I can't make out what he's mumbling, but it seems to get the better of him because he's now shaking his head.

Not sure if it's the night or my age that bothers him more. "How old are you?"

"Too old for you."

I laugh but then scoff when I realize he's serious. "What's too old for me, gramps?"

This time, he chuckles. Taking two bottles from the minibar and twisting the top off one, he returns to give to me. "Here. Water never hurt anyone." He takes the top off his bottle. "I'm thirty-five."

I have no idea why I'm grinning other than I'm enjoying myself . . . *at his expense*. "Thirty-five?" I exclaim in a teasing tone. "Geez, maybe I should be getting you the water and making sure you're hydrating. Need me to go out and get some prunes or maybe I have a piece of hard candy in my purse for you." I take a large sip, then watch as he tries so hard not to give in and laugh.

"Keep going. This is entertaining." I finally get a smile out of him as he sits in a chair facing me. It's short-lived as he drinks his water, slow at first till he finishes the entire bottle. Keeping me on the edge of my seat, I sit waiting for him to elaborate, but he doesn't. I'm not sure if he's trying to get me riled up with the great buildup during the silence, but it's impressive how he doesn't feel the need to fill the void. Seems to be a party trick he's mastered.

I'm too weak to stay silent for too long, so I ask, "Is the plan to stare at me all night?"

"It's not the worst plan I've been involved in." He grins. "You're not here for the race, so why are you in Miami?"

The accusation stings, and my head jerks to the side, averting my gaze. He sees me too clearly. I shift in my seat, thinking I'm playing it cool, when I know every move I make is a sign of discomfort. Forcing my eyes to return to his, I reply, "I came to support my family." Silence. I bite the inside of my cheek and chatter on, "I was working in Canada, so I haven't been able to travel across the world for the other races."

"Makes sense."

Nothing about his response sounds like the matter is settled. Is he politely letting me off the hook? I'll accept the reprieve he's giving, releasing a breath. A coffee table, pestering silence, and a million secrets lie between us. "I'm sorry for dragging you into my mess tonight."

"You can always call me." He's so sincere that my heart skips a beat. Sitting forward, he sighs, then scrubs his hands over his face before resting his forearms on his legs. "I don't know what to think about you. You don't hate me, but you also don't like me. We're not friends, so what does that make us? Enemies?"

"You're just too tired to fight with me."

He chuckles before sitting back and sliding down a bit in the leather chair. His eyes still never leave mine. "So we stick with enemies or somewhere in-between?"

"The unknown might be easier."

"Nothing with you is easy, it seems." He cocks an eyebrow as if he's waiting for the perfect comeback, but I'm out of snark at this hour.

"Corbin cheated on me with the wardrobe assistant on the film we've been shooting in Vancouver." My throat feels dry, so I take another sip. "I guess they have been sleeping together the entire time because he wasn't sleeping with me."

His deep sigh says it all. I'm just as exasperated by this cliché of a tale. "Sorry to hear that."

"He would say all the right things if I broached the topic, constantly reassuring me, but something was off. I felt it in my gut." I glance over his shoulder as if I'll find the strength in the corner of the room. I don't, so I look into his eyes instead, which are much more comforting. "When I told him I have no desire to live life without sex with my partner, he accused me of cheating on him or wanting to. The thing is, sex wasn't all I was missing from our relationship."

"Love?"

Hearing that word both rattles me and calms my rapidly beating heart. It's out there . . . "I don't know that I ever loved him." Shame still coats a part of my psyche, trying to convince me to be the bad guy and take the fall for the failure of the relationship. In the past, I might have . . . I did. I don't have the energy to fight for something that never was.

"We were a match made in Hollywood. We auditioned together for a movie and were cast as a couple. I guess I was naive enough to believe it was real in the beginning, but I think we've been method acting ever since."

I take a breath, and my heart is already lighter after exposing the truth, even if it is in the middle of the night. "I remember looking at him when he told me my career would be over if I broke us up. You know what?"

With Cash's gaze traveling from my eyes to my mouth, he asks, "What?"

"I didn't care." I shake my head as my resolve from that day returns. "I couldn't force myself to care about a career that would tie me to Corbin Darian forever." I release a breath like I've released my guilt for not trying harder to make that relationship work. It feels good to finally get this off my chest. I've been living in a state of what-if for days, and I'm so much closer to the answers. But Cash's continued silence after my final confession makes me anxious, like I'm waiting for a judgment to be laid upon me.

Somehow, from the paddock to now, I care what he thinks of me. I care what he thinks, period. I don't struggle to hold his gaze as my sudden connection with him runs deeper than the green of his eyes.

He finally shifts, licking the inside corner of his lips. "How long has it been since you've had sex?"

Shock . . . offense . . . annoyance forces me to my feet. "That's it? That's all you got from everything I said?" I walk toward the balcony, needing fresh air. "I haven't told a soul any of this, not even my best friend, and that is your burning question? The only thing you care about is my sex life?"

My wrist is caught when I pass, and he pulls me back just enough for our gazes to lock. "Don't get all haughty on me, babe. I've already proven myself as trustworthy tonight. Is that not enough?"

"You don't owe me your trust. You don't owe me anything."

"Except a phone, right?" he replies so quickly, though his expression remains neutral under the strain of the circumstances.

Both of us are stubborn enough not to look away from the other but smart enough to let down our guards when it's a lost cause. I angle toward him, not comprehending this deep-seated need I have for him to give me understanding in return. To open up to me and share a secret? His own sad story? To say something that makes me feel less vulnerable right now? But he doesn't, so I say, "I exposed myself and—"

"Your secrets are safe with me. I won't share them, and I won't use them against you. But I also need you to do me a favor."

Crossing my arms over my chest, I stand in disbelief. "You completely disregard everything I told you to focus on your own interests, and now you have the nerve to ask *me* for a favor?"

"Stop overthinking everything you say and do. You'll never be happy if you're always living for someone else's approval or worried about what they'll think of you," he says so easily sitting atop a pedestal looking down on me like I'm nothing more than a fan in the audience.

"I'm just picking up the vibe you're dropping down."

"Come here."

"No."

"Marina." It's not a question. By his tone, it's definitely a demand.

My arms tighten over my chest, holding tight to my newly formed defenses. "No."

"God, you're so fucking stubborn." Reaching forward, he grabs me by the hips and pulls me to him.

A squeal instead of a protest escapes as I land in his lap. Any other guy, I'd be clawing his eyes out. Cash's eyes are simply too nice to ruin. But otherwise, they'd be toast. "What the hell are you doing?"

"Getting you to listen."

I'm not about to tell him I've been called stubborn a time or two, but he has a point. I sometimes get caught in my thoughts instead of seeing what's right in front of me. So to spite the alcohol that wants to muddy my mind, I try to think clearly and be levelheaded about this. "Fine. Tell me what you want to say so badly."

"Stop wasting time trying to figure out what went wrong because the answer is always going to be that your ex is just an asshole. So don't second-guess what you did or didn't do. And don't hold it against every other guy out there because he doesn't speak or act on our behalf. He's an idiot for letting you go. A million other men are smarter than that."

Trying not to fall apart in his arms from the sweetness, I melt instead—my heart, my defenses, and my willpower not to kiss this man. Why does he have to be so good to me? If he keeps this up, I won't fight against this wave of emotions and give in to his tide instead.

"Can I ask you something?"

"Forty-two."

My head jerks. "Whoa. Forty-two inches?"

He chuckles, rubbing my hip like he has no intention of giving me up anytime soon. I love it. *Damn him.* He says, "The meaning of life, but thanks for the compliment."

"Is that a compliment or a threat?"

"Hmm. Guess we'll just have to find out." My laughter releases like bubbles in champagne, making me feel lighter in his arms. "What were you really going to ask?"

It's not in the words he said, although they hit close to home. They were a home run, in fact. But it's the way he sounds; he knows what I'm going through, and he's been there before from personal experience.

Is that why I trust him?

Is that why I remain on his lap?

Savoring every second and every word he shares?

Yes.

I tap the end of his nose. "What do you suggest I do?" I ask, booping the tip. "And it better not involve sex with you."

Clicking his tongue, he grins. "There goes that plan." He reaches up to tuck my hair back from my face. His smile disappears as his fingers linger on the shell of my ear. A rise in his chest spurs other body parts to rise along with it. "I . . . uh . . ."

"Eight months." I suck in a breath and release it easily

around him. "I think it's been eight months since I had sex or anything else that would . . . would—"

"Would?"

"Release some tension."

I almost expected him to laugh out loud at me, but that's not what he does. His fingertips slide around my ear, then lower to my collarbone. He traces an imaginary design across my chest, leaving a wake of goose bumps behind, and whispers, "That's too bad."

"Yeah, it's a tragedy." I wriggle on top of him because we've come this far already anyway.

The right side of his mouth lifts. And though that just adds to his appeal, that part of him hasn't captured my attention. He's hard and large, and I move again to feel more of him. My lids threaten to close, my body willing to take the chance that pleasure could be found through rubbing against him. With the heat of our connection spreading into my chest, I do what I don't want to, touching his cheek with the tips of my fingers and whispering, "I should go. Nothing good happens after two a.m."

Leaning in, the scruff of his cheek scrapes against my face, and when he reaches my ear with his mouth, he whispers, "All the more reason to stay."

Stay.

One word that has me throwing caution to the wind. I wrap my arms around his neck, trying to satisfy a craving I've kept at bay since I met him.

Why does he have to be so nice?

Why does he have to care?

Why does he have to be so ridiculously sexy?

Damn him.

7

Cash

I KNEW she didn't hate me.

What I didn't know was how badly she wanted me. If I had, I would have skipped to the point at the paddock. I kiss her, sliding my fingers into her hair, savoring the sweet pressure of her lips, the subtle flavor of wine and desire mixed, and then lean in as she pulls me closer as if it's possible.

With every swirl of her tongue . . .

Her body pushing against me . . .

And the taste of her has me deepening the connection.

It's that first taste of this incredible woman that seals my fate. Kissing her will never be enough. I can rattle off ten reasons she's a bad idea, and the bottom line will always be the same. Despite what we might want, we can't fuck around together. That's the hand we've been dealt.

Too much is at stake.

When I run my hand along the bare skin of her lower back, dipping my fingers under the edge of the dress that sits high on that incredible ass, she has me ready to throw everything away.

My dick strains against my pants, not giving a fucking care that I'd be her rebound. "We can't do this, princess."

I know it.

She knows it.

The whole fucking world knows nothing can happen between us. It would break too many rules and anger the owners. Pulling back, I cup her face and say it again to remind myself what's on the line if I cross this one with her. "I can't risk ruining my career."

"For a woman," she says with deprecation sneaking in.

"For anyone."

Grabbing my wrists, she leans forward until our foreheads are pressed together, and closes her eyes. "We got carried away is all."

I caress her cheek, then lean back to get a better look at her. When she opens her eyes, I whisper, "It's easy to do with you." There's no fight in her, no snappy comments or rush to get away. She softens her shoulders and leans against my hand. "You make it hard to walk away, Marina."

I'm gifted a smile. It's small, but I'll take everything she's willing to give. "It's the right thing to do," she whispers, not sounding any more convincing than I do.

I grin so stupidly big and chuckle lightly. "Sure doesn't feel like it."

"In the moment. But once we forget how good that kiss was, it will be like it never happened."

I push her hair back from her face. "I won't forget." A fire burns between us, but knowing better than to act on it, I take a breath, hoping to cool things down.

"Why does doing the right thing feel so wrong?" She

reluctantly pulls away with a heavy sigh. "I've not acted like myself this weekend."

"If this isn't you, I can't wait to see the other side, then."

That lightens her mood, and she's smiling when she gets up and crosses the room. Other than leaving, she can't get much farther from me. "I have a feeling you're one of the reasons I'm acting like this." Her eyebrow peaks as she watches me.

Rubbing my thumb over my bottom lip, I chuckle again. "I'll take the blame anytime for you."

Her smile is the biggest I've seen since we met, but it fades with our laughter. Suddenly, even seconds feel like too much time, and space has been left between us, and questions rush in. "What are we doing, Cash?"

I think about it. I'm exhausted, yet nothing I can say will relieve the worries that have snuck into her tone. "You tell me."

"I should have gone to my room instead of coming to yours. Why did you let me stay?"

I sit back in a chair, resting my arms on the tops of my legs as I rub my brow. I can't answer carelessly. One thing leads to another with her, and my words could be used against me. It was okay in daylight when I was sharper, but the timing is off tonight. "You looked like you needed a friend."

Walking to where she removed her shoes and left them earlier, she picks them back up, leaving the pair to dangle from two fingers. "We're tired and—"

"Nothing good happens after two a.m."

Something comes over her, tempering her smile but not making it any less potent. *Pride maybe?* "Exactly," she replies.

She's making moves, grabbing her purse from the dresser, and angling to leave. I walk over, catching her just before she reaches the door. Her hand is on the knob when I anchor mine above her head, keeping it closed just a moment longer.

Turning around, she tilts her head and smiles up at me. "Can I help you?" A giggle frequents her throat.

"Yeah." I run my knuckle under her jaw, taking in her pretty face. "You all right?"

"You don't need to worry about me, hotshot. I always land on my feet." She's an actress and a good one by how she has everyone else fooled, but I see through her, especially when her gaze falls to the wall beside us.

I lift her chin between my fingers until her eyes meet mine again. "I'm not talking about the song and dance you put on for the rest of the world, Marina. I'm talking about the inside, the part you hide from everyone else."

"What makes you think I'm hiding?" She struggles to hold eye contact, and slow blinks give her the reprieve she needs. Her lips part as frustration creeps in, and she pulls away, only stopped by the closed door behind her. "I'm not hiding."

I lower my arm, straightening my back. "Okay, you keep telling yourself that lie, and you might start believing it."

I'm poked in the chest before I can stop her, and then she pokes me again. "You don't know me any more than I know you." She turns away, tugging open the heavy door. "I don't know why I trusted you—"

"Because you couldn't trust your family."

"I can trust my family," she snaps with her voice rising and whips back after slipping into the hallway.

I lean against the doorframe, watching her heavy step her way down the hall, sulking. "Okay."

She stops again because now she's really fired up, and from what I've witnessed of her personality, she doesn't give up. "Stop saying that. You don't know anything about me or my family."

"On a personal level, I know a little." I dip my head and watch as she crosses her arms in protest, her shoes in one hand and her bag in the other.

"Oh yeah, what do you know?"

"I know there's an expectation put on your shoulders. You're the star of the family, the baby that got all the attention, and you don't want to let them down now that you're all grown up."

"Isn't that everyone? No one wants to let their family down. Try again."

Flipping the slider to keep the door from locking behind me, I walk a little closer cautiously, not wanting to send her running toward the elevator. "I saw you at dinner. I heard you tonight. You pretend for them." I stop with two feet left between us and say, "But you open up to me."

"That was clearly a mistake I won't be making again."

"That's too bad. I quite like that side of you, the more vulnerable, real part of you. The one who doesn't wear a crown on her perfect head parading around the place like she's the queen."

"Don't you mean princess?" she snarks, pursing her lips.

The hour doesn't call for controlling every emotion, and I start laughing. "Yes, princess."

Her arms lower, and she releases a sigh that sounds like it's been held for years waiting for this moment. "Why do you have to be such a jerk?" The defensiveness is gone as teasing weaves through her words. Coming closer, she grins up at me. "You're a powerful man, one of twenty on the racing grid, but you're standing here making sure I'm okay. Why is that?"

"Because you have a great ass."

I'm whacked on the chest with her bag. "You're the worst, Cash!"

I catch her by the hips before she slips out of reach again. Leaning down, I whisper in her ear, "Trust me, babe, I'm the best you'll ever have."

The warmth of her breath hits my neck, and when she turns, her cheek slides against mine. Her lips reach my ear, and she waves the green flag with two whispered words, "Prove it."

I kiss her, cupping her face and holding her steady. I'm pushed, shoved toward the room with more strength than I expected her to possess. Grabbing her waist, I lean back with a laugh. "How long did you say it's been?"

She fists the front of my shirt. "Are we going to do this or not, Ryatt?"

"Well, since you asked so nicely . . ." I scoop her up and put her over my shoulder because I'll happily get us back in the room much faster.

A hard smack to my ass accompanies her laugh. "Cash!"

"*Shh*. People are sleeping." Using my foot, I push the door back open and lock it once we're inside.

After a huff, she snarks, "Any day now."

"Safety first. Women have been known to sneak into my room to seduce me."

"To seduce you? You mean groupies?"

"Women who call you at all hours or show up at your work—"

"Wait." Her body stills over my shoulder, and she lifts her head up. The woman's got great abs. "Are you insinuating that I'm a groupie?"

"Those are your words, not mine."

"For the record . . ." She holds a finger in front of my face, the middle to be precise. I rub my palm over the round of her ass because the beads, and let's face it, her fucking insanely sexy body has me wanting to grab a handful.

"What are you doing?"

"Nice beads."

"Uh-huh . . . "

I carry her into the bedroom and stand at the end of the mattress. Just after she lands on the mussed-up bed, she says, "I didn't sneak. I was invited the first time and forcibly transported the second." She takes a breath and says, "And if this is your idea of seduction, you're hanging out with the wrong women."

"How would you do it if you can't get a word in edgewise?"

Lifting up on her elbows, she asks, "Seduce you?" Falling back in a fit of giggles, she flails her arms around the crumpled sheets before relaxing and looking back at me. "I don't have to seduce men, so it's not a skill set I've developed, but if I had to pick one thing, at the moment, I'd have the bed made to make it more enticing to stay."

I toe off my shoes. Whether she decides to stay or go, I'm getting in that bed. What happens after that is her decision. "I was sleeping when you called to have me rescue your ass."

She slips off the edge and turns her backside to me. With a pat, she asks, "This ass? The ass you're obsessed with?"

"Fuck me," I growl, reminding myself to be a gentleman. "That's the one." I release a sigh, equally exasperated and getting hard watching her walk toward the bathroom. What the fuck have I gotten myself into with her?

Trouble.

Bad decisions.

"Don't go to bed without me." She closes the door before

I can respond, reaffirming that this woman never hears the word no.

I run my fingers through my hair, debating if I should go through with this. My dick has already made its decision, but that's how I got off track last time.

A woman.

My kid.

My career going up in flames.

I don't think I'm the guy who will break her heart. She needs to have something on the line for that to happen. When it comes to me, she's safe in that area. "Hey, Marina, I think—"

The door slides open, and words cease to exist when she leans against the inside frame wearing one of the undershirts I left in the bathroom. "Hope it's okay I borrow this?"

"Yeah." I gulp like a teen whose fantasy came to life. "Sure."

Her hair is looser, and her curls have softened over the hours, as if she's run her fingers through the strands like I did. Her legs are tan and somehow look even more shapely coming out from under my white tee than the beaded blue dress she was wearing. It's her face that's utterly captivating, though. Washed free from makeup, she's prettier than when made up. An ache in my chest reminds me to breathe, so I suck air into my lungs, unable to take my eyes off her.

She smiles, and I know my world will never be the same. "I think you're right."

"About?" I ask, lost to whatever we're talking about.

"It's late." Ah. "We're not thinking clearly." Walking toward the bed, she stops on one side while I remain standing at the foot like an idiot. "Do you still want me to stay?"

"I do," I reply without hesitation.

Her smile is softer as if the night's gotten a hold of it, her lids heavier as she climbs into bed. She slips under the covers and lies back to watch me. I start on my shirt and unbutton it. The air around us has shifted, the energy winding down instead of running off adrenaline. "I'll leave before you wake up," she whispers, "I promise."

The intimacy is thick, making me shift in the newness of it. I don't spend time with women like this anymore if I ever did. We're not caught in foreplay or the aftermath of having sex. I don't know what this is, but I'm not opposed to experiencing it with her. "You don't have to rush out of here."

Her smile returns, making me not give one fuck of a care what tomorrow brings. Tonight, I want this with her. I want to hold her, to kiss her, to listen to her fall asleep in my arms.

With only my boxer briefs on, I climb into bed and slide next to her. She caresses my cheek, staring into my eyes. "The bad boy of racing isn't so bad when you get to know him."

"I've worked hard for that reputation. Don't ruin it for me."

"Your secret is safe with me." I catch a genuine grin shaping her expression just before she rolls onto her other side, facing away from me. I lay my head on the pillow and wrap my arm over her, pulling her frame against me as she molds her body to mine.

I kiss her shoulder because I want to, but I shouldn't because I know the truth.

I'm already in too deep.

I'm so screwed.

I bolt upright to the sound of banging on the door. My eyes burn from the daylight flooding through the doorway from the wall of glass in the living room.

The blinds are open.

Fuck.

Memories of Marina pushing the button come back, but there were other bigger distractions for me to remember some minor details, like closing them again.

Marina.

I reach out but find nothing except twisted sheets beside me. "Marina?" I get up as the banging continues and make my way toward the door. "Marina?"

There's no sign of her in the bedroom.

Maybe that's her.

Maybe she went out for coffee.

Maybe she grabbed some breakfast for us.

No shoes.

No bag.

No beaded dress.

Unless she left my shirt in the bathroom, that's also gone.

I scrub my hand over my face and then look through the peephole. *Shit.* This can't be good. Popping the locks, I open the door. "Noah—"

He barges in.

"Come on in," I add, moving out of his way since he seems to be on a mission.

He stops just inside the living room and turns back, crossing his arms over his chest. "What the fuck are you doing?" As if he can't stand still, he lowers his arms, his phone in one hand and the other fisting at his side. He puts more distance between us when I come closer.

What little control he appears to have over his anger is slipping. "What the fuck, Cash?"

"Good morning to you, too." Morning . . . *oh shit*. "What time is it?"

He glares at me. "My sister aside—"

"Your sister aside?" I ask, searching for my phone. It clicks just before I enter the bedroom. *Fuck.* He knows. "I can explain, but I need—"

"I don't care what you fucking need. Do you know the damage you've done?"

Holding up my hand, I say, "Five minutes. Give me five minutes, and then you can yell all you want, but I need—"

"This isn't about me, Cash. This is about the team, the Westcott name, the—"

"It has to wait five minutes." I dash into the bedroom and find my phone on the dresser right next to the charger, but it's not plugged in, and it's dead. "Fuck!"

"I tried to call," he says, standing in the doorway.

I'm trying not to lose my shit, but I want to slam the phone against the wall. I plug it in instead. "What time is it?"

He huffs but checks his phone. "9:15."

My stomach twists into knots, waiting for the screen to tell me it has enough power to make the call. Maybe Noah understands there's something more pressing because he stands there, not making a sound.

Green on the screen has me scrambling to call the number. The phone rings, so I put it on speakerphone to keep charging.

"What's going on, Cash?" Noah asks as if we're friends again.

My heart thunders in my chest, making me wish I could

pace the floor. "I need to talk to my son." It rings two more times. "Please pick up. Please pick up." When the phone answers, the words race from my mouth, "I overslept. Can I—"

"Leave a message after the beep." *Beeeeeep* . . .

If this phone weren't the only connection I have to my son when I'm traveling, I'd crush it. I hang up and drop onto the end of the mattress, sinking forward and covering my face with my hands.

"Talk to me," Noah says, his tone leaning toward concern now.

I can't make myself sit straight as disappointment races through me. I look up, covering the rest of the distance. "I was supposed to talk to my son at eight this morning. She only gave me that one chance to reach him."

"Sorry to hear that."

"She uses every opportunity to get back at me." I push up, dragging myself back into the light of the living room. I sit on the couch as he takes the chair Marina possessed for too short of a time last night.

"I know you like to talk to him before a race, but you can't let this define your day."

"I won't." I don't know whether I even believe myself at this point.

He taps on his phone a few times, then sits on the coffee table in front of me. "I hate piling more shit on top of you, but the media is having a field day this morning, and my brothers are fucking furious."

Marina.

I still play dumb, glancing between the phone and him. He picks it back up and reads, "The bad boy of racing wins the heart of racing royalty."

Scrolling, he flashes a photo of Marina and me . . . Fuck.

We're holding hands as we exit the nightclub. "Beauty and the Bad Boy."

He says, "You're not rested. It was careless and—"

"I can explain."

"You better because they're discussing the procedure to fire you."

Fuck my life.

8

Marina

"GET IN, MOVIE STAR!"

The tires had barely stopped screeching when an unfamiliar car came to a stop in front of me. Normally, I'd run in the opposite direction for safety, but fortunately, I knew the voice. Poppy Stanfield. *Prom queen to my homecoming crown. Blond to my brunette.* Voted most likely . . . *that's all*, just "Most Likely."

And she hasn't changed a bit. I love that about her.

Bending down, I peer into the car and am greeted with my best friend's smile.

"I thought you were trying to kidnap me, Pop."

"I am. Get in, and let's go." She waggles her sunglasses on her head. "Though I'm only taking you to the apartment." Looking every bit the troublemaker with a wicked smile, she asks, "Unless you want to go on a spontaneous road trip? I'm all for that."

"Love to, but I have filming tomorrow. It's the only reason I'm back."

She pops the trunk. "You standing around here all day, or are we getting you out of here?"

"Sounds like you're breaking me free from the penitentiary." I drag my suitcase to the back and load it into the trunk. When I slam the trunk closed, I hear my name being called in the distance. I jump into the car and say, "We've been spotted."

"It's so kind how you include me in the chaos of the paparazzi when we both know they don't care about me one bit." She's pulling away from the curb faster than is legal in an airport zone. I look back and laugh. "I'll always come to the rescue like Thelma and Louise."

"Can we skip that ending, though? That was brutal."

"Yeah, no cliff diving for us. So . . ." She glances over at me. "Apparently, we have lots to discuss."

In an act of desperation, or maybe it was despair at that moment, I sent her a simple text: *Corbin's been cheating. I don't know how I feel about it. I'm stuck in a bathroom in Miami. I'll be back in Vancouver tomorrow. Chat then.*

Okay, maybe not that simple since it contained the facts of everything going on in my life, but if it got her here in my hour of need, I'm not complaining. "How did you get here so fast?"

"I contacted Lauren, and she gave me your flight details."

"How are you here? You have a job in Seattle."

"I did, but that guy was an asshole, and I was tired of putting up with his freaky requests."

"What was the line?"

"He told me to get fresh lionfish with a dollop of Indian red chili made with buttermilk and served over grits." She's shaking her head as if she's offended all over again. "That's not a thing and shouldn't be. The flavors alone would be bonkers. I'm all for fusion, but it can't just be adventurous. It needs to make sense on the palate." She flails a hand between us. "I couldn't do it. I couldn't cross that line into Bonkersville. So I'm currently looking for a new job."

"I'm sorry, Poppy. He was awful to you from the beginning." Realizing she used the opportunity to come see me makes me lean over and hug her shoulder. "Thanks for coming to see me."

"I want to be here, so don't worry about it. Lesson learned. There was a reason he couldn't keep a chef. That was a year of hell I don't intend to repeat." She laughs, clearly doing fine after leaving her private chef gig. Glancing my way again, she has one hand on the steering wheel and the other anchoring her sunglasses on her head. "But let's talk about you, Ms. Westcott."

"I'd rather not."

"Yeah, you're not getting off that easy."

I laugh lightly, leaning my head back as I watch the world go by. "I haven't been getting off at all. Guess that's why Corbin was cheating."

"Corbin was cheating because Corbin is a cheater. It has nothing to do with you. Doesn't matter if you were having sex with him or not. Just be glad you weren't now that you know the truth."

I roll my head to the side, bringing my feet up on the seat and wrapping my arms around my knees. "You're right. Guess that's why I'm not upset. Upset enough, I suppose."

Reaching over, she rubs my forearm. "It's only a blow, Mar, because you were blindsided by the news."

"You never did like him."

"I liked him fine. I just didn't love him for you."

Somehow, this doesn't make me feel better. Go figure. "Why is that again?"

She shrugs. "He puts off ... he just puts off."

"It's called arrogance."

Tapping the tip of her nose, she says, "Ding. Ding. Ding." Sitting forward, she squints at the signs ahead before relaxing back again. "Twenty minutes to the apartment."

"Thanks for picking me up."

A wide smile spreads across her face. She's always been beyond gorgeous, but when she smiles, the whole world takes notice. "I'm glad I could be here. You still have that spare room, right?"

"I do." She's visited me a few times, but it will be nice not to be alone in the aftermath of the fallout from Corbin.

"Why'd you go to Miami again?"

Shifting my purse back to my lap, I dig through it, looking for lip gloss. I want to be ready just in case cameras are aimed at me when we arrive at the apartment complex. "Just a quick weekend in Miami to watch the qualifying race."

"I'm sorry. Let me be clearer. *Who* were you doing this weekend?"

I balk, but then it trickles off, and my cheeks heat, remembering how good Cash looked last night. His hard abs. That strong jawline. He listened when he didn't owe me a thing, much less any of his time. How he held my hand and me so close in protection from the paparazzi.

Slinking in my seat, I rest back, staring out the window. "You know I'm not doing anyone."

Gripping the steering wheel, she seems to have something on her mind. Poppy has never been good about keeping her feelings hidden. I suspect she won't now either. I just have to help open that door for her. I ask, "What is it?"

"You know I'm a vault when it comes to you. I would never share or sell any secrets."

"I know." I nod, truly knowing I can trust her like my

own family. After being best friends since we were little, she's family. "I'd tell you if something was going on." I scrape the gloss wand across my lips and look at her again. "Why do I get the feeling there's more going on here?"

"Your flight was early, right?"

Running my fingers along the hem of the shirt, I reply, "I barely arrived in time to board at six thirty. I got there right before the doors closed."

I look down at the tee I stole from Cash, grinning like I got away scot-free from a bank robbery. Wonder if he woke up smiling like I did. Hope so since it's race day. "Though it's nothing big, I did . . ." I stop speaking when I lay my eyes on her. Her knuckles whitening, her eyes fixed forward, and a weird vibe fills the car. "What's going on, Poppy?"

"You've missed the news this morning." She glances at me and then back at the road again.

I push up to right myself and take a deep breath. My stomach twists in knots from the thought of my private life becoming gossip. "Did the story about Corbin come out?"

"Um. No." She cringes and hands me her phone. "I know you don't have social media for all the right reasons, but you need to get online."

Taking the phone, I'm nervous about seeing what I'll find. "I had all my notifications like Google Alerts off as well. What is it? Just tell me."

"Open my phone."

"I don't think I want to," I joke, but my laugh is riddled with nerves. I do it because, good or bad, we face our demons.

Even though it's only been seconds ago, entering her code is the last moment of peace that I'll have.

"'Beauty and the Bad Boy?'" My eyes flick to the next article on the screen. "'Bad Boy Image Gets Makeover by

New Love Affair.' I don't understand. What is this?" I ask, scrambling as I scroll to the next article. My gut knows. This is a nightmare in the making.

And then I see the photo . . .

I cover my mouth to keep my jaw from dropping. Everything captured in that bright light moment in time makes Cash and me look like a couple. "Oh no," I say, unsure what else I can.

"How are we feeling? Happy? Devastated? Caught in a news cycle?"

I can't stop staring at the two of us together, looking like I never did with Corbin. "It's nothing. I swear." I glance up at her. "I would have told you."

"You didn't have a chance since it happened last night, or did I read two o'clock?"

I want to laugh, to tell her all the good things about last night, but I know what these stories mean. Our lives are about to be turned upside down.

"We didn't have sex," I blurt like someone who's most definitely guilty. "I don't need to defend myself."

"No," she says, "not to me or anyone."

"Then why do I feel sick to my stomach?" I wrap my arms around my middle, wanting to curl inside myself and disappear. My eyes begin to water as reality sinks in. "I've made it so much worse for myself." Dropping my head into my hand, I squeeze my eyes closed. "And for Cash." All the good we shared is gone in the daylight. While I was flying, oblivious to the gossip splashed all over the internet, he's been dealing with this directly. I jerk up and look at Poppy. "He's going to hate me. More than he does already."

"He hates you? Why would he hate you?"

"I dragged him into this mess when he should be concentrating on the race today."

"Is this the club you were at when you texted me?"

"One and the same. I called him to save me." She's polite enough not to verbally judge me, but her eyebrows shoot up, and eyes stare ahead like she's in disbelief. As if it will make it any better, I add, "I had a few drinks and calling him seemed like a good idea at the time."

Her mouth straggles down at the ends. "Um. All right ... Well, since we can't turn back time and make a better decision, how can I fix this? Lauren?"

"Lauren's going to kill me. I'm shocked I haven't heard from her yet."

I pull my busted phone from my bag and turn it back on. Twenty-two texts and fourteen missed calls. "Yikes."

"Nothing is unfixable."

I glance over at her, and trepidation fills me as I pull up my contacts list. "I should call him."

"Are you sure?"

"No," I reply, already calling. "I'm not sure, but I—"

"Hel—" His voice cuts out, replaced by silence, so I pull the phone from my ear to stare at the screen. "Cash? Can you hear me?" I put it to my ear again, but the line only crackles, and then the screen goes out. "Cash?" I scramble to push buttons, but nothing brings my phone back to life. "Dammit!"

"What's wrong?"

"My phone died."

She grabs her phone from the charger. "You can use my charger."

"No, it's the phone. It's broken."

"How'd you break your phone?"

Some of the emotions I felt when Cash knocked it from my hand awaken. "Long story." I rub my temple in an attempt to soothe the rising panic taking over.

"It's going to be okay, just use mine." She must sense my anxiety because she reaches over again to pat my shoulder. "Call him back. Do you know his number?"

Shaking my head, I lean back on the headrest. I close my eyes, wanting to wake up to a new narrative. I can't wish it away, though. This is my reality. And now I've dragged Cash into it. "I don't have his number. I don't have anyone's number. That was my phone's job."

"Yeah, I get it."

We ride in silence for a few minutes as a million things run through my mind, everything from what Corbin is going to say to me, how he's going to spin this to his advantage, and how mad Lauren's going to be . . . is already. She knows every story before it breaks publicly. I'm surprised I didn't have a barrage of messages from her this morning. Maybe she's too busy trying to clean up this mess before dealing with me.

I finally say, "I've really made a mess of things, Pop."

"Nothing that everyone won't forget when the next story breaks." I appreciate how calm her voice is, and in the confines of the car, maybe my world won't come crashing down. "You know how this stuff works."

"I do, but I'm not usually the one in the middle of the storm."

"This storm will pass." A comforting smile engages her face. "But since we're in the middle of it . . . You and Cash Ryatt, huh?" She fans herself with her hand. "How hot was that?"

I laugh, just a little at first, but the release feels so good that I stop holding so tight to being upset. "He's so frustrating, borders on rude, can be offensive—"

"Gorgeous—"

"Absurdly attractive." I peek over at her. When her grin

splits her lips apart and she laughs, I continue. "Big, making me feel small in stature but not little in presence. He listens." My gaze drops to my lap. My fingers fidget with the hem of my shirt again as I remember the myriad of emotions he evoked.

"So how was the sex again?"

I burst out laughing again. We've known each other our entire lives, and there's a reason we're best friends. Poppy Stanfield never disappoints. "I swear, we did not have sex."

"Are you sure?"

"Pretty sure, Pop."

"I feel disappointed." She looks at me quickly. "How did you not throw yourself at him? You must have the willpower of a saint."

Memories of last night hit me.

Kissing him.

Groping his shoulders, ready to mount that man.

But when he placed that kiss on my shoulder and then wrapped his arm around me, holding me against him in bed, I've never felt safer or more cherished in my life. It doesn't make sense. He barely knows me. He barely likes me. *If* he likes me.

Doesn't matter.

I know he hates me now.

9

Marina

Surprisingly, acting like nothing is wrong doesn't actually make the gossip go away.

How very disappointing.

A broken phone also doesn't keep someone determined to get ahold of you from calling you either . . . I take the phone from Poppy, resting my case and point, and place it to my ear. "Hell—"

"What have you done, Marina?" My eldest brother has never been one to beat around the bush, but wow, I've never heard him so mad. He's a lawyer, so time is money, I guess, even when it comes to family.

I brace myself for the onslaught by sitting on the couch. "I can explain, Loch," I start, after just finishing telling Poppy everything, and I mean everything. From the argument in the paddock to the ride to dinner, the bathroom, and then how Cash held me like I was the only thing that mattered last night, I didn't leave out a detail.

Closing my eyes, I touch my lips, remembering how the

pressure of the connection was just right, how I not only got lost in that kiss but wished it could go on forever.

"Please explain," Loch says, leaving the fight for the courtroom instead of with his sister. He can be a softy when he wants to be.

I reply, "It's not as bad as it seems."

"It may not be, but we have two sponsors on the verge of leaving, and that's only from the implication of you two sleeping together."

"Marina, this is Harbor." If a call could end like a needle scratching across a record, that was it when Harbor took over for my eldest brother.

I flop back on the couch, not quite ready for the next lecture I'm doomed to receive. "I guess you're all there."

"We are." His tone is relatively calm, but I know him. He's good at neutrality, at least acting so. It's a characteristic he got from my father. Me, not so much. It's not a trait the youngest in the family usually inherits. "We've had the press hounding us since before the sun rose here in Miami. It's a race day, so I can't say I was sleeping, but I wasn't prepared for this shitstorm either."

I feel awful for so many reasons, but upsetting my family was never my intention. "I'm sorry." I say the only thing I can think of, though I know it won't make anything better. "I'll do whatever you need me to do, whatever it takes to make this better."

"It's not that simple, sis." There's a pause, and I can only imagine he's digging his fingers through his hair. That's something Cash does as well. *A guy thing?* Probably just to get their temper from escaping. I hear shuffling on his end, and he says, "I've taken you off speakerphone because I'd like to hear your side before I fire our driver for seducing my sister."

Seduce? People use that word? Guess it's more polite than the alternative. "Cash didn't seduce me, Harbor. He did do me a huge favor, but as you can see online, no good deed goes unpunished."

A loud noise has me pulling my phone from my ear. Eyeing Poppy, I laugh anxiously in silence.

Poppy mouths, "What's going on?"

I shrug, but then I hear, "Honey, it's Mom."

"Hi, Mom." I put her on speakerphone. "Poppy can also hear you now."

"Poppy? How are you, dear?"

Leaning toward the coffee table where I set the phone, she smiles at me, and replies, "I'm good, Mrs. Westcott."

"You're grown. Call me Delta, please."

"Mom, this is business," Harbor says in the background. I can only imagine he's pinching a nerve in his forehead right now.

"I know, but since we're all here . . ." More shuffling, then she says, "Can you hear us, Marina? I'm putting you on speaker."

"Yes, I can hear you."

"Dad and your brothers are here with me."

"Hi, honey." My dad's voice pops in, sounding so supportive as always.

"Hi," I reply again, unable to hide a giggle. How can I not laugh? This is a serious situation, and the whole family is involved now. At this rate, I'll be on this call all day. "Let me just start with the facts. When my friends abandoned me, I called Noah last night—"

"I had a missed call from her when I woke up," he says in the background, supporting my story, which I appreciate. "Sorry for not answering, Marina."

"You were sleeping," I reply, "I understand."

"Marina," my mom asks, "why did you call your brother so late?"

"Why did you go out at all?" Loch barges back onto the call with a sigh. "You're in the spotlight now. You're a celebrity. Anything could have happened to you, Marina."

I thought he was angry, but beneath that emotion lies the real one—*worry*.

"I didn't think it through. I just wanted to have fun." I hate sounding so careless or oblivious to the dangers my family sometimes faces. But what can I really tell them? I wanted to escape my life for a night, not to think about the impending humiliation I'm facing. I can't. That's a conversation I'm not ready to have with them. Although hearing the concern straining my oldest brother's voice has me reconsidering.

Just thinking about Corbin cheating because he didn't love me, he didn't want me, but worse, he wasn't attracted to me . . . my eyes water, but I refuse to let any tears fall over him. Hoping this is enough for us to move on, I reply, "I'm sorry. It was dumb. I'll do whatever you need me to so I can make this right for you."

"It's not about making it right for us," my dad says.

"Are you okay?" Harbor asks me.

"I left the club as soon—"

"We'll get to the play-by-play," Noah interjects. "Are you okay, Sis?"

The collective silence on the other end has me getting up and pacing. I take a deep breath and stop to stare at the Vancouver skyline. Their concern ripples through the conversation, and I don't want to worry them more than necessary. "I'm fine. All good."

A shushed balk from behind me has me turning back.

Poppy stands with her arms crossed over her chest and whispers, "Tell them about Corbin."

Covering the phone, I whisper, "I'm not adding more stress to the situation."

"They already think the worst because they don't know the truth."

The betrayal I feel streams through my veins as I stare at her in disbelief. Apparently, this is the line in the sand for her, my dating life, where she's taking a stand against me but on my behalf. *Go figure.*

I hate that Cash has been put in this fishbowl because of me, but now is not the time to drag Corbin's sins into this. I sit by the phone again and say, "The paparazzi were waiting for me like vultures who found their dinner."

"They got paid anyway," Poppy adds.

I cringe, glancing up at her. I think this might go smoother without the added commentary. I know she means well, so I just continue, "I hid in the bathroom and called you, but when you didn't answer, I didn't know what to do."

"How did Cash get involved?" Harbor asks.

"I called Liv, but she couldn't leave because the kids were sleeping."

"So you asked for our driver's number? There was no one else?" he says with a heavy sigh. "No one else you could have called to help you? Like me, for instance, your parents, Loch, and not the driver of a fifteen-million-dollar car with millions more than that on the line depending on how he performs today?"

"Well . . ." My throat dries, but I try to swallow. "When you put it like that. I had just enough drinks to think it was a good idea at the time." Shamefully, I look down and close my eyes. "I know it wasn't. I'm sorry for getting him involved."

Do I tell them that I was planning to only text him? That when I asked for the number, it wasn't my intention to plead for help? Time was a ticking bomb in that bathroom when panic set in as if having me under fire would be a victory for Corbin's team. I called the number because I knew Cash would help me.

Lauren should have never planted that seed. Nothing good has come of a plan I had no business being a part of. It's not like her to make missteps like this, but it's not like me either. And me repeatedly saying I wasn't thinking is just no excuse.

"She was right for helping you," Noah says of his wife. "We were just blindsided by the news this morning. I have more fires to put out, so I need to go. We've all been hit hard with this story today."

"I'm sorry." I'm out of justifications because I never had a good one to begin with. Maybe it wasn't a fear of being asked about the cheating. Maybe subconsciously I sabotaged myself as well as Cash.

Cash . . .

I feel awful for the damage I've caused him.

Harbor says, "Don't talk to the press. Have you spoken with Cash today?"

"No." I'm not sure if I should ask or if it will make things worse, but I do worry. "Is he okay?"

I'm met with silence before someone clears their throat. "He was . . ." *Loch.* "Upset this morning. But he's also a professional who performs under pressure every time he's on the track. Today will be no different. He needs to stay out of his head and focus. That easy."

"That easy," I reply more for myself. "You didn't ask, but we never . . ." *Why is this so hard to say to them?*

"We understand, Marina." Harbor saves me the pain of having to spell it out in front of my parents.

I slide forward in the chair and pick the phone up again. Taking it off speaker, I hold it to my ear. "I'm sorry about the sponsors."

"Sponsors are like skittish kittens. They thrive on threatening to pull out their money. It's their way of feeling like they have control of the situation," Harbor says with conviction set in his tone. "Unfortunately, I need to go and deal with this mess." He pauses, and for some reason, it concerns me.

"Hello?" I say, making sure they're still there.

"Marina," he says, "you need to keep your distance from Cash and the races in general until this settles down."

I'm being grounded? Well, this is humiliating. I dip my head and rub my temple that's starting to throb. I gather the strength anyway and ask on an exhale, "Are you asking me?"

"No." The answer is blunt, though I know it wasn't said maliciously.

Why does it feel like I just had the rug pulled out from under me? "*Oh . . .Okay,*" I whisper, "if that will help."

"Yeah," Harbor says, "it's for the best, Sis."

I hate this, the pressure they're under, the tension between us, the mess I caused. My heart has sunk deeper into the pit of my stomach with this news than initially getting in trouble. "I understand."

Loch says, "We'll have you out again, but let's just put a pin in any visits until we can get ahead of this story or it fades. Just for now."

"I understand. I didn't mean to—"

"We know," he adds. "We need time to get things under control."

"Of course."

Goodbyes are heard from the other end as I hang up and give the phone back to Poppy. I feel better that they know the truth but sick about how much trouble I've caused them.

As much as I'd love for this all to be swept away with the tide tonight, I know it won't be. I look at her, still slumped in the chair. "What do I do? How do I make it better?"

"I'm not sure you can without risking more bad publicity."

A knock has us both looking toward the door. She asks, "Did you order something?"

"No."

"Hm." She pushes up and goes to answer it. Signing for a package, she waits to say anything until the door is closed and locked again. "A hand-delivered package." Showing off the purple ribbon wrapped around it, she lets it fall over the side again. "Fancy."

We stare at the white box and silky bow when she sets it on the table. It's not big, but big enough to be dangerous. "Is it safe? Should we call the police?"

She laughs. "I'll open it." Taking it, she tugs the ribbon first and then lifts the side flap. A sealed box with an image of a rose gold phone slides out. "Ooh, this is nice. Who's it from?"

I grin, taking it from her. Biting my lip, I'm not sure if I'll make it worse by telling her or if I should keep my mouth shut. There's no way she's going to let this slide, though. I know Poppy too well. For what it's worth, if I were her, I wouldn't let it go without knowing who sent it either.

10

Cash

"HEY, buddy, how are you? Miss you."

"Miss you, Daddy." My chest tightens hearing Cullen's voice, the strain of sadness weaving through it. "When do I see you?"

He's the first one I called after coming off the track, straight in here, hoping to catch him. "Tomorrow. I can't wait."

"Do I get ice cream?"

"Yep. What flavor?"

He giggles, filling the holes the time apart has left inside my heart. "Bubblegum."

"It's good, right?" I walk to the back of the room, leaning my head against the wall with the phone cradled in my hand. It's not that I need a five-year-old's approval, but I want to keep the connection with him, hoping he understands why I leave so often during the season. "How'd I race today?"

"You had a race?"

Forget the media mess this morning, the questions asked about Marina and me, despite the excitement in my son's voice, I'm gutted by those four words alone. She's broken our agreement before, but hearing that my kid didn't even know I was racing . . . I should expect this from her, but that doesn't ease the blow that he didn't know. "Yeah." I struggle to sound positive, but I do it for him. "Came in sixth."

"You got points."

"I did. Hey, so have your stuff ready tomorrow when I pick you up. I'll be there at two o'clock, okay?"

"Okay."

Normally, I'd touch base with Terpidy, but I'm too angry to stay calm, and anything above a whisper pisses her off, so I let it lie for now. "I love you, Cully."

"Love you, Daddy."

I hang up and stay in the peace of the room for a moment longer. "I did it." I fucking did it, putting points on the board for my team. After the disappointment I could see in their eyes, if I'm being generous, I hope this can redeem me in light of the situation with their sister.

Marina has been on my mind too much—the softness of her skin, the curve of her hips, the pink of her lips that I couldn't resist. Fuck, I can't do this.

Off-limits.

I've been warned . . .

Since I'm still in my racing suit, I push off the wall and start stripping it off, anxious to get out of here. But if I'm going to face cameras on the way out, I need to take a shower.

"You did it." I recognize the voice as two hands clap down on my shoulders. *I had gotten so close to escaping the track without another lecture.*

"I made a deal." I laugh as Noah comes to walk beside me as I exit the paddock.

"You kept it. It's unheard of," he says, looking up at the sky behind his sunglasses, "to do this well as a new team."

We keep walking, but I sense there's more he's not saying. I stop and cross my arms over my chest. "What is it?"

He stops, shifting a bit. "You did great with the post-race press, but we need to steer clear of any questions regarding my sister. If they ask you about last night or her, tell them it's not something you're commenting on. It's better to leave it vague than to give them something to feed off."

We look around, noticing eyes that wouldn't typically be on us as other teams tilt their ears to eavesdrop. P1 racing has the biggest bunch of gossips. Always has.

Walking again, Noah keeps his eyes ahead. "We talked with Marina earlier. She regrets dragging you into her predicament."

"She doesn't need to regret anything."

"My sister has . . ." I glance at him, wondering if he's going to throw her under the bus. Other than my mom, there's no one in my family to choose to speak to anymore. I've had photos from my childhood sold to high bidders, stories that I thought were once great memories tainted as I read about them in the press.

I feel like the Westcotts are genuine in protecting their own, but there's money on the line, so you never know. Money changes everyone, everybody I've known.

The harsh lines of his expression stagger into sympathy when he looks back at me. "She had expectations placed on her that I never had to deal with growing up. She's in the spotlight now, but she always was at parties and school. It's not of my family's doing. The world took notice of Marina Westcott early on." He pauses again as if searching for the right words. "She can hold her own, but she shouldn't have to all the time."

I appreciate hearing the respect he has for her. I know they're close, but I like that they're friends. "Can I be honest with you?" he asks.

"I hope you're always honest with me, Noah."

He nods. "I worry about her. She's pulled away the last few months, which is unlike her. Did she talk to you about anything that might be going on?"

Her ex.

The cheating.

Going out seeking revenge.

"You should probably ask your sister," I say, walking ahead.

He stops. "Does that mean you know something?"

Turning back, I keep walking but throw my arms out. "Not getting involved in Westcott family business except as a driver. Have a good one."

"Yeah, have a good one."

Slipping through the rest of the paddock and avoiding any press hanging around, I weave to the back where I see the car waiting for me. My bag is already loaded into the back when I slip inside the vehicle with Duncan, my trainer, behind the wheel. As soon as I put my seat belt on because he's a stickler for safety, he drives toward the exit. "You earned that spot today," he says with eyes on the road ahead. "You should be proud."

"I feel . . ." *Accomplished. Redeemed. Proud.* "I feel good about my performance."

"The work we've been doing physically and the focus

you have with your mental game are paying off." He glances at me. "How are you holding up after the grilling?"

Chuckling, I reply, "It wasn't bad. Only a few questions about last night. I think once I stayed quiet on the subject, they realized they needed to get something from me. I can talk racing all day long."

"Figured you were hearing about the incident enough, but I need to know where your head is at or if we need to make some adjustments."

"It's not an incident, so no adjustments are needed. My head is in the race. Twenty-four seven."

"Okay. I'm trying to help you avoid what happened last time."

My anger rises, and I scrub my hands over my face. I shoot him a look, unable to hold back anymore. "Fucking hell. Nothing happened, Duncan. The woman needed help. That's it."

"I laid off you this morning. Got you through your warm-up without a fucking word, Cash. You may have been over there with the owners, but I didn't give you a hard time."

We're friends. *Real friends.* Been through hell and back together in this career. I need to remember that. He's always had my back and helped me crawl out of my lowest point ever a few years back. Duncan is one of the reasons I'm back on the track.

"Sorry." I take a deep breath and exhale slowly. "Last night has been made into a bigger deal than it was. If I would have known this is how it would play out, I would have fucked her." I feel shitty the second the words leave my mouth.

Rubbing my brow, I say, "I shouldn't have said that."

"Why?" His eyes dart over to me quickly before giving me the space I prefer.

"Because she doesn't deserve to be spoken about like that." What am I doing? Making it worse? I can tell him anything, and he won't hold it against me, but he can also see right through me. Fuck.

"It's okay to be into someone. We just need to make the appropriate mental adjustments."

The car stops at the hotel, and I pop open the door. With one foot already out, I look at him. "I'm not dating anyone. I'm not fucking anyone. I don't need any mental adjustments." I get out but duck my head back in. "If you're going to be on the jet, be ready in one hour. I'll meet you in the lobby." I shut the door and walk into the hotel.

I don't know what's happening, but everyone seems to have lost their minds in Miami, including me. It must be the heat and sunshine. New York is calling.

As soon as I drop my bag on the floor at the door, I toss my wallet and phone on the coffee table and flop into a chair. Studying the hotel room, I see most of my stuff has already been shoved in my suitcase by the door, but a few odds and ends remain.

Getting up, I start gathering the rest of my belongings. I'm ready to get back. It's only a few days, but I'll take the much-needed break. Bonus: I get to see my son. I retrieve my toiletries to shove in my smaller case when my phone vibrates against the glass table. I hurry back to see a familiar number on the screen, and it creases into my cheeks.

Fuck me.

A grin is the last thing I should be doing when I see that number. I pick it up and answer, "Hello?" With a shrug popping my shoulders, I move to the windows with an endless Miami beach view.

"Hi. This is . . ." She sounds like she's taking a breath to brace herself. "This is Marina. Marina Westcott."

"I know. Otherwise, I wouldn't have answered."

"Oh," she starts, a lilt lifting the word. "Thank you. I didn't know how you'd react to me calling. I was . . ." This is not the woman I met in the paddock, the woman who set the place on fire, refusing to let me get away with an obvious stunt. The fight in her has subsided.

When she pauses at a seemingly silent impasse, I ask, "How are you?"

"I've been better. You?" A gasp is heard. "Oh my God, you came in sixth. Congratulations! It was an awesome race."

I find myself grinning for real this time around. "You watched?"

"It was on a TV nearby," she deadpans. I recognize that snark.

Chuckling, I ask, ready to list a thousand places. P1 racing is a top sport in the world, so I'm not surprised it was on somewhere in her vicinity. I am surprised she stopped to watch, though. "Oh yeah, a restaurant? Sports bar? Lobby of your hotel?"

"Um, uh." She's quieter than a mouse. "My apart*mmm*."

"I missed that. Where again?" I grip the phone to my ear just in case the connection is bad.

"My apartment, Ryan." Ryan? *There's my girl . . .* Wait, not my girl. She is not my girl. I look back like Duncan might have overheard me because I'm fucking paranoid. He's not even here. *Fuck.* I run a hand through my hair. No adjustments to be made in my life to accommodate a girlfriend. *Been there. Done that.* Not ever going back while I'm racing on the track.

"So what you're saying is that you purposely watched me race today?"

A huff covers the distance, reaching my ears before she adds, "Happy now?"

"I am actually." Though I know better, laughing after all the drama today still feels good. Looking down, I shift my feet, then move to sit on the couch. "So . . .?"

"So I called even though I was told not to—"

"Who told you not to?" Images of punching someone in the face for that bad advice come to mind.

"Everyone."

"Ah. Sounds familiar." I lean back on the couch, setting my feet up on the edge of the table. "I heard the same."

Lighter laughter trickles from the other end. "I wanted to tell you that I'm sorry for involving you. I should have known better with all the paparazzi there. Those photos didn't age well in the light of day."

"At least they got my good side."

"I don't think you have a bad side."

My brows shoot up. Thinking I misheard her again, I laugh. "You buttering me up, sweetheart?"

"Maybe."

I turn on the speaker and set the phone down next to me. Staring out the windows again, it's nothing but blue skies from where I'm sitting, but I'm still cautious. I have to be. "So the call had a purpose?"

"I wanted to thank you for the phone."

"Okay." I kind of wish I had a photo of her that wasn't shared with the world, one just for me. I'd be looking at it right now instead of the blank screen. "Go ahead."

A burst of laughter comes with a reply, "Thank you, Cash, for the phone."

"You're welcome."

"It will be a constant reminder of how I was right, and you were wrong." Her giggle populates like champagne bubbles through our connection.

"I bought the phone so you could see the mess we made online like I have to."

"It's quite the mess." As our laughter dies down, she adds, "I've been banned from the track." Her tone is softer, her words more forgiving.

The punch comes with the admission. I'm not surprised, but it's bullshit. "Forever?"

"For now."

I nod, though she can't see me. Sitting up, I say, "Good thing we don't exist in each other's worlds." Nothing about that feels genuine. Even I don't believe the lies I'm spewing.

"Yeah . . . good thing." A quick pause is cut short. "I should let you go."

"You don't have to." No adjustments. Life is smooth right now. Don't wreak havoc on your career over a woman. "I didn't mean it how it came out."

"How did you mean it, Cash?"

"You're there, and I'm here, and . . . we've just not run into each other before."

I can't see her, but I'm nodding like this makes sense. It doesn't, not to me. I'm pretty fucking sure it doesn't to her either. I lower my voice. "Look, Marina, I'm not upset about last night. I let myself down in other ways, but I don't regret the time with you."

"Do you mean that?" Her breathy and quiet voice matches mine.

"I mean it. Fortunately, it didn't fuck up my race. That'd be a different story."

"You did better today."

The truth should probably sting, but it doesn't. Smiling again, I ask, "Are you taking credit?"

"Never, but *ifffff* I had anything to do with it, you'd tell me, right?"

I chuckle. "I'll tell you, babe." A knock on the door gets me back to my feet. "I need to go. I have a flight to catch."

"Thanks again for the phone."

"No problem." If a conversation could be dragged out, this one fits the definition. I'm not eager to hang up either, though. I put the phone to my ear again and walk toward the door, but before I answer it, I say, "Hey."

"Yes?"

"You have my number, Marina. You can call me anytime."

Her emotions feed into her voice, and she lets a laugh escape. "Like a secret only we share."

"Anytime you feel the urge."

"Same goes for you," she adds. "Take care, Cash."

"You, too."

We hang up, and it's impossible to wipe the stupid grin from my face. I open the door and immediately walk away so Duncan can't see me. "Almost done packing."

"Need some help?"

"Need? No. But I'm happy to let you grab my suitcase." I chuckle, feeling lighter than I have in a while. He doesn't need to know the real reason.

No one does.

It will be a secret only Marina and I share.

No adjustments needed.

Marina

MONDAY . . .

LYING BROWN EYES.

> *Each strand of hair strategically placed.*
> *Smarmy grin that makes me sick to my stomach.*

"Cut." The director strides across the set to stand in front of me. "You're supposed to be in love with him, yet I'm getting black widow vibes instead. Do you need a break, Marina?"

Although a break would give me a brief reprieve from looking at the asshole formerly known as my boyfriend, I choose to be a professional. "No. I'm ready."

His brows pinch together. "You sure?"

"I'm sure, Gerald."

Patting Corbin on the back, he tells him, "Great job. Keep it up."

"I will," Corbin replies with a fake-ass smile on his lying

face. Turning to me, he whispers, "I'm the jilted lover here, so you better pull it together."

"Jilted?" I balk in his face, then whisper, "You? You're an assh—"

"Quiet on the set," a voice rings out, the clapboard slamming closed right after.

Corbin dips his head and then looks up slowly. For a method actor, he sure did struggle to believe he was already taken. "I love you, Debra."

"What is love but something hopeless romantics speak of?"

"Love embodies us, perfumes the air, and . . ." His goofy grin falls as he looks back at me. "Love is all I have to give."

I turn my back to him and close my eyes, lowering my head solemnly just as I remember the script instructing. "Love isn't enough when I've already said yes to another." Turning around, I poke him in the chest. "Why couldn't you tell me before I said yes to Nathaniel? Why did you lie when I asked you if you felt anything for me at the lake last summer? Why did you date Rosie if you loved me so much? Why, Clark?"

"Because I was too shy, too weak, too confused, so I let you go, hoping it would pass. But it hasn't."

Looking him straight in the eyes, I say without hesitation, "You're too late. My heart already belongs to another."

"Cut." Gerald's footsteps echo in the space between us until he appears in the spotlight with us. "Great job. How are you feeling about it?"

"Better than ever." I smirk because I'm not perfect and since sarcasm isn't appropriate, it comes out in my facial expression.

Corbin says, "There was a line that I feel Marina could have delivered—"

"Have a great night, Gerald," I say, walking away.

Gerald announces, "That's a wrap for the night."

Grabbing my water from my chair, I hurry toward the sound stage exit.

"Marina?" Corbin calls out, closing in on me. "Wait up."

Why the heck would I wait on his command? He's so out of touch with reality. Picking up my pace, I head toward my trailer. I open the door, but it stops hard in his hand before I can close it. Glaring at him, I grind my teeth. "Let go."

"We need to talk."

"We don't need to do anything. If you'd like to say something to me, have your people contact mine." I bat my eyelashes with a fake-as-he-is grin on my face, then reach down and yank the door. When he doesn't release the door, I snap, "Leave before I scream."

Staring at me, he dares to take a step up. "You wouldn't—"

"And then security escorted him to his trailer," I tell Poppy over dinner later that night.

We're sitting at my favorite burger place in Vancouver and keep eating as if this is normal for our everyday lives. It's not, but it's nice not to carry the burden of caring so much.

She shoves another fry in her mouth and shakes her head. "This is going to get out of hand fast if you're not careful."

"I was careful." I roll my eyes. "Before the other night with Cash." Swirling a fry between us, I then jab the air. "But it got out of hand when he cheated on me."

"Now he thinks you cheated on him as well, and you didn't."

"I don't care what he thinks. We're broken up." I take a gulp of beer, then set the glass down. Dragging my finger up the pint glass, I collect the condensation on the tip. I look around to see if any eyes are on me. There always are, but none that feel intrusive. The privacy I'm given here is one of the reasons I like this place so much. And the burgers and fries can't be beat. "I'm over Corbin Darian and catering to his whims, him stealing my mascara to make his eyes pop for the fans, and his dumb excuses."

"What excuses has he given?"

"None. That's the other problem I have." Poking myself in the chest, I reply, "I'm not even warranted a pleading for forgiveness conversation, worth lying to my face to keep me in that relationship. I don't matter enough for him to even call me over the weekend. So I can't give him more than he's given me."

Her gaze stretches across the room and she appears deep in thought as she chews her food. When she's done, she looks back at me. "I'm sorry you've had to go through that on your own. I wish you would have told me."

"I did when I knew."

"I wish you would have told me what was going on all along. As your friend, we could have plotted his murder. Now we're stuck with him until the end of the movie." She cracks a smile, prompting my own. "Also, tell me about the mascara. I'm always searching for a great one."

Laughing out loud, I cover my mouth, so the restaurant isn't exposed to me eating. "I can hook you up," I say behind my hand. When I can finally speak freely again, I lean forward, and whisper, "I talked to Cash yesterday."

She does a double take, and her mouth drops open. "What the hell? Why am I only finding out about this now?" Her lips twist to the side, and she raises her brow. I've seen Poppy genuinely angry twice, and this isn't one of them.

I giggle but still shrug, playing it off like it's no big deal that I talked to the man I claim I can't stand. I can stand him ... too much. That's also becoming a problem.

Two fingers are snapped in front of my face. "Marina?" My gaze darts to hers and she says, "You lied yesterday. You really do like him."

My spine straightens in offense. "No, I don't."

There's that brow again. "You sure about that?"

I dip a fry in ketchup and eat half, keeping my eyes on the condiment on my plate. "He's positively awful." I smile to myself while forcing my shoulders to shudder. "He broke my phone." I glance up with all the intensity I can muster for effect. With her eyes set on mine, though, she's not just staring at me. Poppy can see right through me.

I continue because the guilty always ramble. "He's intolerable. Sure, he helped me out of that club and kissed me like I've never been kissed before, but that doesn't mean he's Mr. Wonderful." Cue eye roll for added drama.

Resting her arms on the table, she whispers, "Again, are you sure about that?" She taps her chin. "What I recall from prior mentions of Mr. Ryatt, 'absurdly attractive' had a small part in the conversation."

"Very small, Pops. He's almost impossible to look at," I lie between my teeth. Looking away from her again, I can't stop myself from grinning as I think about him now.

"You do realize you're an actress, right? Like this is the profession you've chosen, yet look at you. You're smiling like a sixteen-year-old when the hot quarterback asks you out. And since I was a front-row witness to that event, I recognize it." Lowering her voice, she says, "Since we both remember how horrible that turned out, I have one warning for you."

Tilting my head, I ask, "Which is?"

"If he'll break your phone, you better be careful with your heart."

I nod because she's not wrong. "Wise words."

"If it makes a difference, though . . ." She twirls her finger between us. "It sure is good to see you happy. I feel like it's been a while."

"Too long. Ironic since I was supposed to be happy with Corbin."

"You weren't happy with him. You were . . ." The bill is dropped off. Poppy slaps her credit card down too fast for me to cover it. "It's on me. I appreciate you letting me stay with you."

"Thank you."

And then it's swiped away by the server almost as quickly. As if there was never an interruption, Poppy continues, "You were waiting."

"Waiting for what?"

"I'm not sure." She sounds as perplexed as I am. "I just know you're not where you're supposed to be."

I could reply with a snarky comment, but I don't. Instead, I let her words sink in. She's right. I'm not where I'm supposed to be—in my career or in life—and it has nothing to do with where I'm currently seated. Glancing at my phone, I think about my earlier call with my agent. "Lauren said I blew the hard work she'd put into Corbin's team. They were signed on for a reconciliation on the red carpet that would have apparently had the world swooning. Now they're going in a different direction."

"What direction is that?" Her high pitch reflects my annoyance as well.

"I have no idea. I have a feeling I'll be blindsided again."

She reaches over and covers the top of my hand. "I hate that and Corbin, but listen to me, Marina. I respect Lauren, but she's not always right. You don't need to have a red-carpet reunion with a cheating asshole. You need to find your happiness again and live life for you."

"I could ruin my career if I do that."

"You could ruin your life if you don't." Sitting back, she adds, "You don't have to live by everyone else's rules." She smiles. "Don't let anyone define you. Only you have that right."

Poppy's my best friend for a reason. Through thick and thin, ebbs and flows of life, she's always been there for me and I for her. I laugh, then roll my eyes. "Fine, you can stay as long as you want."

She giggles. "That was easy."

"Seriously, though, it's good to spend time with you. With you around, I feel more myself again. It's like my backbone had caved to be a good girl, as I'm called too often by producers and Hollywood types."

"It's more fun being a bad girl anyway."

I sit back again when the card is returned. "Maybe it's time for an image change."

"You don't need to change. You don't need to lie. You just need to live for yourself. Screw everybody else and their opinions." She signs the bill and hops off her barstool. "Come on, let's get out of here. I saw a cute shop down the street. Let's go shopping."

The eyes that spied us earlier follow us out the door. Out on the sidewalk, I loop my arm with hers, already feeling better in the sunshine. "I never made a good bad girl."

"You've never tried before."

"The role was already cast," I say, eyeing her and then laughing.

"I'm not as bad as I could have been." She stops and readjusts her bag from her arm to her hand. I slip on a pair of sunglasses when she says, "Maybe it's time for us to switch parts?"

"That's not an entirely bad idea. If we can't beat 'em—"

"Make them regret ever meeting you."

My jaw drops open. "That escalated quickly. I was going to say make them regret underestimating me."

Her shoulders jump just as she loops her arm with mine again. "That works, too."

I'm not arrogant enough to think I'm special. Women are cheated on all the time. I've even been cheated on before. But it's different when it's played out in front of the world. The thing is, I'm the bad guy in the media right now. So if they're going to brand me with a scarlet letter, I might as well make it worth it.

While Poppy looks at shoes, which is the last thing I need to be buying when thinking about my collection at the apartment, I pull out my phone and text Cash: *Is Ryatt your real last name?*

12

Cash

Who is this?

Staring down at my phone, I send the text with a grin, knowing full well who it is. I finish filling the two glasses with ice, then check for her reply: *Very funny.*

My phone rings.

I'm both surprised and impressed by the bold move of her calling me, and answer, "Hello?"

"I don't think Ryatt is your real last name."

"It's not."

"What?" The shock in her voice resounds through the connection. "It's not? Do people know this? Is it public knowledge?"

"It's not a secret, but it's not something I advertise either."

There's a pause, but then she asks, "What's your last name?"

"You don't do any research, do you?"

"I do plenty for characters or restaurant reviews.

Research on people I know is something I avoid if I can. I'd
rather know the real them."

"Sounds like you're catching on to the manipulation of
the media."

"If I didn't prior, I do after the other night. Today is the
first time I feel like I can breathe a little." The sound of her
breathing rushes forward as if she's sat down. "There was
only one encounter. I consider that a win."

"What happened?"

"A photographer jumped out of the bushes when I was
walking on the sidewalk earlier. Scared the crap out of me."

"Their behavior is out of hand. He would have been on
the ground had he done it to me."

"Well . . ." Soft laughter echoes across the line. I like her
voice, but I love hearing her laughter. "I did throw my iced
coffee at him, but that was pure reflex."

I fill the glasses with chilled tea and pull a cup from the
cabinet. "Tell me you didn't help clean him up."

"My manners got the best of me."

A disappointed sigh releases from my chest. "They'll
never learn if you're kind to them."

There's only a brief silence before she says, "I don't want
to turn into some harder version of myself. I get why it
happens, but I'd rather be kind than miserable."

"See, it's not a stretch for me, so I guess that's one of the
many ways we differ, babe."

A huff hits my ears, and she says, "I'm starting to think
you're not as bad as the rumors make you out to be."

"Guess you'll never know."

That gets her laughing. "I don't know. Maybe this is blossoming into a beautiful friendship."

The suggestion of being friends with her isn't as bad as I
thought when we first met. I say, "Warren."

"Warren?"

"That's my real last name."

I don't know why I imagine her with a big grin on her face—victorious or sincere—but I guess I'll never know. "That's a good name."

"Thanks."

"Do I get the story behind Ryatt?"

"One day. Over drinks, maybe."

"That sounds more like a date, Mr. Ryatt. Are you asking me out?"

There are times in your life when you are surefire set on an idea because it feels right. This feels right.

Then reality sets in.

I rub the back of my neck, glancing up at my mom and son out on the terrace finger painting together. "I spoke out of—"

"I'm just kidding," she says, not sounding like she was joking at all.

Fuck.

"The team. Your brothers—"

"So many reasons would make dating a bad idea." It's not hard to catch the strain of disappointment in her tone.

I feel the same, but my son's legacy is important to me. "I'm sorry," I add as if that will change the downward turn this conversation has taken.

"No. No need to be. I should go, though."

I fill the cup with apple juice and sigh. "Yeah, me too." Sucks it had to end this way. "Take care, okay?"

"You, too. Bye." She hangs up so fast that I don't get to say goodbye on my end.

Women are so fucking complicated. I leave my phone on the counter and take the drinks outside. "Who's thirsty?"

"Me," Cullen says, raising his painted hand. His blue

eyes match mine, his hair straddling between Terpidy's brown and my darker blond. It just started changing this year. It was all me until he was four. Not an ounce of this kid could be denied as mine. I would never, but thinking back, Terpidy got what she wanted until I lost my contract.

Suddenly, pieces popped up online, suggesting that some model out of Brazil was the father. Since his eyes and hair were the opposite of mine, she struggled to sell that story to the press once they got photos of our son.

We didn't have a downfall. We had a reckoning with reality.

We have nothing to do with each other except co-parenting. Now, he and my mom are the only family I have and need.

I set the cup down in front of him and place my mom's glass on her side of the table before sitting beside my son. "Drink up, buddy." I point at his paper. "I really like this bird."

"It's a bear."

"Oh wow. Yeah, I can for sure see that. Ferocious. Are those the ears?"

He giggles. "That's his teeth, Daddy."

"Ah." I face-palm and laugh with him. I'm not the best at this stuff since I didn't have a father figure around to show me how to be a dad, but my mom always encouraged me, even if I was shit at something. She made me believe that failure was success in practice. I can only hope to parent as well as she did. . . still does.

"How about we wash our hands, Cullen?" my mom suggests.

He's already getting up before she finishes asking the question. He walks inside, and she gets up to follow him but stops just inside the door. "If you ever want a night off,

Cullen can stay at my apartment. I'm happy to host a sleepover."

"If that is something he wants to do, we can arrange that, but you don't need to take him for me."

"I know you don't get a lot of time off, and when you do, you have Cullen—"

"I want to spend time with him. I don't get much as it is with being on the road all the time during the race season."

"I know. You're a great father, Cash. You're also a good man and a great catch. I just want you to know that if you don't want to be alone, you don't have to be."

"What brought this on?"

"Just haven't seen you smile like that in a long time. I thought it might have something to do with that phone call you were on."

Cullen yells, "Grandma," from the bathroom.

She looks in that direction and back at me. "I better get that kid washed up before he makes a mess."

Eyeing the paint that missed the paper and ended up on my outdoor table, I say, "Bigger mess?"

She laughs. "Yes, bigger mess than he already has."

When she disappears inside, I'm left alone with my thoughts and the same smile I wore while talking to Marina before things turned at the end. I go back inside and grab my phone. Returning to the terrace, I look out over the city as the day starts fading. The weather couldn't be better, but I noticed my mood improved considerably when I spoke to her.

She put herself out there and called. The least I can do is text.

Me: *You know . . . if we ever find ourselves in the same place again, we could have dinner together? And so there's no confusion, this is me asking you out on a date.*

Not leaving me to suffer, she texts: *If we found ourselves in the same place at the same time, it only makes sense to eat together. Who are we to say no if the opportunity presents itself?*

"There's that smile again," my mom says, returning to sit at the table.

Cullen races outside and into my arms. With his arms wrapped around my neck, and mine around his torso, we hug. He says, "Bear hug. Roar."

I dip my face into his shoulder and close my eyes. "I love you, buddy."

"Love you, Daddy." He pushes off me and runs to where his cars are set up on a rug closer to the door.

Catching my mom watching me, she gives me a smile in return. "Is she worth mentioning? Or something passing by."

"I'm not sure." I am sure of one thing, though—my mom is right. This smile feels different from what I'm used to. Cullen has me grinning in pride, love, and happiness just from being around him.

Marina . . . this smile feels different. It has hope entwined. And now I sound like a fucking poet. I should kick my own ass for even having that thought.

That doesn't stop me from texting her back: *It's a date.*

Marina: *Same place. Same time. You're on.*

I managed to open communication back up by being honest. Should we be dating? Fuck no. Did I consider the repercussions before asking her out? Yes, I did. In detail? Nope. I led with my gut.

With my son playing with race cars and my mom soaking in the evening sun, I realize I've never played it safe. And my gut has never led me wrong.

"Is this what we do now? Call each other each night like they did in *When Harry Met Sally*?" Marina asks the next night. East Coast late since she's on the west coast of Canada eating a salad and watching *The Bachelor* finale with her friend.

"I never saw it."

"You never saw it?" Her question is riddled with sheer astonishment that I'd have the audacity not to see every movie ever made just in case we decide to talk about it one night.

With Cullen already asleep, I lie in bed clicking through the channels before I decide to turn off the TV and listen to the sounds of the city and her instead. "It's from the eighties, right?"

"Barely." She huffs. "What am I going to do with you, Cash?"

"Shortcut to the plot so we're on the same page."

"They were old friends who call each other each night before bed to talk about their day."

Even on the ninth floor, sirens can be heard. It makes it difficult to sleep when on the road due to the silence. "I suppose it's one way to pass the time."

"That's all our conversations mean to you? Come on, Warren. Work with me here." I like the way she's taken up calling me by my last name. I won't tell her that, but it's not bad hearing it from her. She says it like it matters to her, like I do. Dumb, I know, but it feels personal with her.

"What do you want me to say? I like that you can't stop calling me, like I'm now on speed dial as your late-night, run-through-the-day friend?"

"Yes." She laughs right before the sound of a large crunch.

I crack up. "I'm good with that." Getting up, I carry the phone into the kitchen. I'm not usually a snacker, but hearing her eating has made me hungry. "I just meant that I like our calls, Marina."

"No babe or sweetheart tonight, huh?"

Chuckling, I grab the milk and set it on the counter. "It's been a long day. I'm off my game." I grab a bowl and fill it with granola before adding milk. Asking her out seemed to be the magic to building a friendship. I wasn't looking for one, but I'm not upset about this direction. "Catch me tomorrow, though, and I'm all over it, babe."

WEDNESDAY...

"HELLO?" *11:19.* I've been lying in bed waiting for her to call for the past hour. I was starting to believe she wouldn't, so I'm glad she did.

"What do you do all day?" Marina Westcott is the nosiest person I've ever met. And I don't mind one bit.

"Sim driving."

"What's sim driving?"

Propping my pillow up on the headboard, I sit up. "Simulated. The tracks, the—"

"You fake drive when you're not actually driving? Why don't you just go drive a real car instead?"

"There are too many rules in place. We can't be on the tracks except for qualifying and the race. Otherwise, we'd have an advantage."

"Interesting." The sound of snoring hits me.

"Brutal." The woman gives no repreives. "Sorry for keeping you up," I tease.

"I'm kidding. I'm kidding." She laughs, then asks, "So your life is all about driving? Nothing else? For fun?"

"That is fun to me." I take a sip of water. "What do you do all day?" The quizzer has rubbed off on me. I don't mind answering all her questions, but she has me curious about her day-to-day.

"Ah." She perks up instantly by her tone. "If I'm on set, it's all day. I could be there for twelve hours or more. If I'm not required to be on set, it's a free day, though I have to squeeze in rehearsals at some point to be prepared the next day."

"So work? That's it?"

"Sadly, yes. Not so sadly, I have an audition this week that I'm excited about."

I love how joy takes over her tone. She's complicated to figure out but not when she's happy. She exudes it from two thousand miles away. "You like auditions?"

"No, it's not the audition. It's the potential of where it could lead. Excitement captures her breath. She releases it and says, "Musicals and plays are fun for me, so best of both worlds."

I understand the feeling well and grin. "That's how I feel when I get behind the wheel on race day. Like a kid doing what he loves again." I get up as she starts munching on chips and head into the kitchen. "You're going to cause me to gain weight and get disqualified."

"Sorry, it's dinnertime here."

"You're having chips for dinner?"

"Well," she says, taking a sip of something. "We also had

tacos, but that was at happy hour. It's worn off now. What's your favorite food?"

"I'll show you next time I see you." Wondering who she's happy-houring with, I ask, "Who is we?"

"If we keep making all these plans, we'll be too busy to enjoy them. Me and Poppy. I'd say you'd like her if you met her, but do you like anyone?" She punctuates her question with a lighthearted laugh.

I could fall into character and lie, but it's starting to feel natural to let my guard down with her. "I like you."

When the phone goes quiet for too long, like five seconds or something, I pick it up to make sure it didn't drop the call. "Hello?"

"I'm here." Everything about her tone has changed. *Shit.* Did I fuck up by telling her the truth?

"Why so serious?"

"Not serious. I just think that was a really sweet thing to say, Cash. Just when I get used to the grump who doesn't say much, you surprise me."

"Sometimes I surprise myself." Like every time I share something I don't typically tell anyone, but feel free to do so with Marina. "Remember that reputation I'm trying to up—"

"Yeah. Yeah. The whole bad boy thing." Her laughter trickles through her words. "I've been starting to question it. What made you so bad that they decided that title fit the best?"

I start to wonder if she can be scared off at this point. Nothing has worked so far. "A few accidents. An arrest. Bad relationship. The list goes on."

"I think it needs to be revisited. I just don't see you as bad as you want to be."

Chuckling, I say, "You could start a campaign."

"On it."

———

Thursday . . .

I hate Thursdays.

Four days with my son isn't enough.

He's had me serving him ice cream well after bedtime and jumping in puddles because who cares about expensive shoes when I can ruin them with Cullen. Watching him go-kart at an indoor track in Jersey was the highlight. He's going to be better than I've ever been.

I wish he could see me race, at least once, in person. I can already hear Terpidy arguing that it's too disruptive to his schedule. I could challenge that argument, but that won't change the fact that I need to respect her as his mother.

"Hop up, buddy." My mom takes his backpack while I lower down so Cullen can jump onto my back. As much as I love his curiosity, I don't think I can have another thirty minute conversation about the cracks in the sidewalk.

We start walking again. "We're booking it today," she says, eyeing me with a reserved smile.

"I can slow down."

"You don't need to do me any favors. I can keep up with you kids."

I chuckle, knowing she's the original speed demon in the family. I drive cars. She wears through sneakers.

Cullen's hand shoots out and points across the street. "Daddy. Candy!"

As luck would have it . . . It's not the candy I see, though. It's the woman shoving a piece of chocolate in her mouth.

The same woman I go to bed thinking about every night. That's when our eyes meet. Even from across the street, I can see that pretty face blush and a smile creasing her cheeks.

I cross the small two-way street and step onto the sidewalk with her. She's more beautiful than I remember, even with a spot of chocolate coating the corner of her mouth. I say, "Same time."

Her smile blooms for me. "Same place. A happy coincidence."

13

Cash

THE SUN IS ALREADY TOO low to shine in Marina's eyes, but they're still bright blue, staring into mine. "Not sure if you know this," she whispers, leaning in, "but someone is hanging on your back."

"There is?" Since Cullen is holding on, I reach around and pretend to discover him. "Wow, there is." Cullen giggles, his arms tightening around my neck. Playfully coughing because I'm not looking to scare my kid, I choke out, "Save me, Marina."

"I'm afraid there's no saving you." The little lift at the corners of her mouth has me catching my breath. Why do I feel like that will happen every time I see her?

Tilting around, she smiles at Cullen. "And who are you?"

"I'm a sloth."

"A sloth?" she replies in delight. "I love sloths. Did you know some are three times stronger than humans?"

Out of the corner of my eye, I see Cullen's arm fan out. Full of pride, he says, "I'm strong. My daddy says so."

"That's right, buddy." Glancing at Marina, I add, "You do not want to arm wrestle this kid. He'll take you down in seconds flat."

She steps back, looking between us with her hands up in caution. "Thanks for the warning." Her laughter blends with his, and I can't help but notice how open he is with her. His mom always calls him shy, but maybe it's the people she's bringing around him. *Fuck, more to worry about.*

Holding out her hand, Marina steps closer again. With a wide as sunshine grin, she says, "I'm Marina, and who are you, sir?"

He wiggles on my back in laughter. There's something about shaking hands that he finds so fun. He's been known to mimic me at headquarters when I've brought him around. Taking her hand, he shakes it hard. "I'm Cullen Ryatt, son of legend Cash Ryatt."

Oh shit. I chuckle this time with my hands out. "I swear to God, I did not teach him that."

"Uh-huh. Sure you didn't." Rubbing her bicep, she plays along. "Wow, you are strong. Thought you were about to take my arm off there."

Cullen loves the attention. He takes after his dad and mom that way. Terpidy and I both have sizable egos. There's no doubt we won't be able to save Cullen from the same fate.

"Hi," she replies, shifting on the sidewalk and closer to me. Strands of her hair blow wildly in the air when a gust of wind picks it up. She tries to gather it unsuccessfully. "What brings you down this street?"

As if it tells her anything, I glance down one way and then back to her. "When the weather is nice, we walk this way to drop him off at his mom's place."

Tucking her hair behind her ear, she glances in the direction my gaze sent her, and then at Cullen and me. "I didn't even realize you lived in the city. I mean, I knew you were here from our calls, but . . . I don't know." She shifts again. "I guess I just didn't imagine it." This time, she nods and tucks her fingertips into the front pockets of her denim. "Well, I should let you—"

"Come meet my mom." I signal to her by sending a look across the street.

Her reluctance reaches her eyes as she peeks across the street again. "Your mom. *Oh.* Um, okay."

"Don't be nervous." I lean in and whisper, "Unlike me, she's really nice."

Cullen giggles again.

We're just about to cross the street when a car comes rushing by. My arm swings out in front of her. She doesn't say anything, but judging by her restrained grin, she's definitely entertained. I shrug. "Habit."

"It's a good habit to have." She bounces on her toes a few times. I chuckle because the sugar seems to already be coursing through her. "If he's allowed to have a piece, I have a lollipop or chocolate?"

"I want candy," Cullen says, patting the top of my head like a bongo set, solidifying that candy is exactly what he doesn't need.

Should I say no? *Yep.* Will Terpidy be pissed that he's hopped up on sugar? *Absolutely.* Am I going to deny my kid this little ounce of childhood joy? *Nope.* "Lollipop, please."

"Yes!" He fist-pumps the air, causing Marina to light up even more. She's too beautiful for her own good.

The woman walks around in everyday life like she's a mere mortal. Her ex is stupid for letting her go, but he's a fucker for making her believe he deserved her love. If she were mine—

"Do you like grape?" she asks him, pulling a purple-wrapped lollipop from her bag.

"If it's candy, he likes it." His body vibrates from excitement.

Reaching around, I hold him under his bottom to secure him to my back. He thanks Marina without me having to remind him. *Progress.*

"You're welcome."

Holding another up to me, she asks, "What about you, Warren? Do you have a sweet tooth?" Nothing about my thoughts is appropriate right now, which is what she intended. Innocence has taken over her expression with wide eyes and batting eyelashes, but that flirtatious smile on her face gives away the underlying entendre.

If we were alone . . . I run a hand over the back of my neck, then shift. "I have a penchant for sweet things but not candy." I shoot her a wink.

I'm gifted with pinking cheeks and a breath that holds her chest captive a few seconds before being released. She clears her throat. "Well, um . . . maybe I should go meet your mom." Fanning herself with the small bag, she looks down the street as if looking for an escape. I don't blame her. This is a lot, and talking about my family isn't something we've gotten around to yet.

It was all fun and games, light and surface.

We cross the street. With my eyes on my mom, I can tell by the just so slight raise of her eyebrows that she knows this is the woman I've been talking to on the phone. As if my face heating didn't already give it away. I feel like a kid again. I always hated introducing girlfriends to my mom. Her opinion matters, and they don't stand a chance if she doesn't like them. Let's see how this goes. "Hey, Mom, this is my friend Marina Westcott. Marina, this is Laura Warren."

"Westcott?" Glancing from me to her, my mom asks, "As

in Westcott Racing?"

Pinching her fingers together, Marina replies, "In name only. My brothers are the stars of that operation. It's their baby." They shake hands. "It's very nice to meet you, Ms. Warren."

"You can call me Laura."

We start down the street together like we're on a casual Sunday stroll, the two of them making small talk about me, the nice weather, and how cute Cullen is. "I don't know much about Cash." Looking at me, she asks, "Are you an only child, or do you have siblings?"

"One was enough," I reply. "I'm sure."

My mom bursts out in laughter. "He was a handful, but Cash was and still is a great son. He's very considerate, and now we have Cullen." She tickles his ribs, sending him into a fit of giggles again. I'm sure the sugar has nothing to do with it.

I swing him around and land him on his feet beside me. Taking his hand, we walk at his speed, which is almost painful since he's so slow, but I'm not going to rush him the rest of the way back to his mother's. I want to savor every second with him.

My mom looks back at me, grinning like she already knows the whole story about Marina and me. She probably does since we were plastered online. Though she always seemed to know everything when I was growing up without the help of the press.

My mom asks, "You're an actress? Have you been in anything I've seen?"

Debating for all of two seconds whether I should save Marina from any embarrassment the question might have caused, I realize I don't have to save her. She's doing great on her own.

Marina says, "Maybe, but I'm newer to film. I moved from New York to LA, and before I could settle, I landed a few parts that kept me on location. I've been filming a two-movie deal in Vancouver for most of the past year."

"That's so exciting." My mom looks back at me. "Isn't that exciting, Cash? She's a celebrity."

As tempting as it is to roll my eyes, I can't be mad that my mom sees me as her son and not the name brand I've become. "Super exciting."

I receive a solid eye roll from Marina, which I can appreciate. Despite the good time I'm having, dread seeps in. While my mom and Marina keep chatting, I look down at Cullen. "How are you doing, buddy?"

"Great!"

He holds the stick in his hand, the candy demolished and long gone. Knowing we don't have far to go, I stop and kneel in front of him. I like to be eye level when I can. I want that trust built, for him to know how much I love him, for him to see it in my eyes. "Hey, so . . ." I fucking hate saying goodbye to him.

"Hey so." He grins at me.

I take the backpack from my mom and adjust it on his small shoulders, fussing with him, as she calls it. I can't help it. I don't get to do this stuff too often, so I find a way to be present in his life. "You're going to be good for your mom?"

His mouth goes to the side as sadness creeps in, but he reluctantly nods.

I say, "I want to talk to you every day, okay, buddy? Every day."

Cupping my face, he repeats, "Every day, Daddy."

"I want you to watch my race."

"Where are you racing?"

"I'll be in the South of France, and then I'll be back in

ten days." I bring him against me, burying him in my chest.

His arms come around me the best they can, and he holds me in them. "Miss you, Daddy."

I kiss the top of his head and hold him tighter. "I'm going to miss you, too, buddy." I hadn't realized the scene I was making until I open my eyes to find my mom and Marina staring. If I were to ever scare off a woman, having a kid with another will usually do it.

But it's not fear in Marina's eyes. It's tears. She looks up at the sky as if she can will them away. Between saying goodbye to Cullen and seeing her staring at me like I just hung the moon for her, my chest constricts. I don't let many people into my real life, but I'm glad she's a part of it now.

Standing back up, I pick him up and anchor him on my hip. Sure, he can walk, but I just want him closer these last few minutes. "I think it's best—"

"We'll wait here," my mom says, tapping Marina's arm with care. She gives Cullen a big hug and kiss, making sure to leave that lipstick mark on his face. I think it's because Terpidy once called her gross for kissing him, even on the cheek.

My mom has never been a vengeful person, but what can I say? The apple didn't fall far from the tree.

Cullen reaches out to hug Marina, who happily obliges his silent request. After the goodbyes, I carry him up the block, stopping at the base of the stairs. We both look up and then at each other. Just to be sure, I ask, "Are you okay?"

He nods. "Are you okay, Daddy?"

"I'll be okay." I give him one more hug and a kiss on the head before setting him on his feet. "Take care, buddy. I love you."

"I love you." He dashes up the stairs and pushes the button.

It takes a minute, but Terpidy opens the door. She looks at him and grins, kneeling to hug Cullen before shooting daggers at me. She scoots him inside the brownstone but stays, leaning her lithe frame against the entry. Crossing her arms over her chest, I can see by the determined look in her eyes that she's looking for a fight. "How many more races do you have left?"

We worked out custody based on our individual schedules, so I'm not sure why she's coming at me with this question. "I have races into December."

"I can't miss the next runway season because I'm stuck here babysitting."

"It's not babysitting when it's your own kid. It's parenting."

She rights herself, her arms falling to her sides. "I need to work, Cash." She's a pain in my ass, but she's still popular in the modeling world. Or so I thought. I guess I didn't realize she wasn't working.

Grabbing the concrete railing, I rest a foot on the first step. "We worked out the visitation schedule through the attorneys. I've paid you more than the required child support because I know you missed a few shows."

"Because Cullen was sick, and I had no one to take care of him."

I practice the breathwork Duncan taught me to lower my blood pressure. This whole issue angered me when it happened, so that she's throwing it in my face again is beyond infuriating. "My mom was available. She offered. You refused. That's not no one," I say, needing to temper myself. "That's his grandmother who loves him and would love to care for him." When she glances down the street from where we came, I ask, "What's this really about, Terpidy?"

Pressing her hand to her chest, she bends forward. "I can't be here all the time. You're off playing in cars and shamelessly sleeping around while I'm here raising your son."

There it is . . . she saw the story. *Will it ever fucking die down?*

Although it's none of her fucking business what or who I do in my own time, as it's also none of mine what she does in her free time unless it involves our son, her irritation tracks. She's got a jealous streak that's caused problems in the past. Ironic since she never cared about me, as she stated in court when fighting for monetary compensation in a judgment against me.

I've grown a lot. Giving in to her tantrums is just one way I don't indulge her anymore. "An entire team and company rely on me. Cullen and my mom do as well."

"What about my dreams?"

"We've worked out the schedule. If it's not a good fit, my mom said she'll take him a couple of nights a week. We can rearrange it to better suit your needs, but unless you let him travel with me—"

"You'd love that, wouldn't you, Cash? To take him so I look bad."

"I would love to bring him with me, but it would have nothing to do with making you look one way or the other."

"I don't want to turn down any more campaigns."

I'm over here trying to do anything I can to have more time with Cullen while she wants less. I can't wrap my head around what she's thinking. She fought me in court when I would have taken full custody. I begged her for it. I believed her speech in the judge's office.

I'll give her the benefit of the doubt because maybe it was true back then. We all change, for better or worse.

No matter what, though, Cullen deserves two parents willing to fight for him. It's clear that I'm the only one left in the battle. "You have my mom's number if you need a break or to take a job. I'll see you in ten days."

She goes inside and shuts the door without any response. A million questions are left unanswered, including if my son is in a stable environment. He appears in the window with a big grin for his daddy and waves.

I wave and give him a smile in return. I couldn't not. Smiling comes easy with him.

Returning to the other block, my mom is nowhere to be found, and Marina sits on a stoop waiting for me. I approach. "Hey there."

She stands on the first step when she sees me, dusting off the back of her jeans. "Hi. Your mom said she was tired and caught a car to her place."

"She runs 10ks," I say with a chuckle. "She wasn't tired. She wanted to give us time alone."

"Well, you shouldn't out her like that. Next time, just play along."

It's the late afternoon cool air, the light that always seems to find itself shining in her eyes when she looks up at me, and a lot about her that has me gravitating closer. I want to rub her hip and hold her close with the other hand. I want to caress her cheek and kiss her.

That would cause a real scandal if anyone caught us. I can't say that dissuades me though.

When I move a little closer, she asks, "So you like to be called Daddy?" She bites her lip while her eyes stare into mine, insinuating everything.

Damn...

She's going to be the fucking death of me.

14

Cash

"I'VE NEVER BEEN one to play games when it comes to sex, but that mouth of yours is going to get you in trouble."

"That's what I'm counting on, *Daddy*."

Fuck me . . . I'm sure my gulp can be heard all the way in Brooklyn. I step back, rubbing the back of my neck before I do more than kiss her on these steps. I'm always in control, but she's got me close to losing my last shred around her. "Yeah, we're not going to do that."

She looks me up and down. "You sure about that?"

The woman is a siren, and my dick has answered her call. The timing could be better than a street in the middle of Manhattan. There's nothing covert about how I shift.

A grin cuts into her expression, and she asks, "You once mentioned your favorite place to eat but never said what it was—"

"Good idea." We start walking, and I keep my eyes on anything but the beautiful woman beside me. Shred is putting it kindly. I'm being held together by the thinnest of threads because of her. Granted, it's been a while. A self-inflicted exile, but that doesn't change the fact that I find her so goddamn gorgeous.

I make the mistake of glancing over and catch her eyes already on me. "How hungry are you?"

"Famished."

"Do you want to catch a car, or are you good with walking?"

"I'm good with walking. It's something I miss when I'm on the West Coast. Not that I don't walk. I do, for exercise, but New York forces you to get dressed and participate in life. It's too easy to stay in bed in Vancouver and LA and order in." I catch the sight of her tongue dipping out and licking the corner of her mouth before I look away, knowing I made a mistake. "Are you okay? You seem . . . I don't know. On edge."

As much as I enjoy her company, it might be too much. I stop and step off to the side closer to the building. "Look . . ." I glance down the street. It's less busy in this section, and I'm not upset by the reprieve. "We could cause another catastrophe if we're spotted together. It's not something I considered with my son because I can usually walk around the city freely." Swaying two fingers between us, I add, "But we're a different story."

"Maybe I look too different in real life for people to notice." She laughs. "But I don't get much attention here either."

"You don't see yourself clearly. You don't see yourself how I do."

"How do you see me?"

I take a slow and deep breath, believing kissing her will definitely be involved tonight. There's just no way around it.

"It didn't take candy to get my attention from the other side of the street."

Softly grinning, she steps a little closer. "No?"

"Nuh-uh. It was you. All you. Your beauty, and the way the last of the sunlight shone in your hair just before disappearing behind a building. Your eyes when you saw me—"

"What about my eyes?"

"The blue burns brighter like where the deep ocean meets the shallow waters when our eyes meet."

Her breath staggers, and the grin fades as she takes one more step closer, the gap too small to change our minds. Marina looks up at me, sheepishly placing her hands on my chest. "You saw all that from across the street?" she whispers.

"That, and you shoving a piece of chocolate in your mouth." I don't whisper. Kissing her is something I want to do, but I know I shouldn't, especially in front of a dry cleaner in the West Village. "Ouch!" I duck out from our proximity in defense mode before she whacks me in the chest again. Chuckling, I add, "You were hot even with chocolate smeared on the side of your lips. It was tempting to lick it off."

"You should have," she smarts, crossing her arms over her chest and walking away from me.

"Challenge accepted."

"Good," she says, like it's a threat.

I can play this game. "Great." I jog to catch up and see her trying so hard not to give me a smile. Reaching over, I rub her lower back. "If it matters, the only reason I didn't is because Cullen was there. I'm sure you understand."

"Of course, I understand. But why do you get me so worked up—angry and . . .?" Her lips purse as frustration anchors her brows downward.

"And?"

As if an epiphany hits her in the head, her hand covers her forehead, and she halts on the sidewalk. Her gaze slides to me when I stop beside her. "I really dislike you sometimes, but I'm so attracted to you at the same time. It's really annoying, actually."

"We're opposites, baby." I shrug and keep walking.

She's not quick to catch up to me, though, which has me wondering if she's going to or if I'm going to eat alone tonight. Hurried footsteps trail me, getting louder and then I'm bumped from behind. "This is what I mean."

This time, I stop, staring down at her because I guess we're not through going in circles. "What do you mean?"

"You walk away—"

"You walked away not one block down." My arm extends in the direction we came from, but I lower it. I'm a big guy. Although she's not the shortest girl around, I'm quite a bit larger. I save the intimidation tactics for the track and leave them in the paddock for the other guys.

Crossing her arms over her chest again, she raises her chin. "That's different."

"How so?"

Her head jerks back as if the question is an affront to her character. I scoff, staring into the distance, trying to figure her the fuck out.

"It just is. I was teasing you."

When I look back, I say, "You argue with me just to argue and to get a rise out of me. You get what you want, and then you don't want it. Make it make sense, Marina."

"Well . . ." She looks as confused as I am. When she doesn't come up with anything, she throws her arms up. "I have no idea."

"Is this how you flirt or a character flaw—"

Her fisted hands fly to her hips. "Wow, now I have flaws? Low blow, Ryatt."

"Interesting how you suddenly know my name."

"Your name doesn't matter." She moves to the other side of me, flouncing her hot self around. "I have your number."

"Phone number? I know since you don't stop calling me."

Fuck. *Too far.*

I cringe, closing my eyes and rubbing my temple.

When I open my eyes again, the hurt I've caused her permeates her pretty features. "I didn't mean it."

This time, she walks away without saying a word. There's no rush to her pace, so I walk behind her, giving her a bit of space before invading it again. "Your calls are one of the best parts of my day." She stops with her back to me. "An hour before, I'm finding a fucking snack and placing my water on the nightstand so I'm ready when you call."

Turning around slowly, she asks, "You do?"

"I do. We talk about everything and nothing, and I look forward to it all day." Her smile blooms again, and I say, "And for the record, the arguing is the only flaw I've discovered."

She seems less than impressed and sighs heavily. "You were doing so good, too." She's about to leave but then pokes me in the chest. "Then you had to open your mouth."

"We all have flaws. If you think I'm Mr. Perfect, you'll be sorely disappointed."

"Mr. Perfect?" She rapidly blinks at me. "I'm full of flaws, and you're Mr. Perfect?" She rolls her eyes and pulls her phone from the small bag anchored on her hip. "I think I'll call it a night."

"No, you're not."

If looks could kill, I'd be in a body bag. "I'm not?"

"Nice phone, by the way, but no, you're not. I'm not letting you walk away from this conversation because it needs to be had."

"Why? Why does it matter?"

"Listen to me, Marina. You can twist this however you want, but it doesn't make it the truth. You won't meet anyone else with more flaws than me. Trust me, sweetheart. Take it as a warning. Save yourself the trouble. But one thing I do know is that I'm trying to be better. I'm trying with you."

As if she's lost the energy for this talk, she says, "You shouldn't have to try. If it's meant to be, it should come easy."

"Bullshit. That's fairy-tale stuff. That's the movies. That's rose-colored glasses. None of it's real. We are flawed and human and not perfect in the least, but if it's worth the effort, it's worth the work."

The silence is shattered when she looks away from me again and says, "My brothers all fought for their wives. *For them.* Not against them."

"I wouldn't be standing here if I didn't think you were worth the fight."

"You barely know me, Cash."

"Yet I'm still here, making the effort."

There's an ease in her shoulders, a breath released, and the swords in her eyes have disappeared. She seems deep in thought, staring at me as if I have the answer we're searching for. She licks her lips, then bites the lower one, but then says, "I was having a good time. I don't even know why we're fighting."

"Because you're not in your comfort zone. You're unsure. So am I."

"Unsure about what?"

"What this is between us. It's new territory." I catch her

hand just as it swings out. Palm to palm, our fingers fold together. "You don't dislike me, babe. It's just something you tell yourself to stifle the attraction."

Even though I'm served an epic eye roll, she never releases my hand. "Okay, I don't dislike you. Happy?"

"Yes."

"I also find you attractive." A shrug and a smile come into play. "So what? A little charming and kind of funny."

"*Little* and *kind of*?" My expression sours, but it's all in good fun now that we seem to be heading in the right direction again.

"*A lot* charming and funny. That's all I'm giving tonight."

"I'm good with that." I move our hands down to our sides and pull her close with the other, rubbing her ass because I may not get another chance. "You're prickly when you want to be but so fucking sexy that I haven't stopped thinking about kissing you since I saw you across the street."

With widening eyes, she catches her breath, and asks, "Really?"

"Really."

Her free hand runs along my ribs, then lower to grab my ass. Guess she's taking advantage of the opportunity as well. "Why don't you?"

"Because I don't want witnesses—"

"Like a murder?"

I laugh. "Yes, like an annihilation of your mouth."

Her lips split into a striking smile, stealing that last shred of my willpower. She says, "Why does that sound so abhorrently sexy?"

Chuckling harder, I caress her cheek. "How is everything that comes out of your mouth a curveball?"

"That's a nice way of telling me I say crazy things. Hey, can I ask you something?"

Something is so insanely attractive about a woman who knows who she is through and through, her confidence shining through her good-girl exterior. I bet she's great in bed—a little wild, a little proper, and unpredictable.

"If I can ask you something in return." We start walking again, the pace slow as if we have forever ahead of us.

"Deal. Why didn't you tell me you had a son?"

"Um. Not sure how we jumped from me being sexy to being a father . . . " The question comes from left field, but I don't skip a beat to answer it. "I didn't hide that information. He's a part of my identity. I'm Cullen's dad. I thought you knew. Guess not. Surprise, I'm a father to a five-year-old."

"First of all, I called the annihilation of my mouth sexy, though, now with more time to imagine that scenario, it's not so much." She tucks her hair behind her ear again, and says, "I want you to tell me the important stuff. I don't want to learn about it online." Shaking her head, she looks up at me. "Every part of my ex's life is online. I'm starting to think I was just bait for the paparazzi for his next storyline. I don't want to share the important stuff of my life with the world. Talk to me, okay?"

Those words alone make us a match made in heaven. "I agree."

With a hop to her step, she turns to face me. "Your turn. What did you want to ask me?"

I love seeing her carefree side. I have a feeling it's not a side she gets to share often. "Why were you buying candy?"

"What do you mean?"

"I don't remember the last time I bought candy, other than for Cullen, but there you are, buying and eating it like it's an everyday occurrence."

"It's not for you?" The bewilderment heard in her tone

has me questioning why I don't. Other than the small fact that I must maintain a certain weight range in racing.

"Come on. We have some blocks to cover if we want to eat before it gets too crowded."

Seventeen blocks, to be precise . . . "Pizza?" She balks. "You dragged me a billion blocks for New York-style pizza in New York City? We could have gotten this ten times over on the way here."

"You don't like pizza?"

She scans the menu. "I love pizza. Just surprised since it's sooo . . ."

"Basic?"

Her sideways grin has me smiling as well. "Normal," she replies.

"What kind of impression do you have of me if you don't think I like normal foods?"

"I don't know. You might be a steak-and-potatoes-every-night kind of guy or as much as you can eat sushi or even a secret lover of fried chicken, but you don't want to admit it."

Rubbing my stomach, I reply, "I love fried chicken. Fried chicken does not love me."

"How often do you deviate into the good foods? And by good, I mean the bad and delicious foods?" Tapping #18 on the menu, she adds, "This one."

"Not often. I'm not twenty-five anymore."

Bumping into my arm, she says, "Are we doing the age thing again?"

"No."

"Wise choice." She steps up to the counter and orders a large pie to go. She's not shy when it comes to food, and I can get behind that. I pay the total, and we step to the side to wait. Groups gather in a line to score a table inside, and I'm noticing eyes on us.

I turn my back, shielding her on the other side of me. I don't think she catches on at first, but then she looks me up and down. "Okay, Everest, you're blocking the view."

"Yeah. There are spies among us."

Her back stiffens, her posture now board straight. "Should I leave and meet you around the corner?"

Selfishly, I don't want her to go, even if I get to see her in a few minutes. Protectively, I say, "I think it's safer if we stick together." I glance out the window of the pizzeria. "Hopefully, it won't be long."

It's a bummer that the tone has changed, that we're both on guard more, and all conversation has ceased to exist. If there are eyes, ears are listening in as well.

The pizza finally comes out the window, and we hustle away from the crowded pizzeria and down a block before we stop. She looks across the street and then at me. "Your place or mine?"

When our eyes connect again, I think we both know that question is loaded with more than dinner plans. But she doesn't hesitate. "Yours."

15

Marina

"Why are you in the city if you're filming in Vancouver?" Cash asks before devouring the last of his fourth piece of pizza.

The man can eat. It's actually impressive. Even if this is the most divine pizza that has ever touched my tongue, I fell out of competition after two large slices. Cash is still going, reaching for another.

"I had an audition this afternoon."

"For a movie?"

It felt like home on that stage today, the feeling still soaring through my veins. "For a play on Broadway."

"That's a big deal."

"That's why I had candy."

His eyes narrow on me from where he sits on the floor, the pizza box a makeshift plate. "I'm going to need more information to make that connection."

I giggle. It might be the beer causing it or the company.

Or both. "It's like a reward to myself. A treat for doing my best."

"Is that what your parents gave you growing up?" The slice is set back on the box. Are these signs of slowing down? I giggle again to myself.

"I feel attacked."

He grins under a muffled chuckle. "You're not being attacked." Resting his back against the base of the couch, he stretches his legs out on the floor. I tried my best to get him to watch a home DIY show, but he wasn't having it for long, and somehow *clears throat* the channel ended up on car racing. Funny how that happens like never in my world. *Until now.*

I take another sip of beer, happy to change the topic before falling back on the couch. "It's not like they bought me the store. It was one treat_"

"It was bribery."

"And I'm okay with it." With a shrug of my shoulders, I add, "It did the trick."

He angles toward me, resting his arm on the couch cushion. "If I won a race, my mom would make me mac and cheese from the blue box. But that still tastes like victory to me."

"What would she make if you lost?"

An endearing smile subtly crosses his mouth, and he replies, "Mac and cheese. From the blue box."

To say I'm eating up every word he's sharing is an understatement. I don't think I could ever be full when it comes to learning these little things about Cash Warren. "I love that." I face toward him, bending my legs at the knee and hugging a small pillow to my chest. "Your mom is very sweet. She spoke to me like we were old friends. It was nice."

"I don't think she's met a stranger."

"I can see how proud she is of you, and she adores Cullen." A frame sits on the console under the TV mounted on the wall. The three of them, all smiles, stand in turquoise waters.

"She's a great mom and even better grandma. She'd do anything for him, which helps me out."

There's more to this man than I ever imagined. Relaxing my head back, I let the pillow fall to my side. "You're very different here in New York versus how you were in Miami."

"Should I be offended?"

"No."

He scoots up on the other end of the couch. Taking my ankles one by one, he rests my feet on his leg. "What did you imagine before you came up here?"

I look around, though I've been picking up pieces of who he is through the decor since I got here. The furniture lends toward darker—black leather but encased in warm woods, metals but balanced with soft pillows and rugs. Even the white walls aren't cold with muted art hanging on them. His home is warm and inviting. And like the size of his appetite, the Tribeca apartment boasts impressive water views with a sunset that I'd pay to see again.

"A revolving door at the entrance with women coming and going all hours of the day and night." I wrap it in a joke, but I really did think he was more of a playboy. All signs—that jaw cut from the devil's himself, the arrogant need for attention, and when those green eyes latch onto yours, you feel like the only woman in existence, to name a few—inferred the same.

With one arm resting across my ankles, he sure is cozy with me around. He chuckles. "I see you think highly of me."

"Not as high as you think of yourself, but a solid to infinity."

"And beyond."

A smile spreads wildly across my face. I'm finding it so easy to feel happy around him in spite of our beginning. "Your words, not mine."

I love the way he laughs—deep and hearty, genuine. The sound is comforting for some reason I don't want to explore. It's too soon to drag feelings into this new . . . friendship? Rubbing my leg, he asks, "How did the audition go?"

My parents ask me about my auditions. Poppy does if she knows about them. My brothers do when I talk to them, but Corbin hasn't since I can remember, and I haven't heard from Lauren at all today. But Cash did. That tells me everything I need to know to trust him with the things that are important to me. "I sang my heart out. The rest is up to fate."

"You can't give away your power like that. I'm sure you didn't walk up and perform unprepared. It's not luck that got you to that stage. It's experience and your drive to be there."

Spoken as a man who has fought for everything, including credit where it's due. "You're not wrong." That elicits a chuckle out of him. "I practiced for a week."

"Here's what I've learned. If you get the part, you earned it. If you don't, you try again another day. But we're not lucking into anything, so own your hard work."

His heartfelt words fill my chest as his hand warms my ankle. I'll blame the beer, but I know it's the company. He's been rubbing me, every stroke awakening a different craving that has nothing to do with pizza or feeling sentimental pride about the work I've put in to chasing my dreams.

Cash said he wanted to kiss me earlier and chose the word annihilation specifically. A shiver runs through me like a live wire. It's been so long since I've been touched, been charmed, been anything that made me feel special. Staring at him, his rugged good looks, the rough of his hands scratching gently across my skin, I see him in a new light that has nothing to do with friendship.

He's so much of everything I want and feel so strongly about—kindness, chivalry, masculine, brute in the sexiest of ways, a great listener, sweet talker, even the arguing is above par. I don't need anyone to bow to me or tell me yes all the time. I want someone I can trust. I want him because this attraction is taxing my abilities to think responsibly. Slipping my legs under me, I slide closer to him, needing to be near him and to touch him. I want him to touch me.

His hand slides around my waist as if we do this every day. I love how big it is, covering the acreage of my back. I love the connection as if he couldn't not touch me in such an intimate way. So much innocence is built in, but always with an edge of possession that if I were his, it might be forever. My insides twist in anticipation of that annihilating kiss, the longing overwhelming as I stare into the intensity of his green eyes.

"I don't know what I'm doing."

"We can go slow."

I smile. "I'm not a virgin."

"Then we can go fast."

The soft lines of his arrogant grin have me realizing I don't have to be so serious. I can be me with him, which means goofy or sexy or however I'm feeling at that moment.

When I move to climb onto him, he takes me by the hips and seats me on his lap. My breath jags when I straddle him, and I confess, "I shouldn't be here, but I don't think I can stay away from you."

"Don't let other people get in your head. You're right

where you belong, Marina." Tilting his head, he leverages me and pulls up so we're just a breath apart. "Do what you want. Do what feels good, what feels right. If that's me, all you have to do is kiss me."

Wrapping my arms around his neck, I whisper, "I call you every night because you've become a highlight of my day as well. You're the escape I can't wait to talk to each night."

"I don't have to be an escape tonight. I'm real and right here, babe."

I slide my fingers through the hair at the back of his head, lean my head against his forehead, and then close my eyes. He slides his nose against mine, a nudge following. My body is already seeking the pleasure I know he'll give me, but my mind won't stop overthinking. "I'm nervous. It's been a long—"

My lips are taken, his pressure possessing but still gentle. I lean into it, kissing him harder, wrapping my arms tighter around him, and rocking on his lap.

His hands are all over—my ass, my back, my shoulders, my ribs, the curve of my waist, and then his fingers are digging into my hair. Nothing stops us. No outside interference. No late hours. No paparazzi stalking us and no witnesses.

There's no rush, but I still have the need to feel all of him inside me.

I pull back to look into his eyes. Our breathing is quick but shallow. His eyes are as wild as mine. "You're so fucking beautiful, Marina."

And here I am, wondering if he wants me as much as I do him, but he answers without me asking. His eyes hold something that latch onto mine. His hands grip my sides, showing no signs of letting go, his body reacting to mine on top of him. "I want you so badly."

I'm flipped to my back and slid so smoothly up the couch until my head bumps into the cushioned arm. He settles between my legs, but his eyes remain firmly on mine. "I've wanted you since the moment I saw you." He slides his hands over my shirt and squeezes my breasts. Dipping his head, he scratches my collarbone with the scruff of his chin as his lips press to my neck. His breath is hot, his tongue slippery under my jaw. He breathes, "Tell me how you want me, babe."

Talking is not something I do during sex. And a questionnaire has never been a part of it. My mind goes blank. "I don't know."

Cash looks up. His hair is messier, his eyes narrowed. "You don't know how you like it?"

I search for the right answer, the one that will get us back to kissing and grinding and feeling good again, but I come up empty-handed. "I . . . um."

"Have you come before?" A thread of judgment weaves through his tone.

"Of course, I have," I reply, my voice pitching. My defenses kick in, and I try to shove him off me, but he doesn't budge. Since he's built like a wall of bricks, my efforts are pointless. "I'm ready to go."

My arms are pinned to the couch, and he pushes up. I can't tell if he's angry or if this is the first stage of annihilation. "You can go anytime you want, sweetheart, but give me the courtesy of the truth."

Tipping my head from one side to the other, I stop and glare at him. "You say I can go but are still holding me hostage."

His hands release me, and he's on his feet, erection and all, which is super distracting because it's quite the sight to behold, even trapped in jeans. "There's the door."

I get up and straighten my shirt by yanking on the hem. Somehow, a few buttons are askew, but it's nothing I can't fix in the elevator. I raise my chin and exhale a haughty breath. I'm mad, but I'm not sure why or even what went wrong. I mean, not everyone comes every time they have sex. I've read many articles that most women don't do that often. I'm not unique or anything, but the way he judged me was unwarranted.

Throwing my arms out, I give up and let them fall to my sides again. "We're just too much fire and too much ice to be together in any civil capacity."

"Civil capacity as in sex?" He crosses his arms over his chest, his shoulders appearing broader in the stance.

"Civil capacity as in not making someone feel like crap for not having an orgasm during sex all the time." I cross my arms over my chest, my feelings bruised and my ego not faring any better. "Or ever," I whisper.

He sighs as if the weight of the world hangs on his shoulders. It might be dealing with my emotions at the moment. He lowers his arms and comes over to me. Taking my wrists, he unwinds my arms and then holds my hands. "I wasn't mocking you. I'm trying to understand what you like and what makes you feel so good that you leave the world behind for a little while and enjoy the ride."

His argument is valid, and since I overreacted, running hot-blooded in my thoughts as he had my body all twisted in desire, I close the distance between us, wrap my arms around his middle, and rest my cheek on his chest. The scent of his soap and cologne is euphoric, and the safety of his arms when they hold me the best feeling I've ever felt.

When he places one singular sweet kiss on the top of my head, I confess my shame, hoping he doesn't hold it against me. "I've only had an orgasm alone."

Two of his fingers slip under my chin, lifting until our eyes meet again, and he says, "We're about to change that."

16

Cash

I SLIDE my hands up her arms and over her shoulders until I cup Marina's pretty face. As if the anticipation in her eyes didn't tell a novel worth of information already, I still need to start with the basics. "Will you stay?"

"You couldn't kick me out after the promise you just made." I grin, but hers falls too fast for my liking. She fists my shirt and whispers, "I'm nervous."

"You don't need to be." I keep my eyes on her lips, then dip my head and lick the corner of her mouth. "Not with me, babe. Not ever." I suck in her breath as her body falters. I'm quick to catch her. It's not the first time a woman has fainted in my presence, but she was a stranger. I have no intention of letting Marina pass out before making her come so hard that she'll never forget it.

Her legs are steady, and her eyes open, meeting mine. The length of her hair falls over her shoulders as she looks up at me like I hung the moon in the sky just for her. I would. For her, I would do it just to see her smile. So I won't let her down now.

I kiss her, knowing nothing could stop me from giving her everything she deserves. Our lips part before we get too heavy, and I brush the hair from her eyes.

She asks, "The bedroom?" This is one invitation I would never turn down.

As I take her hand and lead her down the hall, I'm at a loss for words. There's no reason she should be here. No reason for her to waste her time on me. No reason that I'm being given the chance to be with such an incredible woman. Marina's everything I don't deserve based on my bad deeds in life. So I won't take her for granted.

She stops in the bedroom and then looks back at me. "You have very good taste."

Leaning against the doorframe, I give her a once-over, taking in every inch of her and debating where I'll begin to unravel her. "I agree."

Her cheeks pinken, noticeably even in the dimmer light of the bedside lamp. "I was referring to the furniture and decor."

"I was referring to you."

She clasps her hands in front of her, innocence straining in her posture. Licking her lips, she takes a breath and says, "So . . . here we are."

"Here we are."

"In your bedroom." She looks around again as if seeing it in a new light this time. "This is where all the girls come. Oh God. I didn't mean it that way, though it's probably correct in both entendre." Rubbing a hand over her face, she shakes her head. "Please put me out of my misery and kiss me."

Although I'm amused by the rambling, I won't make her

suffer any longer. I cross into the room and go straight for her, running my hands around the base of her neck and bending to kiss her. It's gentle at first, the tension still felt in her shoulders. But when I encourage her lips apart, and our tongues meet, her body loosens under my touch.

I walk until the back of her legs meet the bed, then stop everything. "I want you to take your clothes off. Will you do that for me, babe?"

A thousand thoughts cross through her eyes as panic sets in. "Like, just strip right here with you staring at me?"

"Yes."

"Whew," she exhales loudly with her hands planted on her hips. I expect her to start pacing at this rate or throwing jabs in the air. "I can do that. Yep, no problem."

As entertaining as this is, it's not exactly what I intended. "You psyching yourself up there, champ?"

Her eyes find mine again. "Sure am."

"If you're not comfortable—"

"No," she starts, on the verge of another run-on sentence, and nods while staring at the floor. "I can do this. It's like acting. I'll just get into character—" She gasps when I capture a whirling hand, stilling it.

When her gaze reaches mine, I say, "I don't want you in character. I just want you, Marina." My voice is firm, but she appears to find understanding in the direction.

Her body stills, but her breathing remains steady. "Okay."

"Will you allow me?"

Her wordless reply comes in another nod, but no nerves are attached this time.

"Turnabout is fair play." I start on my shirt first, tugging it off over my head and dropping it at our feet. The tips of her fingers, the slight edge of her nails start on my chest and lightly scrape lower over my abs. Her eyes follow the trails, then she lifts to kiss just under my collarbone.

Her touch, her lips, the kiss, her . . . it's all so sweet that I can't stop myself from holding her to me, even if just for a moment. I kiss her head, rubbing her back.

She steps out of my hold, and with her eyes locked on mine, she unbuttons her shirt. My gaze dips lower when the shirt travels over her shoulders, exposing her bra and the bare skin of her abdomen. The uncertainty that lived briefly in her eyes has vanished, replaced with determination, intrigue, and conviction as she starts on my jeans.

Pushing my fingers into her hair, I caress her scalp, keeping her eyes up as she goes lower. Not that I'm shy. Far from it. "I can't get enough of how fucking sexy you are, babe."

"In the paddock, I got even madder when you took your helmet off."

I smirk, outlining her lips with my gaze. Fuck me, she's hot. "Oh yeah? Why's that?"

She continues on my zipper, then stands up again. Leaning against me, she says, "I wasn't expecting you to be so attractive."

Laughter escapes me. "It would have been better to argue with me if you didn't find me so devastatingly handsome?"

Running her hands over my shoulders like she already knows I'm hers, she laughs. "Your words, not mine."

"Are you calling them a lie?"

"No, the truth is in there. I just hate that you already know it."

I work on the clasp at the back of her bra, popping it. "Hate is the opposite of love. Is that what it's going to be with us? Love or hate with no in-between?"

Peeling the straps from her arms, I watch the bra slide off her body to the floor. "Seems that way."

She steps back again, standing before me like a present I don't deserve. As she slides her jeans down, there's no shy girl left, only a confident woman before me. She even pulls the lace wrapped around her hips down with the denim.

Placing her hand against me, she steps out of them and looks up at me. "Breathe."

I release a heavy breath that had been trapped in my chest. I'm never nervous about sex. It's second nature to me, but with her, this feels like more than two people enjoying each other's company. I touch her neck and bend to kiss the same spot. "You stole it."

"Turnabout is fair play."

Bringing her against me and feeling the heat of our bodies surging through the shared connection, I say, "It sure is," then kiss her. Deep. Tangling tongues. Kneading her tits until a moan is solicited.

She pulls back to slip my jeans down the rest of the way, my boxer briefs coming with them. Her eyes cover my body before she wraps around me, shamelessly teasing my cock with her body.

Getting a good handful of that beautiful ass of hers, I ask, "Now that you have a new phone, what are you going to hold against me this time?"

"It's not what I'm holding to you but you're holding to me that I'll remember most."

"Trust me, sweetheart, this won't be what you remember most about tonight."

"Prove it."

I lift her and toss her on the mattress. Coming around, she's lost in laughter when I climb on next to her. That quietens her real quick. She reaches out for me, her fingers running along the hills of my bicep and higher as I go lower. Spreading her legs, I settle between them and kiss her lower belly. Her lips call to me with the smoothest skin and sweetest scent. I dip my tongue between them and taste her for the first time.

When she reaches so the tips of her fingers scroll over my shoulders, I look up and whisper, "I'm going to make you feel so good." I slide my hand over her belly and between her tits. "Lie back for me like a good girl."

Her head falls to the pillow, and her hands rest on the cover that she fists her fingers around. I kiss her inner thigh and say, "Relax, baby, okay?"

"Okay," she says, her voice coated in staggering breaths.

Lifting her leg up by the knee, I position it over my shoulder so I can go deep for her. I don't tease. I go right in with my tongue, then lick the length of her entrance and suck her clit. She bucks beneath me, so I reach up and hold one of her hands to the bed. She holds tighter to it as I do another round. But it's when I dip two fingers in and slowly drag them out again that her body lifts, her back arching, her moans begging for more.

I kiss her sweet bud and fuck her with my fingers until she's pulling my hair. "Cash. Pleasesse." The words are dragged from a carnal yearning that taints her voice with desperation.

Please is my weakness, like she is. I suck harder, flick faster, and pump quicker until I feel the tremors quaking her body and taste all of her as she comes on my mouth.

When she sinks into the mattress, all fight gone, I move higher, anchoring my hands on either side of her head before lowering to kiss her just as deep as I did her entrance. The heat of her hands warm everywhere she touches as her arms come around me, and she kisses me with just as much fervor.

I break away and pull a condom from the nightstand drawer. The peaks of her nipples are on display against the pinkish areola, tempting me back to her. I kiss one and then the other, leaving each with a swirl of my tongue before rolling to my side to put the condom on.

Glancing at her, I ask, "How do you feel?"

"Free." She smiles, stretching her arms above her head. "I don't have a better word to describe it."

"You don't need a better word. I get it." I settle back between her legs, this time positioning my dick instead. Kissing her, I bend toward her ear and whisper, "You know what's better than free? Coming together. I want you to come with me, baby. You understand?"

I kiss her cheek as she nods, and when I reach her lips, I kiss her and push in. Her mouth opens, and she sucks in a breath, followed by a calming moan. "Oh wow." The words slip from her lips.

The heat.

The way she stretches for me.

The hold she has.

I'm consumed by her. Obsessed with her. "So tight, baby."

"God, please move. It's too much."

"Since you put it so nicely . . ." I pull out and thrust back in. I kiss her neck and under her jaw, squeeze her tits, and fuck her like I don't know her name. Her body writhes wildly under mine, chaotic in the bond as we both thrust together. But then she pushes me over and slides on top by straddling me.

Pressing her palms to my chest, she finds the stroke that feels too good to stop, and her eyes can barely stay open. I grab onto her ass, encouraging every grind and thrust as I watch her perfect tits bounce on her chest and feel the heat of her body taking over mine ... "Fuck, I'm going to come."

"Wait. Wait. Wait," she says, panic striking her tone. The rocking slows down, every move both delicious torture and pushing me closer to the edge. When she finds her stride again, she leans forward, her touch light but nails sinking into my chest. She holds her breath, and under a curtain of her hair, she cries, "Oh God, yes. Yes. Oh yes."

The sound of her pleasure and the grip of her body around my dick sends me careening off the cliff with her. I squeeze her hips and shove upward several times. "Fuck," I shout, gritting my teeth right after until I hit that purgatory of peace found in the aftermath.

My body gives in, and I lie, eyes closed, with my arms spread wide. Marina cuddles to my side, her leg draping over my thigh. I wrap my arm around her and pull her closer, reaching to kiss her. I'm met with welcoming lips and a blissful sigh.

We lie together in the quickening of our breaths until they regulate along with our heartbeats again. When I look and see her languid smile, my heart beats hard in my chest. I like this ... this with her.

I like her.

She opens her eyes, her smile widening as she sees me already staring at her. Running her fingers along my temple and jaw, she says, "That was the best sex I ever had."

I'm out of snappy comebacks or arrogant remarks. I'm stuck in the beauty of this woman and how easily she's accepted me despite the rough beginning. I'm mad that I need to leave in less than seven hours to make my flight to France instead of having the privilege of waking up next to her. She feels so right. Her arms are where I belong, and she belongs in mine.

She kisses my shoulder. "I set you up for the perfect comment, and you say nothing?"

Choking down the words that would be utterly ridiculous to admit to her, I reply, "What can I say? It was the best sex of your life."

I catch her little fist and bring it to my mouth to kiss. "And the best night of my life as well."

17

Marina

I BLINK, hoping to make sense of where I am.

Closing my eyes again doesn't help. So I open them and scan what's in front of me. Everything is different—unfamiliar curtains hanging over a window I've never seen before. A blanket that's so much more luxurious than mine in Vancouver and not blue like the one at my brother's house where I stay in New York. Even the diffused sunshine trying to sneak in isn't what I'm used to.

Except for the scent in the air. I snuggle the pillow a little tighter and take a deep inhale. *Cash.*

I roll over and prop myself up on my hands but find the bed empty beside me. "Cash?" I call, but I don't hear a response, so I'm louder. "Cash?" I flip the covers up and tiptoe across the room to the bathroom. The door is wide open, same with the bedroom door that leads to the hall. "Cash?" It would be impossible for him not to hear me, which means I'm alone.

To confirm, I grab his shirt from the floor and put it over

my head just before I enter the hallway. "Cash, are you here?" *Nothing.* "Huh."

Standing at the window looking out, I wonder if I could spot him among the busy street from nine stories up. The sun is barely awake at this hour and hides behind clouds. The view of the water calms, though the white caps might foreshadow a storm later.

I move into the kitchen, searching for signs of Cash's existence this morning, but I don't find any. The coffee isn't made, no dishes are in the sink, and the counters look clean except where a Post-it Note is stuck to it.

Where is he? Out for coffee? Grabbing bagels for us? Off to the next country to race? I have no idea, but I hope this note tells me. Otherwise, I'm going to feel like I imagined last night.

My body aches in ways that I haven't ever felt—a little pain but wrapped in pleasure. I smile as I peel the note from the counter.

LAST NIGHT WAS the best night.
    Thanks for a great time.

CASH

I STARE at the yellow paper for at least a minute before the words truly sink in. Thanks for a great time? *That's it?* He's not coming back?

No coffee?
    No bagel?
    No warning of his departure?

With every red flag flying, anger accompanies the disappointment flooding my veins. But more so, I thought we'd have a nice leisurely morning, then I'd go pack and fly back to Vancouver later. Seems I'll be doing the walk of shame instead.

Returning to the bedroom, I debate if I should shower to wash off the humiliation or just get dressed and go back to Lark and Harbor's where I'm staying to do the deed?

I look for a clock unsuccessfully but find my phone on the coffee table. It's early, not even seven. If I go now, I could slip into the house unnoticed. I decide that's the best plan I have, so I pull on my jeans and slip my bra back on under the shirt. Picking up my shirt, I go to put on my shoes and grab my bag on the way out. As soon as I call the elevator, I text Cash: *Revenge for breakfast? I didn't take you for one with a vendetta.*

He doesn't respond, which irks me even further.

I step onto the sidewalk into the cool morning air and order a car to pick me up. I didn't think about being photographed outside Cash Ryatt's apartment building until I see what looks to be a tourist wearing a purple Westcott Racing shirt standing across the street. *Crap.* Ducking my head, I hightail it down the block.

When I see a car matching the description from the app, I wave at them. After confirming it's my ride, I hop in the back and slink down in the seat, hoping to God that person didn't catch me in a photo. It's also a good reminder that Cash is not unknown. Just because he was to me doesn't mean he isn't famous.

I text Poppy, knowing she's asleep on the west coast of Canada since they're three hours behind New York City: *Guess what I'm doing?*

She responds: *What?*

Me: *Why are you up at this hour?*

Poppy: *I was snacking. Why are you up at this hour?*

I didn't know she had a middle-of-the-night appetite, but maybe it's a thing with chefs. I reply: *Walk of shaming it back across town.*

My phone instantly rings. I laugh, needing the light-heartedness right now. "Hello?"

"Do tell."

"Two words." I track my gaze to the driver, who seems too occupied in his own world to be concerned with mine. Whispering, I say, "Cash. Ryatt."

"Holy sh—"

"I know."

"How the hell did that happen? What happened to he's horrible, and I hate him and all that talk about rude, offensive, frustrating?" She takes a breath and adds, "Attractive."

"Absurdly so. Yeah, I remember, and I'm eating my words now."

"What else were you eating last night?"

A bubble of laughter escapes me. "Pizza. That's it."

She fake yawns, and then she laughs. "Boring. Tell me the good stuff."

I stare out the window and begin to recognize that I'm getting close to Lark and Harbor's place. "There was so much good, but then this morning, he ruined it."

"What happened, Mar?" She pushes the joking aside, and her sincerity of concern comes through. "He left."

"What do you mean he left? Weren't you at his place?"

"Yes," I reply, suddenly feeling as lost on what happened as she is. Why did he freaking leave without telling me where he was going? Or if he'll even return.

"He dick-and-dashed from his own place? That's a twist I didn't see coming."

I'm more astonished than she sounds because I lived it. I'm still in a state of awe and wonderment over last night. "Seems so. Also, please never use that phrase again. *Ew.*" The car pulls in front of my brother's townhome. "I need to go. I have to sneak back into my family's place like I did as a teenager."

"That sounds fun. Good luck and I'll pick you up from the airport this evening. I'm thinking wings?"

"You sure do think about food. That's right. You're a chef."

"Yeah, it's pretty much all I think about. Have fun. Safe travels."

I step onto the curb and carefully walk up the stairs. I don't know why I'm sneaking around outside, so I snap out of it and punch the code in like the adult I am. When I step into the secure lobby, I key in the password before entering through the front door into the airy foyer. It's a beautiful home, restored and renovated over a two-year period. I wasn't surprised when it was featured in *Décor Digest.*

My phone pings in my hand before I have a chance to take one step up the stairs. "Hello?" I hear my sister-in-law's voice coming from a darker part of the house.

"Hi," I reply, tracking her from where I think the greeting came from—the kitchen. I enter to find a small lamp glowing from the corner counter and her sitting at a built-in desk in front of a laptop. "You're up early."

She moves her glasses to her head. Lark is effortlessly beautiful, and her soul reflects the same. An accomplished doctor and mom of two, she's always busy. Though I have a feeling my brother also keeps her on her toes. They're an enviable match and a nice balance to each other. I could only dream of meeting someone who fills in the holes that life has left. That completeness must be what contentment feels like. *I can only imagine.*

"Are you working?"

Dragging her hair over her shoulder, she says, "Catching up on work, and I like to be up and awake when the kids get up. We have about ten minutes before the chaos begins." She angles on the side of the chair to face me. "How are you?"

Although I appreciate that she doesn't show any signs of having an opinion on my early morning arrival, I reply, "I'm sorry for coming in at this hour."

"You don't need to apologize, Marina, or explain. Though I'm glad that Harbor left this morning, or you might be bombarded with endless questions." She laughs softly. "No matter your age, you'll always be his little sister."

"He's always been a good big brother. He left early. Where is he off to?"

Swiveling back toward the screen when the laptop pings, she says, "The South of France. Harbor, Cash, Duncan, and a few others took the plane just after five this morning."

"Cash?" Her gaze darts back to me, causing me to shift. "I don't know why I said that. I meant—"

"It's okay." She smiles, pulling her glasses back over her eyes. "I know what you meant." No judgment. No conviction. Just letting me off the hook as if I didn't just royally stick my foot in my mouth. "Will I see you later, or are you flying back to Vancouver?"

"I'm flying out today. I'll be back in the city in two weeks, though, for the premiere."

"That's fun. Are you looking forward to it?"

I shrug, unsure about a lot of things these days. The film not so much, but the men in my life, I'm lost on what to think or feel. Well, not Corbin. He's awful, but Cash has my head spinning with this new information. "Are they racing in France?"

"Yes. They always fly out early to acclimate to the time change, rest, and prepare. All the stuff they need to do before the qualifier next weekend."

It's hard to stay mad at him when work calls, but couldn't he have told me? At least as a courtesy? Especially after last night.

The sun's broken free from the clouds and shining in through the windows. "I'm going to get a nap in and pack before I head off."

"Hey, Marina?" I stop before I reach the hallway and turn back. Lark smiles, easing her shoulders into a gentle slope forward. "They can ban you from the track but not from living your life. I don't think you did anything wrong. I do think you need to hone your sneaking skills again. They're a little rusty."

My heart beats a bit faster. Is she saying what I think she is? Does she know? I don't want to give anything away if she doesn't. "Good advice."

"It was good seeing you again. We've missed you. The kids have, too."

"It's been nice to see everyone these past few trips."

"The door is always open. You're welcome to stay here for the premiere if you'd like."

I smile. "Thanks. I appreciate that. I'll see you later."

Taking the stairs by two, I reach the bedroom and slip inside. With my back against it, I check my phone to see the message that came through earlier. If it's Poppy with her dick-and-dash jokes—*Cash.*

His text reads: *Good morning, beautiful! No vendetta. You were sleeping so soundly, but I still tried to disturb you. I kissed every inch of your incredible body, a.k.a. annihilated you with my mouth, but the most I got was a moan. And an opportunity to suck on your inner thigh. Hope you don't have any nudity scenes ever, but if you do, the makeup team will have a field day.*

Tossing the phone on the bed, I'm quick to strip down my jeans and prop my foot on the bed. I don't think I've ever been as happy as I am right now. Seeing my inner thigh covered in hickeys is just the sweetest thing ever.

Who knew bruises would make me smile so much.

Cash made the effort. *For me.*

I crawl onto the bed and snuggle under the covers in his shirt, which still has the faintest scent of him, to read the rest of the novel he wrote to me in text. *Is it wrong to miss you? If it is, I don't want to be right. God, is this what happens when you sleep with the girl of your dreams?*

No. It's what happens when you start having feelings. I don't type that response, but I see you, Cash. And I raise you one heart blooming with emotions on my part.

I read the last bit: *I can't wait to see you again, babe. Cash xo.*

I didn't take him for an exes and ohs kind of guy, but I like this side of him. Quick to send him a reply, I type: *I can't wait to more than see you again. Marina xo.*

With the phone held tight to my chest, I close my eyes, dreaming of when I get to see him next.

18

Cash

TRYING to stay awake has become a game, one I'm losing.

Even sleeping most of the flight to France didn't help me recover from the night with Marina.

No regrets.

How could I? When I said it was one of the best nights of my life, I meant it.

I try to listen to the engineer at the front of the room discuss the changes he's made to the car. My mind wanders while I stare at the screen, pretending to pay attention.

My thoughts drift back to the taste of her as she came, dragging my tongue along the inside curve of her breasts as I kneaded them. Her head tilting back, exposing her neck. I tasted and savored every inch I was given access to, and then deep as she chanted my name, begging for more.

I shift in my seat, the hard-on not a welcome addition to the meeting. I need to stop thinking about Marina.

Cold showers.

Rotting eggs.

My personal life making headlines . . .

That does the trick.

It doesn't take away the awkwardness of the current situation, though.

Brother one: Angling to the left, I tilt back in my chair and stretch, eyeing Harbor on the phone and wearing a path into the tile at the other end of the office.

Brother two: Noah tried to talk to me when we first took off this morning, but I told him I wanted to rest and put on headphones, purposely blocking him out. I almost felt bad, but considering what I did to his sister, I thought it best to stay away from idle chitchat about what we've been up to.

Brother three: I'm sure I'll see him later in the week. Loch tends to fly in the day before the qualifier. I'll be on the lookout to avoid him at all costs. He's the least predictable when it comes to how he'll react if he finds out about me and Marina.

I worry less about her parents. They're not always at the track, and they let their grown kids lead their own lives.

Although there are no signs whatsoever of anyone knowing a single detail of what I've been up to, the truth is that I feel like they can tell I slept with her. Now that it's safe to stand, I whisper to Duncan, "I'm getting a bottle of water." I try to catch my reflection in the window on the way out to see if the words guilty or sister-fucker are written across my forehead.

I don't notice anything, but that doesn't mean I'm any less culpable about what they would deem a crime against their family.

But she was divine.

Fuck. I can't do this. I start thinking about anything that will keep those memories from popping up, but when they're that good, I know I won't win this battle.

Pulling open the fridge, I grab the water and drink some before spotting the balcony. Maybe the fresh air will wake me up or get my mind back on track. I sit on a lounge chair and take another gulp of water.

Exhaustion is the enemy in this sport. I'm starting to think it's a good thing she's banned from the race. Otherwise, I'd be even less focused if that's possible.

The low-key night at home I had planned didn't go that way. I'm definitely feeling the drag in my bones today. This morning I was a fucking mess, rushing to throw clothes into a suitcase. I forgot half my stuff. The thirty minutes I dedicated to a failed attempt to wake Sleeping Beauty might be to blame.

I take her need for rest and recovery as a feather in my cap.

"Hey." Looking up, I see Duncan coming outside with a cup of coffee in hand. When he leans against the railing and rubs the bridge of his nose, I know something is on his mind.

"How's it going?"

"Good. Good." He looks out over the paddock, his eyes trained on something in the distance, something that's not me, so I know a lecture is coming. "How's it going with you?" He finally glances over.

"Should we jump a few steps ahead and just get it over with?"

"If you're up for it." He sips his coffee, then rests his arm on the railing so he's fully facing me.

I stand and rest against the railing as well. With a good seven feet between, it feels like a space that's safe to discuss my personal life. "We might need to make some adjustments."

He nods, but a smile appears as well. "We can do that. Same girl?"

"Nothing happened that night. I know it's hard for everyone to believe, but it wasn't anything like what was reported. It wasn't a thing."

"And now it is?"

Angling forward, I study the track at turn one, wondering if I should be saying anything. It's for me, better for my performance if he's in on what's going on in my life. Glancing over my shoulder to make sure no one's coming out or can hear us, I turn to him and lower my voice, "I want it to be."

I don't know how I expected him to react, but it wasn't grinning like he just got secret intel about winning the lottery. "This is good, Cash. Cullen aside, it's been a long time since you've spent time with someone who makes you happy." He stands upright and drinks coffee. "I think we're going to do runs each morning."

"Why?"

"If we start the day with a run, I want you to let your mind cover any thoughts regarding anyone or anything else. Just run it out of your system. Then you'll be present in meetings, unlike what you were back there."

I twist the cap of the bottle and stare at him. "That's the adjustments? Run her out of my system? I don't think it's possible."

"I CAN'T RUN." I suck in a harsh breath. "I can't think." I rest my hands on my knees and continue gasping for air.

"Took five days, but it finally worked like a charm," Duncan says, not huffing half as hard as I am, though we just completed the same run. *Fucker.* He pats me on the back. "You're ready for tomorrow."

I watch as he walks ahead into the sunrise while I collapse on the ground, arms wide, hoping to breathe normally again one day. I thought he had won his case until I stared at the sky. The first thing to pop into my head is Marina—the photo she sent of her staring up at the sky in Vancouver and how she said no matter where we are, the universe still connects us.

She doesn't tend to hide much, especially her feelings, which I learned early on.

I can handle all her moods because the one thing I'm learning about Marina is that she'll tell you when she's happy or mad, frustrated, or even sad.

I'm not as open, though my emotions have been known to get the better of me. Always learning. Always trying to be better. Sometimes I'm too tempered for her, but I don't mind being her yin to my yang.

What she doesn't realize is if I let my mind go to a place of jealousy or anger on her behalf, that director that had her slathering on sunscreen for the camera the other day or the ex that keeps hanging around her trailer like a . . . well, like an ex-boyfriend trying to win his girl back, then I'd be leveling them both with my fist.

She can fight her battles. I've been at the receiving end of her sharp tongue. So it's not that she needs me. She wants me like I want her.

Fuck.

Why the hell are my thoughts so wrapped up in her?

Focus, Warren.

My phone buzzes, so I pull it from my pocket and sit up. Duncan. I snap, "What?"

"Get your ass down the hill. You're going to eat, then

we're heading into the gym. Neck to help against those G-forces and legs today."

I hang up and start jogging down the hill. When I finally grab the bottle of water he's holding for me, he says, "Your endurance has improved quite a bit. You can thank me later."

I'll save that task for Marina. I'm already thinking about all the ways we're going to fu—

"Come on. Let's eat," Duncan says, waving me toward catering.

―――――――

"I'M NOT SORE ANYMORE," Marina drops casually into our call.

"That's too bad. I liked you walking around with the memory of me." I slide lower on the bed until my head hits the pillow. "But it was a good run."

"Trust me, I still have the memories." She giggles, and I find myself holding the phone closer to my ear so I don't miss any sounds. Then she says, "We need to make new memories soon. When will I see you again?"

Although I know I head home after the race on Sunday night, I have Cullen the following four nights and then Brazil after that. *Fuck.* I palm my brow and drag my fingers into my hair. "Other than video?"

"A new territory for us to explore soon, but I want to see you in the flesh," she says, her voice trilling into suggestion.

"What's your schedule?" I put her on speaker and flip over to my calendar.

"I return to New York on Thursday for a three-day press blitz and the premiere."

"We can't see each other then?" I can ask my mom to

hang out with Cullen, get a room somewhere, and meet her, even if I can steal an hour of her time.

"I worry about being at the center of a press junket and how I'll sneak around with the media stalking me and my ex, like we're still a couple. That news hasn't broke yet."

I flex the fingers of my left hand several times. "It's not obvious? He's been partying, and you've been seen with me." She sighs into the phone. It's a topic she hates discussing, but we need to address it. "Smoke equals fire, babe."

"I can't answer that. All I know is his team has kept it hush-hush. I have no idea why when they could have used this for their benefit."

"Why do you have to worry about them? I don't worry about the guy three cars back. I worry about what's ahead."

Soft laughter reaches my ears. "Hollywood is complicated, I guess."

"Did you hear back about your audition?"

"No." She hums. "These things take time. My agent will reach out to them next week if we don't hear anything before then."

Marina has me thinking differently about things I never really gave a chance to for whatever reason. "I was thinking we could go to a show sometime, one you've never seen or even one you love. I've never been."

"You've never been to a Broadway show? How's that possible when you grew up so close to Manhattan?"

My childhood isn't something I think about often. "Single mom who worked all the time didn't have money for things like that. Even my karting was sponsored by a few of the local businesses since we couldn't afford it. I worked my ass off doing shit chores for every dollar they'd pay toward my fees or equipment. I outgrew my helmet every year. Stuff like that is expensive."

She's quiet, but I can tell by the slight of her breathing that she's still there. "I guess this is another downfall of not doing my research."

"I appreciate that you haven't. No one needs to know that much about someone else."

"It's just . . . my heart, Cash."

"Don't feel sorry for me, okay?" I hate that I snap, but I never needed anyone's pity. I especially don't want hers now.

Taking a deep breath, she shuffles the phone by the noise on her end and then says, "I've been feeling a lot of things, but not sorry for you. I've met your mom. I know what a support she's been. You have each other and Cullen. Your family is . . . not everyone is so fortunate. I feel the same about my family. They've been there for me no matter what."

When I stare through the open curtains and into the night, yachts dot the harbor like stars in the water. "That's my mom. If there were more hours in the day, she would have been sweeping the deli and the corner store floors with me."

"My heart wasn't hurting for you. I was taken by your story. When you're ready, will you share more with me?"

This woman has me opening like an oyster presenting a pearl for her. I don't understand these feelings I have for Marina. My chest always tightens when I think about her, or I have a damn erection. There's not much in between, so I don't understand what's happening. I just know it's not like how I've felt about others. I feel good. She feels good, more than good.

With the qualifier being tomorrow, I'm going to bed earlier, but there's still time to talk to her. Depending on the time difference, I usually talk to Cullen in the mornings, but my nights are reserved for Marina. "How much time do you have?"

"Two hours until I return to set, so I have time."

I click the remote to close the curtains and turn out the lights. "None of the kids I used to race with made it to this level. Some moved over to Rascal Racing, though. They've done well on that circuit—"

"But it's not the same as Principle Racing."

"P1 Racing has more money and prestige. They never did know what to do with a guy like me. I had more street smarts than pedigree."

"I think you're pretty smart," she says, adjusting and sounding more relaxed. "You're dating me." She starts laughing again.

I don't. Not because I don't think she's ridiculously cute because I do. More so that she's right. I was smart enough to see through the act she puts on that everyone else falls for. "One of the smartest things I've done in a long time."

"Aw, Cash. I was just teasing, but that's so sweet."

"I know you were, but it's true. Hey, Marina?"

"Yeah?" She's breathier now. "What is it?"

"I'm not seeing anyone else." She says she doesn't look people up online, but sometimes reputations precede us. "I just want you to know that we talk about our dating even though we've only gone out once, maybe twice if you count Miami."

"I count Miami."

Smiling, I shift to my side to get more comfortable. "I do too."

There's a pause, our breathing keeping us company. "I'm not seeing anyone either. Since you're not and I'm not . . ." she whispers, leaving it open for me.

I don't need time to think about us. It seems that's all I do lately. "How about we don't see others together?"

"You're such a sweet talker, Mr. Warren. You got yourself a deal."

"Sweet like candy."

"Mm, my favorite, like you."

The woman's insatiable for me. It's all good since I feel the same about her. "I have just the thing for that sweet tooth of yours."

"Oh yeah?" she purrs, knowing exactly where I'm going with this. "When do I get to taste it?"

"Soon, I promise."

As soon as we hang up, I change my flight to New York. I think a detour to Vancouver is in order.

19

Marina

"What happened?" I ask, rushing inside the trailer.

Poppy hops up from the couch and looks at the TV on the wall. "Seventh place in qualifying."

Relief washes through me as I shut the door and lock it. I don't want any uninvited guests entering. "That's where he was in Miami."

"Is that good? Seems good since it's out of twenty."

"Cash and my brothers were happy. It's in points positioning."

She sits back down and blinks at me like she's working through a calculus problem. I've seen the look since Noah's tutoring is the only reason she passed that class. "I hear you speaking, but none of that makes sense."

"You win money if you get points." I strip off the robe I wore, crossing the studio lot. "I think." Tossing it on the bed, I rush back to sit beside her. "Have they done any interviews?"

"First and second drivers. How are there so many cute race car drivers in one sport?"

Figuring that's rhetorical, I bite my lip and lean forward, stabbing my elbows into my thighs. "There he is!" I jump to my feet while she ramps up the volume.

"Two races in a row in seventh. It worked well for you last time in Miami. How are you feeling about tomorrow?"

Cash looks straight into the camera, and that gaze caresses my soul. My breath stops hard in my chest, and I can't swallow. All I can do is stare at him and that gorgeous face of his.

He says, "You know I don't get into predictions, Chuck, but I'm feeling better than I have in a long time."

"Get some rest, and we'll see you on the track tomorrow. Cash Ryatt," Chuck says, turning to face the camera.

A woman puts her arm around his back to guide him off camera . . . It's not jealousy I feel, though. I trust him, and that's her job. She's a little handsy, but I am too with him. Okay, maybe I'll casually mention it next time we talk. Or not, and I'll be supportive instead.

Oh geez, I'm doing my head in. I turn around to Poppy. "He was good, right?"

"Really great." She stands and clicks off the TV. "He looks happy. Is that because of you?"

"A girl can dream." I feel delirious like anything is possible after seeing him. The hard edges of his usual expression are absent even in the seriousness of the interview. I slip off my shoes and climb onto the bed at the back of the trailer. As I stare up through the moonroof, the weather couldn't be more perfect, but it's Cash who makes me feel invincible. "How is it that I feel like I could walk on the clouds right now?"

"Because you're in love?" Poppy calls while approaching.

Leaning her shoulder against the small closet door, she says, "You guys talk every night."

"You hear me?"

"I hear you laugh sometimes. I can't hear anything being said." Crossing her arms over her chest, she smiles. "You never seemed this happy before. And look at him. It's moving fast between you two. Should I worry?"

Sitting up, I rest back on my hands. "No." I feel so certain about Cash that saying anything less would feel like a disservice to our blossoming relationship. "As fast as it seems in hours and days, it's been weeks and feels right in other ways."

"Are we rhyming on purpose, or did love make you do it?"

We both crack up. "Love makes a person do silly things."

"It sure does."

A knock on the door has both of us going to the front of the trailer again. She opens it to see the assistant director. "We are wrapping you for the day, Marina. We plan to get some exterior shots, so you're free to go."

"Thank you," I say. Turning to Poppy, I laugh. "Let's get out of here before they change their minds, and it's another fourteen-hour day."

We hurry to get our stuff, and I change clothes. Since the wardrobe girl is fucking my ex-boyfriend, I need to drop these in the box outside the door. I want no contact with her.

We do the deed and get in the car. As soon as she starts the engine, she says, "I have a few interviews in LA."

Although the news comes as a surprise, I'm happy for her since she's started to worry more about her career. "That's great." She backs out of the parking spot and drives toward the gate. "When do you leave?"

"Tomorrow morning. I'm going to set you up with some meals."

"You don't have to do that."

She smiles when she glances my way. "I want to."

"I'm not going to complain. I love your cooking." My selfish side asks, needing to prepare for her absence. "How long will you be gone?" I like having my best friend around. She's not only a comfort to me but she's also fun to talk to and watch TV with before we retire to our rooms each night.

"I promised my parents I'd visit after LA, so I'm flying to Beacon right after."

"You'll still make the premiere next weekend? I really want you there."

Smiling, she glances my way. "I wouldn't miss it. Anyway, I have to make sure they pamper the movie's star, and I'll be there for any wardrobe malfunctions."

"Are we expecting a wardrobe malfunction?"

"It might boost the career if you reveal a little nip."

I burst out laughing. "That will do nothing but get me shunned in Hollywood, so let's hope there are no nip slips."

"I'm your girl."

Her words remind me of the conversation I had with Cash last night. I'm his girl, and he's my guy, to put it simply. We're more complex than that, but it's fun to feel this excited about being with someone. *I miss him.*

I even miss the soreness.

He touched parts of me that had never been reached before and woke my body up to the possibilities. Getting him off my mind has been impossible, which has miraculously dulled all other concerns. "Poppy?"

As memories of his face between my legs swirl around my head, my face warms, and heat creeps across my chest.

She glances over with worry, threading her brows together. "What is it?"

I press my hands to my cheeks, hoping to cool them down, but grin stupidly at her instead. "I need to tell someone, and I know we can tell each other anything, so I—"

"Oh my God, Marina, you're freaking me out. Is this good news? Just tell me."

"It's not a big deal." I cackle in delight. "He's huge . . . *it's* a huge deal."

Looping around toward the street that leads to the apartment, she laughs and reaches over to feel my forehead. "Are you feeling all right?"

"Better than ever."

"Okay then, spit it out." The puns just come without even trying. If she only knew what she was saying.

"There was no spitting involved."

"Marina, what the hell?" She bursts out laughing. Slowing for a red light as soon as she stops, she says, "Tell me every dirty detail."

I can't keep it to myself any longer. "He gave me the best orgasms of my life."

"I knew it! I knew something was up with you all glowing and walking on sunshine." Her mouth then falls open. "Wait, as in plural?"

I nod erratically. "As. In. Plural."

"Oh wow, Marina. Lucky girl." She glances at me once more before driving again. Taking a turn into the garage, she's grinning as if she's the one who scored. "I miss sex."

This time, my mouth falls open. "How long has it been?"

"Too long. I was up before dawn and falling into bed at midnight at that last job. There was no time for a social life."

I smirk. "You don't have to be social to have sex."

"True," she replies with a laugh. "But it's nice to catch a name."

She's laughing when her phone lights up on the console between us. We both glance down. "Ugh. It's him. My old boss wants me back." Gripping the steering wheel, she shakes her head. "The new guy can't get the wheatgrass shot right."

"Isn't it just wheatgrass?"

"I always put a few special ingredients in it."

Although my eyes go wide, I'm not as surprised as I appear. "Should I ask?"

Turning into the parking garage, she replies, "Probably best if you don't." With a burst of laughter, she adds, "It's a few drops of pineapple juice to cut the grass. Pun intended." She pulls in our assigned spot and cuts the engine.

I trust this woman with my life, but for a split second there, I had my doubts. "Sounds really good actually."

"Glad you think so. I'm making some for you. We've been eating like crap lately. We both need to get premiere-ready." We get out of the car and slam the doors shut.

"What would I do without you?"

When we walk toward the elevator, she says, "Apparently have multiple orgasms. I think you're doing just fine without me."

Later in the night, I want to call Cash, but I know he's strict with his schedule the night before a race. Miami excluded. But I do text him, so he knows that I'm thinking about him: *Congrats today! I know tomorrow is also going to be amazing.*

It takes about two minutes of me staring at the phone, but then I receive a reply: *Thanks. I'm feeling good about tomorrow. I'll try to call you after the race. Sweet dreams, babe.*

Me: *Sweet dreams.*

As much as I love our nightly calls and text exchanges, I'm feeling lonely. Sleep is going to be my friend tonight instead of dwelling on the fact that I won't get to see Cash in person for another week. That is, if I can slip away during the time I'll be promoting the movie.

WATCHING Cash come in fifth and move up in the rankings along with Westcott Racing has me wishing I had someone to celebrate with. I know he won't see it for a while since he can't have his phone on him, but I text Cash anyway: *So proud of you! Congratulations!*

I also send a congrats to the family group text, letting them know I watched from Vancouver. I get quick replies from most of them. Harbor is celebrating with the crew in the paddock. I want to be there, but being a distraction is not something I want to be responsible for.

Lying on the couch, I watch the reporters scramble to interview the team members and drivers as they get out of their cars. Any flash of Cash has me sitting upright until the interviews die down and the sports channel switches to baseball. No interview with Cash is disappointing, but the happiness I feel for him is like it was my own win. He did amazing today. I want to shout it from the rooftops.

I also don't want the cops called on me, so I don't shout. I lie on the couch smiling over my boyfriend's great performance on the track today instead. I just wish I could be there to celebrate with him.

SOMEONE KNOCKING on the door startles me awake. Still groggy, I look ahead where night lies on the other side of the sliding glass door. Behind me, the knocking continues.

I have no idea how long I've been asleep, but something isn't right.

I tap my phone to see the time when I stand. 11 p.m. *What the hell?* Who would be here at that hour? And more importantly, is it safe, or should I call the police?

Since Poppy isn't here, I walk over so the person won't hear me closing in. I peek through the peephole, my heart stopping fast in my chest.

Oh my God.

Oh my God.

Oh my God.

Hurrying to unlock the bolts and latches, I finally free the door and swing it wide open. I jump right into Cash's arms—legs wrapped around his hips and my arms around his neck. "What are you doing here?" I ask, covering his face with kisses.

"I was in the neighborhood."

20

Marina

I'M PINNED between a brute wall of muscle and one made of sheetrock when Cash carries me back into the apartment and kicks the door closed. With his mouth attached to mine, I hear the click of a bolt before he pulls back to look me in the eyes. "Goddamn, I missed you."

"How are," I start, still needing to catch my breath, "you even here right now? You were just in France."

"I chartered a plane."

"You chartered a private plane to come see me?"

His gaze is latched to my mouth while my body is weighted on one of his hands. Leveraging the wall for support, he brings his other hand to my mouth. Caressing my cheek, he runs the pad of his thumb along my bottom lip. The pressure is gentle with a commitment to more. My breathing deepens just seeing the intention in his eyes, my heart racing like he did on that track today. "I missed your mouth so fucking much. Your eyes when they stare into mine with the same hunger that has me wanting to fuck you so hard right now." Glancing down, he sports a wry grin. "Those tits. I've gotten off from the memory of them, but I need the real thing again. I need you, babe."

"You flew ten hours to have sex with me?" I don't mean to sound irritated, but I'm so wound around him that I can't grab anything that makes sense.

"Do you hate me?" The question comes as a challenge, and he doesn't move a muscle as he waits for my answer.

"God, no." I run my fingers eagerly through his hair. "That's the sexiest thing I've ever heard." I smash my mouth into his, and our lips part, our tongues greeting as if it's been years and not days or weeks. Nothing is tentative as we twist, curve, and caress each other's mouths.

Pulling back once more, he investigates the living room ahead. "Bedroom?"

"Door on the right." He's already moving, pushing open the door and charging into the dark room. The light from the living room reaches far enough to find the bed.

As soon as he sets me down on the mattress, he's tugging his shirt off. He's a masterpiece made for display, a man made of marble muscle and a perfect specimen to inspire artists and my tongue.

Is it wrong to want to lick him, to smell him, to drag my nails over his hard abs? The instinct to own him as much as he owns me grows wildly in my chest as if he's planted the seeds himself.

I bounce to my feet, then tug down the hideously unattractive and holey, guacamole-stained sweatpants I'm wearing. When I lift the Beacon University T-shirt, tortilla chip crumbs sprinkle over my feet. Yeah, not embarrassing at all. "Maybe a little warning next time please."

Judging by the look in his eyes, I'd say stained clothes and crumbs are the last thing this man cares about. "And miss this? Catching you in your natural habitat." He chuckles. "Never."

Shame should have me apologizing, but this is me on my days off, which aren't many. "I haven't showered today."

"I can't wait to taste you then." *Why is that so hot?* My bra clasp is released, but then he stops. Reaching forward, he cups my breasts, then dips down to lick one nipple until it's pert and then the other. A quick blow of cool air breezes over the peaks, hardening them even more. All I can do is hold his shoulders as my head swims from the deliciousness.

The sides of my undies are dragged slowly over my hips and to my ankles. With tan muscles and broad shoulders exposed, the fly of his jeans is left open. Cash kneels, then dips his nose between my legs with a deep inhale.

It's naughty and intense, sensuous, and draws me closer to him—physically and emotionally. He'll take me as I am, appreciating all of me as if every part and side is beautiful to him.

When I look down to watch, his eyes are already set on mine. Dragging two fingers between my need for him and my lower lips, he teases me. "You're so wet for me, babe."

Bending, I cup him by the jaw and kiss him. "I'm so everything for you, babe," I whisper when we part again.

I don't hide myself while standing naked before him this time. There's nothing but desire in his eyes when he looks at me. I feel sexy and revered when I'm with him. The need to make him feel just as incredible is strong within me.

Taking his hands, he stands. I hold one and change places with him. "I want your clothes off," I say, using his words for my benefit. "Will you do that for me?"

Cash grins, toeing his shoes off and pushing his jeans

and the rest of his clothing off before lying on the bed on propped elbows to watch me. "Don't keep me waiting."

I'm not nervous, though I'm beyond my skill set. The art of seduction isn't something I've been inspired to master until now. I climb on and straddle his legs. "I want to please you."

Reaching forward, he runs the tips of his fingers under my jaw, landing on my chin. Holding me there, he says, "You already do."

His words are intoxicating, but the look in his eyes mesmerizes me. I've never felt craved before, but it's potent in its effect. I bend over, taking his erection in hand and licking the tip without foreplay. Cash groans and falls flat on his back. The heat of his touch scorches the shoulders of my skin, feeling heady from the sensation.

Using my hand to cover the base of his erection, I go down, knowing I can't cover the length of him with only my mouth. His cock is as epic as he is, making it so tempting to mount him and chase my own needs.

But when I hear his moan of hedonistic pleasure that I brought him, that *I* elicited, I go as deep as I can, then drag my tongue along the base as I come back up. His fingers weave into the hair on the back of my head, and when he finds a rhythm that matches mine, pleasure builds, and his groans keep coming.

"Keep going," he says, his voice rough with need. Picking up speed causes him to breathe harder, to squeeze the hair fisted in his hand tighter, and his hips to punctuate his erection into my throat. "Such a good girl."

I want nothing more than to have him fall apart because of my doing. I bob over his tip, using my tongue to cradle the ridge. I suck and pull and drag my teeth, causing him to lift as if the pleasure is too much.

"Fuck, Marina." He rips his dick from my mouth and grabs me by the arms, pulling me up his body. "Tell me you're on birth control. Say it, babe."

With my hands pressed to his chest, I know the thirst he feels inside needs quenching. My own core throbs as if my heart has sunk lower. I struggle to still, the need too much for me not to rub myself shamelessly against his leg. "Do you need me?" I ask, a reckless game at play between us.

"I need you." He grabs his erection, stroking. "I need you so much."

"I'm yours." I lift enough for him to position himself beneath me. Sitting up with his chest against mine, he holds my hips above him. "I'm all yours, Cash—Ah!" I'm released, and my body slides down his massiveness. There's no time to acclimate. The burn from stretching around him becomes foreplay as he kisses my lips and swallows my gasp.

He fucks me with reckless abandon, and I lose myself in every thrust that pushes air from my lungs and kiss that revives me each time. *Hard. Raw. Carnal.* There's nothing kind about our physical connection, but I can't stop myself from begging between *mercy* and *more* with every push and thrust.

"So good," I breathe into his ear as I bounce on top of him. The buildup is fast, the coil wound so tight that I won't be able to stop from unraveling too soon. I dig my nails into his shoulders and wave my surrender flag as my body falls into the abyss. "*Ooh . . . Cash . . .*"

I'm held so tight that the thread between the two worlds I'm straddling snaps, sending me in both directions, the ache and the satisfaction becoming one. "Ah," comes in a whispered release before the lights dim.

Three more intense and restless pushes have him falling with me. "*Fuck.* So good." *And then the peace of darkness comes.*

As wrapped up in the moment as we are in each other—arms and legs tangled messes, panting, and racing heartbeats—I can feel his beating strong in his chest, so I lift my head from his shoulder, wanting to see his eyes only to find them on me already.

I run the tips of my finger along the lines of the corners of his eyes and kiss the side of his lips, working my way over until our mouths are together again. "Hi," I whisper, closing my eyes and savoring every second of this with him. I'm exhausted but ready to conquer the universe. It's a weird dichotomy.

But when I open my eyes, there's no question about this overwhelming feeling. The realization steals my breath just like he does.

Kisses are trailed along my shoulder and neck until he reaches my lips again. Just shy of kissing them, he says, "I need to leave in twenty minutes."

"Wait." That was not the sweet nothing I expected to hear. "What?" I do a double take, fully engaged with my senses again.

Pushing my hair back on one side of my face, he kisses my cheekbone and my temple. "I need to be in New York by nine o'clock."

Disappointment devastates the night I thought we had ahead of us. "No." My arms tighten around him, and I hold him as close as I can. "You can't leave."

"I'm sorry," he whispers against the shell of my ear. "I have to pick up Cullen by nine."

I lean back and look into his green eyes again. "You flew completely out of your way just to see me for an hour?"

"Yes," he replies, grinning unapologetically and glancing down at the connection our bodies still hold. "But there were ulterior motives involved."

I take a deep breath, not able to embrace being upset. How can I when he made me a priority? "That's quite the distance to travel for a booty call."

"Worth every hour and mile. The sex is spectacular." Kissing my other cheek, he says, "Like the woman herself." Then he looks me straight in the eyes. "You are amazing."

Beyond the words and compliments, my heart feels most grateful for him. We kiss without caring about the time or the world outside. We kiss deeply, our bodies bonded more than physically. And then we let silence momentarily come between us, enjoying the here and now. But then I spot the time across the room. "We still have fifteen minutes."

I'm flipped onto my back, and he buries himself deep inside me. Despite the time ticking away, we're slow and calculated. Our eyes stay fixed, and our hearts fastened. It's not about hard or slow, or days together or apart. It's just us, consumed in each other.

Cash steals a few minutes in the bathroom before returning to kiss me, where I was left a bag of naked jelly bones on the bed. I use the last of my strength to push through the familiar soreness beginning to return and wrap myself around him again.

Carrying me to the door like a bag of groceries he doesn't want to drop, he unplucks his lips from mine and says, "I hate this."

"You just said," I start to tease, but my heart's not in it. "I hate this, too." I drop my head on his shoulder and breathe him in. "I'll see you next weekend."

"Next weekend, then." Cracking the door open, he keeps me hidden behind it as he leans his head against mine. "I wanted to tell you something." I don't interrupt with careless words when I'm feeling so sad. I just need to hear him and memorize his voice, though I know I'll be talking to him soon. "You're beautiful, not just in looks, though that's stellar, but the way you make me feel, the way you treated my son and my mom. I saw you smile at something on the TV at my apartment, and it was as if the sun had risen at night." I'm not sure, but I think I hear him gulp, or it's me trying to choke down the emotion I'm holding in. We're both struggling to swallow as he shares his soul with me.

He says, "I can't stop thinking about you and that chocolate." I laugh, but it's not as free since I'm having to let him go. "The way you bounced from joy or the sugar. I'm not quite sure, but you're so fucking adorable and filled with life, the life I've been missing from mine. I feel alive when I'm with you, when I hear your laughter, your voice as you drift to sleep, the vivid detail you go into over the minutest thing. I love every word out of your mouth, the breath that you breathe, the smile that always reaches your eyes, and the way you flip from rose-colored glasses to anger in the snap of a finger."

"My heart feels too big for my chest."

"Mine too, babe." He kisses my temple and then leans back, his gaze roaming my face, taking me in until it settles on my eyes. "I don't want to date anyone else. I only want you. I love you, Marina."

My lips part, but no words escape, nor breath, or a single sound. My own feelings are so large, too much to restrain in the confines under the current situation. "I love you, too. So much."

I worry I'm living in a fever dream and afraid to wake up, but every kiss and touch is so real that I'd choose this reality over life if I could feel like this forever.

And then he says, "The press will have a field day when they find out."

My back stiffens as my feet land on the floor again. "My brothers are going to kill us both."

He sighs, the bubble sounding like it's burst. "I'm not sure what to do about that."

"I'm tired of the world having a say in my relationships and my professional management team advising me on how to behave. I just want to be with you and to always feel like this."

A lopsided grin creases his mouth. "How's that?"

"Happy."

21

Cash

I DASH up the stairs and ring the doorbell. It's not a huge place in the West Village, but it's nice, and Terpidy and Cullen have it all to themselves. I'm late, and she's not going to let it go. She never does, though I'm rarely five minutes after the agreed-upon time.

The door opens, and I'm greeted by Cullen's toothy little grin. "Hey there," I say, bending down to hug him.

"Hi, Daddy." He reaches behind him and grabs his bag, but I slip in and get it to carry myself.

"Cash?" Terpidy calls from behind the half-open door. It swings open, and she looks me up and down. I catch the slightest of eye rolls before she catches it herself.

Standing, I say, "Hi." Fighting with her is the last thing I want to do, especially with our son between us.

"I have a job in Paris on Monday." I could point out the lack of pleasantries or the basic courtesy of a hello. Her career had already skyrocketed when we met. The girl who partied one night in Monaco and then in LA after the

Oscars isn't the same woman now. She has no tolerance for me like she once did.

Justifiably.

I was a real beast of an asshole once we soured, which didn't take long. Not that she was any better. We were one and the same that way and never meant to be more than a few drunken nights in Ibiza. What we were or weren't doesn't matter now. Cullen does, and for him, I'm trying to be the father he needs. "I leave on Sunday for Brazil. I can see if my mom is available." Glancing down at Cullen, I smile. "That'd be fun, right, buddy?"

He shrugs.

She covers his ears. "If she can't, he'll be with a babysitter all week. I'm not turning this job down. It's a big campaign, and the money is great."

Got to love being made into the villain. It's a no-win for me. Damned if I say I can't. Damned if I stop her from leaving him with a stranger. "I'll take care of him."

Kneeling so I'm closer to his eye level, I ask, "Do you need anything for the week? Or do you have all your stuff?"

Another shrug.

I'll buy what he needs.

Straightening back up, I bring him with me, settling Cullen on my side. "When will you return?"

"I don't know."

"You don't know? What kind of fu—" Deep breaths. *In through the nose. Out through the mouth.*

Terpidy kisses Cullen's cheek and gives him a slight smile before stepping back into the house and holding the door between us. I'm still staring at her in disbelief as my thoughts scatter, searching for answers she won't give me.

She says, "You still have the key if he needs anything?"

"Yeah," I reply dumbly, not saying a damn word about

what she's about to do to him. "Say bye to your mom, Cullen." The phrase more for him than her as we walk into the unknown of when he'll see her again.

He says, "Bye, Mommy."

I'm still staring at her, wondering if she means days, weeks, or never returning.

She smiles at him. "I'll see you soon, okay?"

"Will you?" I say, unable to keep myself from asking.

"A week at the longest." Her smile for me is smaller but just as genuine as the one she gave him.

My chest loosens from hearing her say that, and I nod. "Okay. Just let me know."

I set him on the ground when we get a few blocks down, finally feeling like I can breathe normally again. I don't know what she was thinking. She can play games with me all she wants, but not with him.

Scrubbing my hand over his head, I say, "Your hair looks lighter."

"Mom says it's from the summer sun."

Or me, but I'm not going to quibble over it. "Yeah, mine gets lighter during the summer as well." A little quibble, but who's counting? "Ice cream?"

He giggles. "It's morning."

"Exactly." I tap his nose, seeing this as an opportunity instead of a burden. In a few months, he'll be starting school. I need to make the most of his freedom. "We make our own rules."

"Why am I adding beef bouillon to marinara?" I ask my mom, who's walking me through a recipe on speaker. She lives two floors below mine, but the guys are cooking tonight. Day four on our schedule was packed with the aquarium and shopping to make this meal.

"It adds a nice depth of flavor, and I think it makes it heartier." She says, "Check your meatballs."

Cullen cracks up anytime we say the M word, so he's in a fit of giggles on the couch.

"Okay, I added it." I bend down to check the meatballs in the oven, which are looking good. Making this meal is a bigger production in time and steps than I expected, considering we could have just ordered it. I know it will pay off, though, and it's been fun to cook with Cullen.

I was always at the track until after dark, so I didn't get skills from my mom back then. I'm taking advantage of her expertise now. We're not Italian, though, so we're going off instinct versus accuracy.

"Thanks, Mom. I think I have it from here."

"Happy to help." She's been a help and is set up to take Cullen when I leave for Brazil.

Grabbing a beer from the fridge, I twist the cap and flick it into the trash can I've pulled out from the cabinet. I don't drink often since my profession is taxing on the body, and it's in my contract that I can't consume alcohol within five days of a race. But I don't head to São Paulo until Sunday, giving me five full days of padding. And because I've earned this after all the kid fun we've had this week.

"Mom drinks wine," Cullen says, climbing on the barstool on the other side of the counter.

I don't dig the tale-telling, but I let my curiosity get the best of me and anchor my hands on the cold stone. "A lot?"

He shakes his head. "Mostly Sundays." Um, that's odd. He swivels in the chair and asks, "May I have juice?"

"Yeah, sure." I get an apple juice from the fridge and hand it to the kid. "Every Sunday?"

"Race day." He hops down after scoring a juice box and runs back to the couch to watch his show.

I don't know what to make of that, but the garlic bread needs my immediate attention.

———

"GUESS WHAT?" Marina says as soon as she answers.

I waited until eleven, my time, to call her. My tired body sinks into the mattress. I'm more exhausted from the past few days with Cullen than from my high-intensity, high-risk job. "What?"

"I'll be in midday but head straight to wardrobe and makeup. I have an afternoon packed with interviews and a late-night talk show. It films early, though, so I'll be free by dinner. Hint. Hint."

"Subtle."

"It's my specialty," she says, laughing,

I chuckle as well, both of us knowing the truth. "Would you like to have dinner with me, Ms. Westcott?"

"And Cullen. We can go somewhere fun that he'll—"

"If you'll take me, I'm overdue for a grown-up conversation. Anyway, he probably needs a break from me. He called me grumps earlier."

"He wouldn't be the first."

I feel like the sympathy I was looking for isn't going to be found on this call. "He's worn me down, Marina. The kid doesn't need sugar. He's wound up on life."

She giggles. "Kids are great like that, but if you want me all to yourself—"

"I do." I smile even though she can't see me. "He's been begging to spend the night at my mom's." It sounds as if my son prefers Grandma's, and I'm okay with this. "She bakes cookies for him every time he stays over."

"That will do it." A little moue crosses the miles, and then she says, "Will you bake cookies if I stay at yours?"

"I'll bake you anything you want, babe." She sniffles, so I ask, "Hey, what's going on?"

Her breath is unsteady, but she says, "This press tour and premiere are supposed to be a pinnacle in my career, but I'm just happy I get to see you again."

Damn, it's like she reached in and squeezed my heart. "I thought I was supposed to be romancing you?"

The softest of laughs is heard, and she whispers, "I've been sentimental all week."

"I like that about you. And I can't wait to see you again, Marina."

The call isn't long as she has an early flight, and Cullen has officially made me feel like an old man. I don't know why I felt the need to pack in so many activities this week, but I think a few slower days are called for starting tomorrow.

I woke up with newfound energy and hopped on the treadmill to knock a few miles off this morning before Cullen wakes up. I hit my limit right around four, but I also find the treadmill boring as shit mentally. I prefer the runs with Duncan when we're on location for all races.

I don't hear from Marina until around two o'clock. She sends me a quick clip of her in hair and makeup before leaving to do interviews. I text: *You're beautiful. Break a leg.*

She replies: *I love you.*

I will never leave her hanging: *I love you. Knock 'em dead!*

Cullen and I head out to the park just after three because he's bouncing off the walls. He needs wide-open spaces to let his imagination run free. He talked me into buying a balloon that he lost two point three seconds later when he released it in hopes of bouncing it like a ball.

Tears followed when it got too high for even me to catch . . . and that's how he ended up with four more balloons tied to his clothes. I've held his hand the entire walk home because he then worried he would float away. I promised to always keep him grounded, like my mom did for me.

When we're two blocks shy of the apartment, he's mood snaps, so we detour into the deli for a snack. Food is always a good decision when it comes to Warren men.

Warren . . . Sometimes I regret being talked into his using Ryatt as the surname. It was all ego naming him Ryatt.

Holding Cullen's hand in one of mine and a sandwich in the other, I take a bite, which is a quarter of the sandwich. Food fixes bad moods. Mine included.

I ask, "How are the Goldfish?"

"Fishy."

I laugh, watching him pop another orange cracker into his mouth. "Fresh catch." A happy kid once again.

When we get upstairs, a familiar silhouette haunts my doorway. "Do I need to call security?"

Marina laughs as Cullen starts skipping toward her and gives her a hug. "Nice balloons." She glances at me. "Daddy must have been a pushover today."

"For the record, I was the hero."

"You're always a hero in my book." I lean in to kiss her, but then stop when our eyes connect. She glances at Cullen and then raises an eyebrow.

Right.

I move to the side and punch in the code to unlock the door. "Want to come in?"

"Thought you'd never ask."

Pushing the door open, I hold it while they walk in, then grab the small bag before she has a chance to carry it.

Cullen skips inside, chatting with her and telling her about our day and the aquarium.

She's smiling, bringing the whole apartment to life with her vibrancy. I want to stare at her beauty and watch as she moves about the space as if the thought of her living here isn't so far-fetched. I want to touch her, kiss her, welcome her home, but . . . I take a breath. I've not been in this position before with Cullen. I'm not sure how to maneuver with this circumstance, so I'll restrain my need to be close to her and pretend we're only friends.

As soon as she frees the balloons from his belt loops and a buttonhole on his shirt, he begs her to let him set them free on the terrace. She looks at me for guidance, crinkling her face. "I'm not sure if that's allowed."

I collect the strings and knot them together. "You can show Grandma when she gets here, which is any minute now. Why don't you grab your bag so we won't keep her waiting?"

As soon as he dashes down the hall, I grab Marina and kiss her. The sweetest caress of our lips still produces the heat that's always burning between us. We don't linger, but our breathing is quickened when we pull back. The sound of shuffling has me retreating into the kitchen, and I catch sight of Cullen coming out of his room with his backpack. My gaze pivots to Marina who is standing where I left her but touching her fingers to her lips.

Happy as a clam around her, Cullen asks her to read him a book, but a knock on the door derails the activity. "Hi, Laura," Marina says, raising her hand beside her.

My mom comes in and beelines for her. They greet each

other with a hug and make small talk as I give Cullen a hug as well. "Be good for Grandma, okay?"

"I will. Promise."

My mom doesn't even give me a chance to ask her if she'd like to stay a bit before she's hugging me and walking out with Cullen. "You two have a great night."

"Love you guys," I say from the door. As soon as it's closed, I turn back to my girl. "So . . ."

"So," she replies. "Do you have plans?"

Coming closer, I take her by the hips and kiss her neck. "I have all sorts of plans for you, babe."

"I had an idea."

I lift to see mischievous eyes staring into mine. "Oh yeah?"

My plans involved a bed, the kitchen island, and a shower.

Hers involved cramming into a crowded theater, paying for overpriced cheap wine for her, then hiding in the corner praying the lights go down before we're spotted.

I'll never say no to her, so my plans are back-burnered until later while we watch a play in the standing-room-only section since all the seats were sold out. Marina insisted this was the best way to see a play. I'm not convinced until after intermission, and I see tears hovering in her eyes as she watches the people on stage.

I've missed the complete story because I was captivated by the way every emotion she feels deep inside plays across her face. The magic isn't on stage. The magic is wrapped up inside Marina Westcott.

Not once has she shown this depth of emotion in her films. I need to get her back to Broadway. Selfishly, it brings her closer to me as well.

We slip out before the ovations, which is smart, so hopefully, we're not recognized. When we hop in a car to head back to my place, I ask, "What would it take to get you on that stage again?"

"Being cast for the role." She looks down at her fingers as they fidget with the seat belt. "I've missed a lot of auditions because I simply can't make them or don't have time to film them to send in."

"You're a star."

"In your universe, Romeo." Definitely in mine. She says, "Maybe even in Hollywood. But on Broadway, I haven't established a great track record."

"Will Hollywood get you there?"

"Yes. If this movie does well."

Reaching over, I take her hand in mine and bring it to my lips to kiss. "It will. I know it."

"How was your first Broadway show?"

Let's hope she doesn't want to discuss the plot because all that matters is sitting next to me now. "Magnificent."

We didn't make it to the bedroom, but the kitchen got a solid workout. Yeah, my plans were better, though I won't tell her that. I'll happily accompany her to any play or show her heart desires if I get the pleasure of her company.

Lying under the stars on a warm June night, she takes a sip of wine and asks, "Why did you choose to use Ryatt over Warren?"

I'm not ashamed of anything in my past other than the nuclear bomb that was my relationship with Terpidy and the aftermath. Before her, though, it was my father. Cullen is the bright spot that numbs the angrier part of me these days. "I was offered my first major contract at seventeen. I was a punk-ass kid with a huge fucking chip on my shoulder. I'd been calling myself Crash Ryatt—"

"Crash? Probably not good in your sport."

"Nope," I reply, chuckling. "I was a big gamer in my teens and won every race I entered. It was fun to be someone on that track, to make a name that was all my own."

She sits right up. "Please tell me Cash is your real name."

"Don't worry. It's my real name. Crash was a play on it. Ryatt, as bad as it is, is a play off the word riot. I signed that contract as Cash Ryatt because back then, I didn't want to be a Warren. That gave my father too much credit. And trust me, that deadbeat doesn't deserve an ounce of recognition of my life or my mom's."

She reaches for my knee and rubs gently. "I'm sorry."

"It's okay. I'm not as bitter as I used to be. I mean, the fucker will never be a part of my life or my kid's, but now I just think of him as a necessary evil. And I'm the product of him."

"You're nothing like him."

"No, I'm not. I may have some resemblance, but I'll never be like him. Cullen won't know anything other than I'm the proudest fucking father on this planet." I drink some water and sit up from the lounge chair. "And Ryatt's a really fucking cool name, like a superhero."

Her mouth falls open. "You gave your son a superhero's name. That's going to be hard to top for your future kids."

Eyeing her, I take her hand and grin. "Future kids, huh?"

She wobbles her head, her cheeks turning pink in the moonlight. "If you have more kids, that is," she says, flustered. "I'm not assuming or trying to trap—"

"I know. It's good to talk about these things. We should." Holding her hand a little tighter, I push right into the uncomfortable topic of conversation. Might as well lay it all out there. "For me, I want more kids, but I want a stable relationship to bring them into. What about you? Do you want kids?"

She nods, her smile softening. "I do, but like you, I want the family unit, too." Getting up, she turns and settles on my lap. "You're a great father, Cash. Cullen's lucky to have you."

Readjusting on my lap, I lie back and hold her so I can see the stars shining like a halo over her head. She's the only star in the universe I need.

"I'm lucky to have *him*." I kiss her shoulder and add, "And you."

22

Cash

"You killed it."

"Really?" Marina rolls to her side to face me.

I click off the TV when the show ends and set the remote on the nightstand. Turning to look at her in bed beside me, I feel a sense of pride that I'm not sure I have a right to. I feel it anyway. "Yeah, you were funny and sweet, beautiful, and so smart he couldn't keep up with you."

"You have to say that."

"No, I don't. I'll always tell you the truth." Signaling toward the TV, I add, "You were incredible. Viewers will fall in love with you." I cup her cheek and lean over to kiss her. "Just like I have."

Caressing my hand on her, she says, "You fell for my spicy side."

I chuckle, kissing her neck, and then move across her shoulder. Planting wet kisses over her collarbone, I slide my hand under the covers and much lower between her legs.

Her eyes flutter closed as she rolls to her back and licks

her lips. Moving over her, she butterflies her legs, opening for me like a flower. Sinking into her wet heat, I kiss her mouth, then whisper in her ear, "I fell for your every side, babe."

———

A POKE to my forehead has me swiping away at the nuisance and groaning.

My chin . . . "Fucking hell, gnat, I need sleep."

I swat at it again and then hear a giggle. My eyes fly open to see a smiling Cullen staring at me. "Hi, Daddy."

"Hey, buddy—*oh shit*." I sit up to block his view of Marina sleeping next to me. "What are you doing here?"

He's now covering his mouth and giggling even harder from hearing me swear. "Grandma said I needed clean . . ." *Giggle.* "Underwear."

"I thought we packed some for you." He shrugs. I say, "Go get some in your room, and I'll come with you."

My mom rushes in to guide him by the shoulders out of the room. "Sorry. Sorry. There was an accident and . . ." She doesn't even bother finishing before she shuts the door behind them.

Scrubbing my hand over my face, I then shake my head. Not the way I wanted to wake up this morning.

Marina sits up beside me and rubs my back. "Good morning."

"Sorry about that."

"You don't need to apologize, but I guess we need to start figuring out how this will work. Not only for Cullen but also my family, and eventually, the world since we live in a fishbowl."

I realize I haven't even looked at her. I'm so caught up in

what happened that I'm missing what's right in front of me. Her hair is a complete fucking disaster, and I couldn't be more attracted to her than I am right now.

That she can show up on my doorstep in full makeup and fancy clothes but let me ravage her for hours last night without a single care about how she'd look in the morning —fucking perfection.

She rests her cheek on my shoulder and says, "I need to shower and get going. Busy day of press ahead."

"And then the premiere. Will I see you tonight?"

"I can stay at a hotel or Harbor's since you have Cullen tonight."

Wrapping my arm around her back, I hold her close, and kiss the top of her head. "You're important to me. I'm going to talk to him soon about us dating."

"I'm not going anywhere, so do things on your timeline and what's best for him. I don't mind waiting."

"You're amazing."

She pecks my shoulder again and hops out of bed. "I'm also running late, and it seems you have an underwear emergency."

Getting out of bed, I catch her by the hand before she slips fully into the bathroom. I don't have lines I've been working on. Just simple truths from my heart to hers. "I love you."

She lifts and wraps her arms around me. After kissing me with abandon, she drops down on her heels and says, "I love you so much. You say you're lucky, but I'm the fortunate one."

"One day, I'm going to outcharm you."

Waggling her brows, she laughs. "Guess we'll see." She kicks her foot behind her and laughs as she closes the bathroom door.

I pull on my jeans and hear the shower starting as I slip out of the bedroom. Cullen's room is empty, so I head into the living room. My mom comes to me and whispers, "I'm so sorry. I wasn't thinking you'd—"

"I know. It's okay." I rub her arm in reassurance. "It's new for all of us."

Sitting on the couch with his backpack still on, he says, "Grandma spilled tomato juice on my pants."

"Oh?" I look at her, raising my brow, and laugh. "When you said accident, I thought you meant—"

"It was all me." She touches my shoulder. "I'm so sorry, Cash." She lowers her voice and whispers, "I didn't think running out of here would make sense to him."

"I'm glad you stayed." Moving around her, I give her shoulder a gentle squeeze. "Coffee for the road?"

She smiles, putting the strap of her bag over her shoulder. "An unsubtle hint received." Walking toward the door, she holds out her hand. "Come on, Cullen. I promised you a toy car for that mess. Time to go to the toy store."

"Make sure it's a Westcott Racing car. Can't have my kid supporting the other teams."

"Never," she says, walking out the door. "Don't forget to give me the all clear." She pokes her head back in. "And if you need another night, I'm more than happy to spend time with my grandson. We started a new puzzle, and I've already packed enough clothes."

"I appreciate it. Love you, Mom."

Cullen runs back and jumps into my arms. Hugging me tight, he says, "Love you, Daddy."

I hold him even tighter. Kissing the side of his head, I whisper, "I love you, Cullen. So much."

As soon as I set him down, he asks, "So can I spend the night with Grandma again?"

"Wow," I start, shagging up his hair. "You little traitor. You sure? You're with Grandma tomorrow night, too, because I have to fly to Brazil to race."

He straightens his backpack on his shoulders. "Yep." Running back toward the door, he waves. "I'm sure."

Scratching the back of my neck, I say, "See ya, kiddo." I'm not sure what to make of that. He's five and fifteen at the same time. Damn, the teen years are going to be lonely if he's already over spending time with his dear old dad.

When I return to the bedroom, Marina stands beside the bed, staring at her phone. Her hair is still twisted on her head, and a towel is wrapped around her body. By the way her shoulders hunch forward and she drops to sit on the mattress, I know something's wrong. "Hey, everything okay?"

Silence remains between us, drawing me closer until I'm beside her on the bed. Wrapping my arm around her, I see a text exchange on her phone with Lauren's name at the top. "Is that your agent?"

"Yes."

"What's going on?"

She hands me her phone to read. I start at the top of the messages, "His team has decided to part ways, completely sinking our plan." I glance at her to ask, "Your ex? What plan?"

"Yes. My ex. My co-star on the red carpet tonight." She lies back, then twists her legs to tuck them under the covers again. With her head on the pillow, she stares up at me. "It means his team has decided they're going public."

"Who's they?" I sound like an idiot. "I don't . . . Why now? Why when you guys have almost made it to the finish line without any more major distractions from the movies?"

She sighs and looks up at the ceiling. "Lauren said my

interviews have gone too well according to his team, which puts him in a bad light."

Resting my hand on her chest, I feel her steady heart-beat. "You mean the pity party he was hosting for himself is over? He's jealous. That's what this is about."

"His press hasn't been flattering." Draping her arm over her head, she angles her gaze at me, appearing small and even fragile. "How am I going to survive this? The press will ask all the questions, and I don't have the answers."

I hate that she feels less because of that asshole. Taking her hand, I hold it on my lap. "Why won't Lauren be there to handle it?"

"She has a premiere in LA tonight for one of her A-list clients. She couldn't do both on opposite coasts."

"That's bullshit. She should be here instead of throwing you to the wolves."

Marina finally sits up with a heavy-chested sigh. "I can't dwell on this anymore. I need to go to my fitting, or I'll really be in trouble hitting the red carpet in sweats and a T-shirt."

I've struggled for hours to figure out how I can help her. With our relationship a secret from almost everyone, I also don't know how I can be there for her and not break the rules Westcott Racing has put in place.

I receive two texts from her hours later: *She's wearing the same designer from the same collection as me.*

Me: Doesn't matter. *You'll outshine her.*

And then after that, she texts: *They're engaged and announcing tonight.*

Harsh.

And if effective, it will humiliate my girl at her own premiere.

Fuck that.

She's a fucking queen to be bowed down to. And I know

who I am. Her fucking king. Like I told my son, we make our own rules.

I pull one of my tuxes from the closet and start getting red carpet ready.

———

I HAVE CONNECTIONS, so it wasn't hard to snag a ticket. I'm hoping Marina will be happy to see me. Everything we have could be ruined by a bad decision. This could be my worst of all time, and that's an impressive list.

Stepping out of the SUV, I straighten my jacket and button it. I don't dig these events, but I've been to enough to know what to do. I'm guided forward to the press and start the game, answering questions and taking photos. The positive about not being announced until arrival is that no one is prepared to talk to you.

The downside, they wing it. "The last time we saw you and Marina Westcott together, you were holding hands in Miami." The journalist holds the microphone under my nose and asks, "Are you here to support her as a friend, or is there more between the two of you?"

I step back and reply, "She's a brilliant actress. I'm here to support her and the movie."

Not really into the fame side of things, I start walking ahead until I hear someone from the press corp yell, "Marina, over here."

I step to the busiest part of the carpet and scan through the bustle of people. I have no idea what she's wearing or how her hair is styled. I don't need to, though. She stands out from the crowd.

With my eyes locked on the stunning target, I move around people, cutting through groups until I finally reach the edge of the area where she's posing for photos. They'll never know the smile she's wearing is fake, but I do. It doesn't reach her pretty blues and falls short of the apples of her cheeks.

I stop to catch my breath that she's stolen, watching her own the entire red carpet with her presence. She's wearing a pink dress so hot it's electric with black shoes and her hair falling over one side. I turn to the guy beside me and say, "She's a knockout."

Then he shoves his microphone in my face, and I know I've screwed up. Does it matter anymore? I'm about to blow our cover to smithereens. I walk straight up to her when she turns my way.

Her eyes go wide, and deep pink lips part. I catch the tight blink as if she's seeing things. "Cash? What are you—"

"Whenever you need me, I'll be there for you."

"You're going to get into so much trouble." She smiles. "Is it worth it?"

"*You* are worth it to me, babe."

Looking at the flashes explode around us, she turns back to me and whispers, "You sure you want to cause a riot?"

Sliding my hands around her waist, I pull her close, and say, "Too late." I kiss her with her head tilted back, our names being shouted in every direction while my lips are pressed firmly to hers, and tongues tangling like we're the only two people left on earth.

"Ah, the famous race car driver?" The intrusion of his annoying fingers snapping near Marina's ear has me pulling her upright again and close to my side.

I glance at Marina. "This is the ex?" She nods as I try to stifle my laughter, but I slip. The guy's a good three inches shorter than me, and he doesn't look like he could hold up a fence post already cemented in the ground by his build. Is this really what girls want from Hollywood?

Disappointing.

The frenzy of the media causes chaos on the red carpet as well. Our names being called repeatedly and the tap on the shoulder by a microphone put me on edge. But I'm beginning to worry about Marina's safety if a fight or violence breaks out to capture the story. A lot of money is attached to first pics, and we're chum in the water for the sharks.

The actor says, "I'm sure you heard I got engaged."

I'm slow to turn my head toward Marina, hoping he catches the drift. He doesn't. He's standing there like I give a shit about him or his life. "Why is he still here?"

She laughs. "I have no idea." Turning to him, she says, "Tell me where you're registered, and I'll send you a gift. You didn't want me then; you're not getting me now. Just leave me alone and go live your own life."

Leaning closer, he talks to us like he's sharing a secret. "Well, I just wanted to come over and tell you sorry for breaking your heart, Marina."

"You did no such thing," she smarts as if the mere suggestion offends her. I wish she wouldn't react at all because he doesn't deserve it, but I understand the why of her behavior. I'm also a work in progress.

I step in and shake his hand. "I actually wanted to thank you for being a cheating bastard, or I wouldn't be dating this amazing human now." I pat his shoulder. "So thanks there, Chip."

"It's Corbin." He drops his tone like he knows he won't win. Wise.

He walks away, leaving us stunned by the realization that

he's only just now experiencing the regret of losing something you will always want and love.

Despite the audience, we move inside the theater. Standing in the crowded lobby, she loops her arms around my neck, not giving a damn who sees us. "You're my Prince Charming who came to my rescue."

I love the silky material wrapped around her body. Sliding my arms around her, I hold her to me. "Nah. I'm just a guy who came to support his girlfriend."

"You're acting humble. That's so unlike you. I don't approve either. Where's my Cash?"

"*Your* Cash, huh?"

"That's right. *Mine.* You're all mine." She looks around although we already know we're surrounded by an audience of spies and eavesdroppers. "You know what I really want to do?"

Wiggling her hips in my hands, I hope it's what I'm thinking. "Get some candy and go home?"

"Tempting." She laughs. "I really want to kiss you."

"What's stopping you, sweetheart?"

"They'll write horrible stories about me tomorrow. If only they knew the truth and what really happened."

Running the back of my fingers over the delicate curve of her neck, I look into her eyes. "They're going to write what they write. You can't control it, so you should do what you want and not live by their narrative."

I almost expect an argument. That is her specialty, after all, but that's not what I get. I get her lips pressed to mine and a deepening kiss. If she wanted to make a headline, she's succeeding, and I'm happy to help.

Cupping her face, I love her with my tongue and my mouth, my lips, but most of all, my heart.

After that, we don't stay long. What's the point? To play

their media game? No, thank you. I'd rather spend the rest of the night making love to this woman.

My girl.

My woman.

Along with my son, she's my everything.

We make a quick getaway, but she turns to look at me in the back of the car. Releasing the lip she's been worrying, she asks, "What about my brothers?"

I wish I had that answer, but I kind of said "fuck it" the moment I stepped onto that red carpet. "I'll deal with them tomorrow. It's only about us tonight."

23

Marina

"I NEED SLEEP, WOMAN," Cash says, eyes closed and grinning against the pillow under his head.

Straddling his firm bounce-a-quarter-off ass, I bend forward, this time to lick his shoulder blade and then kiss the divot he's created by having his arms bent to support his head. "Come on. One more time."

When that doesn't rouse him, I rub my bare body shamelessly against him. I mean, it wouldn't be hard to orgasm with him between my legs.

A growl vibrates through his torso.

That's not helping me want him less.

He captures me by hooking his arm around my middle and dragging me off to the side of him. Rolling to face him, I laugh, too wired to lay around any longer.

His green eyes darken but the smile remains. "You're insatiable."

"No lies detected, but I also only have two hours before I

head back to Vancouver." My phone buzzes, but I don't even check it anymore. It's been going off all night.

The messages are all variations of the same thing: what were you thinking, what have you done, you're dating Cash Ryatt, or some other shock-factor headline of a text question from friends, family, but mostly Lauren. I even got two texts from Corbin calling me a whore. *Him, of all people.*

Being called a whore doesn't actually bother me since I'm not one, but also, so what if I was. Women have to love when they're demonized for liking and enjoying sex. Clutches my faux pearls. Heaven forbid she gets off from it.

I slide closer, draping my thigh over his leg. Even this turns me on. "Are you really going to send me sexually needy to a city across another country?

His amusement is lost in the embers sparked in his eyes. His hand covers my hip, and then he says, "When you put it like that . . ."

I'm dragged under him and spread apart with his knee. As his mouth covers the distance of my neck, he sinks into me. Releasing a breath, I whisper, "I will never get over how incredible you feel."

"*We* feel. This is how we fit together, babe." Kissing and then punctuating with suction, he says, "So perfect for each other."

I dig the back of my head into the pillow as my back arches of its own accord, and I moan in pleasure, "So perfect."

———

THE DRIVER LOADS my suitcase in the back and then opens the door for me to climb into the SUV. One foot up, but I stop with the other on the ground. "Mom?"

"Hi, honey. I hope you don't mind me tagging along to the airport."

"Of course not." I lift myself into the back and shut the door. The privacy glass is already in place. A red flag. "But why do I feel like this isn't just because you miss me?"

"I do miss you, Marina. I'm looking forward to when the movie wraps and hoping you'll spend some time at the house in Beacon. Or we can take a trip together and go shopping like old times."

"I'd love both of those," I reply, snapping my seat belt into place. "But why the sneak attack, Mom? I have a phone."

"No attacking. I've seen the articles about you and Cash from last night. Your dad and I would have preferred finding out from you directly."

"I was forbidden to see Cash, so it left us no choice but to sneak around."

A breath fills her chest as she glances out the window. When she turns back, she says, "Your entire family was in the theater waiting to watch and then celebrate the premiere with you."

"I'm sorry." I hate feeling bad for something that feels so right. "Last night wasn't planned. Corbin—"

"How is your boyfriend engaged to another woman, and we didn't know you two were broken up?"

Angling my knees toward her, I toy with the loose end of the seat belt. "A lot happened in a short span of time on that carpet and in front of the press—"

"And the world."

Frustration sets in, and I purse my lips before realizing I'm tired of holding it in. "I won't apologize for what I did with Cash. Corbin cheating on me was embarrassing. Kissing Cash was freeing. Corbin told me I wasn't good enough for him and then called me a whore for being with the man I love instead. Cash treats me like a queen."

My mom's mouth hangs in shock, her hands clasping together over her heart. "I'm sorry. He treated you awful. If I would have known—"

"I don't have any more regrets because I learned what I would never tolerate again and what kind of man I deserve."

No parent wants to hear their child had to go through something like this. Corbin will be dead to her like he is to me. "You've gone through so much," she says. "How are you?"

"It's been a lot, but I'm doing better than I have in years." She embraces me again, and I let her, loving her comforting arms around me. "I'll apologize to the family for not letting you know what was happening. I just couldn't bring myself to go inside that theater after all that happened beforehand."

"The man you love?" She reaches over, stilling my hand with hers. "You love Cash?"

I feel caught, precariously walking a tightrope of protecting what's mine and makes me so happy and sharing with everyone else. My mom isn't everyone else, though. I swallow any hesitation and just say it. "I love him. I'm *in* love with him." And then I wait . . . I don't even know what reaction I expect from her. She's always been on my side while still being a guiding parent with advice.

She sits back, and her gaze falls forward. But then a small smile tiptoes onto her face, and when her hand covers her heart, she says, "I've never heard you say that about anyone you've dated before." Reaching over with arms open, she snuggles me in her arms when I lean closer. "Oh honey, I'm so happy for you."

"You are?" I reply the best I can as I have the daylights squeezed from my body.

When we sit back again, her smile is as wide as the one she wears on Christmas morning. "Love is a beautiful emotion. It's strong and more powerful than any other."

"It's all-consuming. I only want to be with him, to lie in his arms." I stop, my eyes going wide at the realization of what I just confided to my mom. Does a parent want to know that kind of thing about their daughter?

Reading me like a book, she laughs. "You're a grown woman, Marina. You should be in love. You should be making love with someone who matters to you and makes you feel giddy when you see them. We enter this new stage of our relationship if you trust that your dad and I always want the best for you."

"I know you do, Mom. Thank you. I trust you and Dad and our whole family to always have my best interests at heart. It's just hard with so many opinions, and then you add in the fact that they're his boss—"

"You are too. Don't forget."

Part ownership was an amazing gift and could pay off to be a financial windfall with how the team is doing, but in no way have I ever had a say or hand as an owner. "I do forget. It's not like I have a vote."

"Of course, you do. You just have to use it." She pauses to dig her phone out of her bag. Reading a message on the screen, she sets it on her lap just after, seemingly satisfied. "An owner of the team dating one of the drivers complicates things."

She's right. This could make things messy.

Resting my elbow on the window, I lean my chin against my hand and stare out. "I hadn't thought of myself in that position." I turn back to face her. "Tell me it's okay to follow my heart with him."

Her smile is soft, sincerity straining the edges. "I can't do that. Only you can decide if that's the right path for you."

The SUV loops into the airport, and I know my time with her is running out. "I guess I should have listened to my brothers. It was never about Cash but the situation we're now in."

"Your brothers said they would have never banned you from the races if they had known about you and Cash. It's out there now, so we'll move through the storm together as a family and handle the coverage the best we can."

"Thank you."

When the vehicle comes to a stop, the driver gets out and grabs my suitcase.

I unbuckle and lean over to give her a hug. She embraces me like she always has—as if I can do no wrong—and says, "I love you. Take care of yourself."

"I love you, too, Mom."

Just as I climb out, she says, "Think about going to Brazil next weekend. I think it will be good for you to be there."

"Okay. If I can get away, I will."

As I roll my case through the private security doors, I think about everything she said. It wasn't a conversation I would have sought to have, but it was needed.

The media was alerted of my arrival, so when I landed, they swarmed, asked questions that would make even the strongest feel weak, and shoved me twice before security intervened. With Poppy back in New York, I have no choice but to run to the car line and wait my turn.

Fortunately, security shuffles me to the front as the words "cheater" and "Corbin" are tossed out with one or two "slut" and "horrible person." Those words should bounce off me like a rubber ball, but they still hurt when I realize this is what they think of me.

What the hell?

Tears fill my eyes, and with no time to find my sunglasses, they fall. A back door is opened and through watery vision, I squeeze through the chaos. The phone in my back pocket buzzes as I climb inside the car. I don't even care if my suitcase makes it at this point. I tell the driver, "Go. Please go."

How do I go from one of the best nights of my life to dropping my head into my hands and crying?

"Are you okay, miss?"

"No. I'm not." I turn to look outside, but something catches my attention in my periphery. I look at the driver again and see him handing me a box of tissues.

He says, "I'm sorry. That was awful."

Taking the box, I stare at him. As awful as that was back there, here I'm being offered the kindness of a stranger. "Thank you." This is what matters. Not people who make more money off upset celebrities or the paparazzi who make a living off provoking someone to capture their worst in a photo. "I appreciate it."

He nods, focusing his attention forward for the remainder of the drive. My phone keeps blowing up, but I'll deal with that when I'm back at the apartment. I take a deep breath, deciding that taking a moment in the quiet will benefit me more.

The quiet doesn't last long when I get into the apartment, but I leave the other calls for later. I just need to hear one voice to feel better.

"What the *fuck* just happened back there?" Cash answers on speakerphone. I assume he needs room to pace.

"How do you already know what happened at the airport?"

"It's all over social media. I was texted links."

"Are you okay, Marina?"

I'm not okay, but worried I'll anger him more, I whisper, "I'm—"

"Don't say fucking fine. Are you hurt?"

I might need to pace myself. "Don't talk to me like that." I put him on speaker and walk to the sliding glass door. "I'm okay."

He exhales loudly, then says, "I'm sorry. Where is your security? The fuck is going on that you're being pushed in a crowd, and nobody thinks to help you?"

"Airport security intervened. I'm fine. Really. I'm not hurt, Cash. My pride is bruised, but physically, I'm all right."

"Do you have a security team, or does the movie provide a detail to protect its stars?"

Spotting someone in the distance, I squint my eyes. "Oh my God. Some guy has a long lens aimed into my apartment." I quickly shut the blinds.

"It's not safe there. You need to get to a place with active security on duty."

Stuck standing in the dark, I sit on the couch when my feelings start to overwhelm me. "I . . . Poppy's at home . . . alone. I have no food."

A video request rings and I see him trying to connect. I swipe at my tears before accepting and plaster on a fake smile. He's angry, not at me, but I don't want to deepen the emotion. He needs to focus on his career. "Hi," I say, holding the phone up so he can see my face.

The shock of how handsome he is never seems to wear off. I can't take my eyes off him. "I'm coming to get you," he says. "If they can't protect you, I will."

"I can't just leave because some paparazzi pushes me or calls me a slut."

"What? *The fuck*?" I gulp, realizing I probably shouldn't have said that. He rubs his temple as he looks away, almost sounding disappointed in me. When he turns back, he asks, "That's bullshit. You know that, right?"

"I know," I whisper. "But why are you mad at me?"

"I'm not, babe. I just want to punch their fucking faces in."

I don't want to let fear dictate how I move in life, but it's hard. I need to turn it into anger. "So do I right now." I throw my arm out wide. "I thought it was bad after Miami, but now the whole world seems to be on his side."

"There aren't any sides. There are his lies, and your team is doing a shit job of turning this around." He takes a breath as if to calm himself. "I can come get you, and we can spend the week in São Paulo together."

It may not solve my problems, but the offer is tempting. I stand back up, coming to my senses. Carrying the phone into the kitchen, I shake my head. "I can't, Cash. As much as I want to, all that will do is leave it for when I get back or make it worse."

He looks away, natural light shining on his face. His head lowers when he turns back to me. "I'm sorry for causing this. Please let me fix it."

"Causing what, babe?" I clear my throat and stand in the light of the fridge. "Causing me to fall madly in love with you? You're guilty, and there's nothing you can do to fix me, so we just have to adapt."

A wry smile models for me on his face. *Damn him*. He can't even help how attractive he is. "You just have to steal all the good lines."

"Are they working?"

"They sure are." He keeps smiling like he doesn't know how to make another expression. And I love it. The light that gleans in his greens. The lines that form at the corners of his eyes. The way he looks at me like we're in person standing face-to-face. He's so authentically himself it's enviable.

I move into the bedroom and turn on a lamp. "I have good news."

Running a hand over his head, he says, "We could use some."

"If I can, I'm going to take you up on the offer of Brazil next weekend because the ban was lifted."

Surprise shapes his face, but then he smirks. "How'd you get that lifted?"

"I told my family how much I love you."

"Ah," he says with a slight nod. "My flight to Brazil with the Westcott brothers should be interesting."

24

Cash

THEY'VE BEEN STARING at me for over an hour.

Noah shook his head once before looking down in disgust.

Loch has knocked into my shoulder twice. Once while going to the toilet at the back of the plane and then when he returned to his seat on the couch at the front.

It's Harbor I'm most worried about. His expression hasn't shifted out of neutral from boarding to now. I can only imagine what's going through his mind.

Small talk isn't going to win them over, so I haven't tried. As soon as I sat in the seat, I put my headphones on and stared right fucking back at them. They don't intimidate me other than the risk of losing my seat on the grid for having sex with their sister. I fucked around, literally, and I'm willing to find out. I have bigger concerns than them overstepping their role as Marina's brother.

Loch and Noah share a silent exchange. Must have drawn the short end of the stick because Noah gets up and comes to sit across the aisle from me. He pinches the bridge of his nose, then leans forward to rest his forearms on his legs. "I thought . . ." He looks at the ceiling of the plane and then back at me. "We had an understanding? As coworkers, boss and employee, even as friends."

Realizing this isn't going to be quick, I recline the chair. "And what would that be?"

"That you wouldn't fuck my sister, who's also your boss, and ten years younger than you—"

"Nine."

"Nine what?" he snaps.

"Marina is nine years younger than me. Stating for accuracy because so much that's put out is inaccurate regarding us."

If eyes could bulge, his are. "Are you telling me you're not having sex?"

"I didn't say that—"

"Motherfucker." He's fast, but Harbor is quicker to his feet and drags Noah to the other side of a row of seats.

Noah shoulders him and frees himself from his confines. "Did you hear what he fucking said?"

"I did," Loch replies. "But we should hear the full story before judging." I don't trust anyone who remains that calm after how he was staring at me for so long. Loch sits in a swivel seat facing me with access to block Noah if he needs to. I appreciate the effort to hear my side of things.

Harbor sits where Noah was and looks me dead in the eyes. "We have a problem, Cash."

"Oh yeah? What's that?" It's best to let them air their grievances so we can all move past this. I recline even more in preparation for getting some shut-eye on this flight before we land.

"Our sister—"

"Your sister," I say, sitting forward and making sure all three of them hear me loud and clear, "is a grown-ass woman with a mind of her own." Raising my hands, I add, "No one was taken advantage of, there was no manipulation involved, and trust me, we weren't thinking about you guys when we fell in love. So—"

"Love?" Noah asks, standing with his guard fully intact. "You can't love my sister."

My gaze volleys among them as they each take in the news differently. "I do. I love Marina very much." Sitting back again, I add, "None of this was planned. If you would have asked me at dinner in Miami, there was no fucking way I would have seen any path that would have led us here. But here we are."

Harbor sits back, and Noah sits down again. Loch twists his hands with his gaze attached to the floor. The four of us sit in silence until I remember that Duncan is asleep in the back, oblivious to everything that's going down. I'll have to thank him for so nobly having my back during all this.

Maybe I should keep my trap shut while I'm ahead, but it just doesn't feel right to have the only thing they are imagining is Marina and me having sex. I mean, it's what I think about most of the time, but it's not good for them. I say, "Her beauty is obvious, but Marina is intelligent and quick, funny, and a little quirky at times. She has a gentle soul she hides behind a temper to protect herself. I didn't set out to fall in love with her. I just did the more I've gotten to know her."

They're staring at me again, but it doesn't matter. I want the whole world to know how I feel about her. "I hope that helps settle how I ended up in this position. I really had no choice in the matter. My heart was hers the moment we met. Our fates sealed together."

"We're not your girlfriends, and this isn't a slumber party

for your dating life confessions, Ryatt," Harbor replies, stony-faced. "We get it." He puts up a hand to stop. "You . . . love her." He glances at his brothers before turning back. "We do, too. If you hurt her, you're done."

I don't know what "done" means to them, but I don't want to find out either.

Everyone gets comfortable in their own space, and soon, I'm able to get some sleep.

A text comes through as soon as we land from Marina: *I love you.*

I'm grinning, feeling like I got away with the king's ransom when it comes to her. I text: *I love you.*

The feel-good texts end there. Scrubbing a hand over my face, I really needed more sleep to deal with the mess of texts I received from Terpidy. The messages flood my phone as soon as I get in the car after landing. Four messages populate the screen.

TERPIDY: *The shoot has been extended a few days.*

Terpidy: *Won't be home until the following Monday.*

Terpidy: *Your mom said she'll watch Cullen.*

Watch him? Like a babysitter. *Where is the disconnect?* My mom will not just watch Cullen. She'll raise him. She'll love him. She'll take care of him like she did for me.

Terpidy: *I'll try to call him every day. If I don't get through, tell him I love him.*

Try?

I take a deep breath and hold it in for the count of three before exhaling. I don't even know how to reply, and anything I type right now won't be nice. I call my mom to get the details and hopefully cool off. As soon as she answers, I ask, "How are you guys doing?"

"We're good. You have other things you should be focused on." I knew she'd downplay any disruption. The thing is, I don't want her life more disrupted than it is by my schedule.

"I heard from Terpidy."

"Cullen's in good hands, Cash. You really don't need to worry."

I angle away from the other guys in the SUV and lower my voice. "I'm worried. What do you need? What can I do?"

"There's nothing you can do from Brazil other than score points. That's your job and your only focus this week. I have all kinds of crafts and puzzles for us here. We'll also be watching your race."

Watch my race. It's something he's never done in person, and now it becomes my sole mission. "I can fly you down here."

"Oh, I don't know. Going to another country is a lot, from dealing with the airports and a five-year-old to passports and exchanging money."

"I'll fly you private. You don't have to do anything or mess with the busy airports in New York. You can fly private and come down Thursday or Friday to do some sightseeing or hang out at the track." I don't know how good a sales job I'm doing, but I really hope it's working. "You haven't seen me race this season. Please come."

There's a pause when I can hear a show in the background and giggling. Cullen. I smile, missing him so much already.

Finally, she says, "If I can get his passport from Terpidy's, we'll come to Brazil."

I sit up, too anxious to rest back. "I have access to it. That was part of our agreement. The key to his safe deposit box is in the top drawer of my desk in the back room. I'll send you the details of where to get it and the paperwork so Cullen can travel with you. In the meantime—"

"He's in good hands."

"Yep." I'm in complete agreement and so lucky to have her. "The best. I know from personal experience."

When we hang up, I'm left with a huge grin embedded on my face. After years of wanting this more than anything, my son will finally see me race in person. One goal accomplished.

The second?

Marina.

25

Marina

"You left me to fend for myself, Lauren."

"I can have security in place by tonight, but you must take some responsibility. You went rogue by having Cash Ryatt crash the red carpet like he did."

"I didn't do anything but arrive like I was told. He showed up because he cared. He knew that I would be walking the carpet alone following Corbin's engagement announcement." Even her heavy breath sounds argumentative and rubs me wrong. "I was thrown to the wolves last night, but I'm not going to fight with you. We're clearly at a crossroads." Sitting in my trailer alone, I move the steamed zucchini around on my plate, but then stop and set the fork down.

I can't do this. I don't want to be here.

"We're not. I'm team Marina. You know I like a plan in place and for it to go smoothly. I apologize for not being there or having staff available for you. I will be there with you next time."

I'm not cold-hearted, but I am upset. I have no idea where we go from here. I just know I need off this set. "I need your help."

"With what?"

"Get me out of working this weekend. I'm going to Brazil to support Cash at the race." My chest feels freer voicing my thoughts, but to see Cash this weekend will be the cherry on top.

"I'll take care of it." She pauses and then switches gears, her tone even going a bit higher when she says, "Ready for the good news?"

"So ready."

I DEBATED TELLING Cash I was coming for several reasons.

1. I don't want to be a distraction this weekend. I want to be a bonus.
2. He surprised me, so now I'm surprising him. Fair play and all.
3. If for some reason I couldn't fly down, I didn't want to disappoint him.

After getting through the track's security, I hear the whispers and see the hands covering the mouths of gossipers as they stare. Loch walks beside me and hasn't said a word about Cash since I landed. Either I'll get an earful when the guys are together, or maybe I'll be pleasantly surprised.

I'm hoping for the latter, but I'm prepared if it's the former. Well, as prepared as I can be for the interrogation of three older brothers. I used to have them wrapped around my finger, but they caught onto my tricks.

It's still early in the day, and the smell of possibility is in the air, as well as burning rubber. Cash has been in a great mood since his mom and Cullen arrived on Friday. He also qualified for the fifth spot at the start, his best yet.

Since he's been asking me to fly down repeatedly, I couldn't say no, and the break is good for me.

Loch stops and says, "Hey, before we go in there."

I glance around to see how many people are watching us before looking at my eldest brother. "Is this another warning?"

"No. We just care about you. Harbor, Noah, and I want you to know that we respect your right to date who you like."

"Why does it sound like a backhanded compliment?"

Chuckling, he rubs his chin. "It kind of did. I didn't mean it that way, though. We like Cash. If you love him and he loves you, we'll support the relationship."

He's not the sentimental one, so it means more to hear this from him. Though I have a feeling he was specifically chosen for the job. I definitely haven't gotten the full story yet. I cross my arms over my chest and ask, "What are the concerns?"

"He starts losing his focus behind the wheel and you get hurt."

Quirking an eyebrow, I study his eyes. He can't lie. It's both a strength and weakness of his in life and as an attorney. "In that order?"

"No. I figured you would call me out if I put our concerns regarding you first. But that is the bigger concern for us. What if things go bad?"

I let my arms fall to my sides again. "Then things go bad.

You can't protect me from everything. I would have never dated Corbin if you could. So if Cash and I break up, I just need you to be my big brothers. That's all."

Wrapping his arm around my shoulders, we start walking again, and he says, "We can do that."

Noah is the first familiar face I see when I enter the paddock. He gives me one of his bear hugs. Maybe because I was bracing myself and expecting the worst from them, but feeling their support has my heart lumped in my throat.

Releasing me, he states, "I take it you're not here to see me." He chuckles and says, "He's back here." Leading me around the equipment and one of the cars, he pushes a door open.

Tilting with a football in his hand, Cash takes a few steps backward and then launches it into the air. Is there anything he can't do? He's my all-American hero.

The door closes behind me, and that's when someone calls, "Marina?" above my head.

I visor my hand over my eyes to find where the familiar voice came from. When I see Cullen on the balcony above, I smile. "Hi, little man." Laura comes to the railing and waves.

"Hi—" A mass of solid man wraps around me, dragging me under the cover of the balcony. Holding me tight around the waist, Cash walks farther into the shadows.

My neck is covered in kisses, but there's no fear because Cash's scent engulfs me, giving me comfort. "How are you here right now?"

Reaching up, I hold the back of his head to my neck and give him better access by tilting to the side. "Good surprise?"

Cash comes around to the front of me and cups my face. "The best." I'm kissed harder this time. The urge to weaken under him is tempting, just like he is. I'm left breathless when we part, his eyes roaming my face as if I'm a mirage. "You're really here."

"I am." I playfully push away. "But I promised not to be a distraction."

I'm pulled right back into his arms again. "Too late." He hums against my neck and then whispers, "When do you have to return to Vancouver?"

"Tomorrow. Three more weeks until I've wrapped."

"I can't wait to have you to myself again."

I'm so excited to tell him I was cast in the play and will be signing a three-month contract for Broadway, but today is about him. So I tuck that tidbit into my pocket, and I'll pull it out after the race post-celebration.

Taking my hand, we walk back inside, but he corners me under the stairs. "I haven't told Cullen we're a couple. I wanted to do it when you were in town. What about after dinner tonight? I can talk to him one-on-one, and then the three of us can discuss it and see if he has any questions."

"You sure he doesn't know already?" I glance outside, wondering if Cullen saw us already. Add this to the time we woke up to him in the bedroom, and I'm thinking it won't be such a surprise to him that we're dating. Cash has millions on the line for him and the team, and he's made me feel like a champion. "If you feel the timing is right."

"I do. I don't want to hide us around him. It's good for him to see a happy couple in his life." He kisses me, and it almost feels like it's just because he can. When he does it again, my suspicions are confirmed. "I'm so glad you're here. Best surprise ever."

"Mm, I can argue that. Flying across the continent for one hour of sex is a pretty great surprise."

"I flew for you. The sex was just the reward for both of us."

"I need to go, and I won't see you again before the race."

As much as I love the Warren surname, on the track, this legend only goes by one name. I lift to kiss him and whisper against his lips, "I love you, Cash Ryatt. You remember that."

I meet up with Laura and Cullen, giving both a big hug. We spend a few hours walking around, then let Cullen nap in Cash's dressing room since he's warming up and won't be using it.

We're tempted to wake him so he can watch the start of the race, but Laura thinks it will be better for him to be rested. Since we have two hours ahead of us, we let him sleep.

When Cullen wakes during the last thirty minutes of the race, I put on his protective headphones, and we walk to the viewing area on the side of the paddock. I'm nervous, and I'm not the one driving. Holding Cullen's hand, though, is somehow reassuring. I pick him up and anchor him on my hip when we start getting down to the final laps.

"There's your daddy." I point out just as he clears the third turn on the second to last lap. The crew is excited, the cheers keep drawing my attention between them and the TV screens. "Your daddy is in third, Cullen. Do you know what that means?"

He looks at me with that same grin he got from his father. "He wins?"

Tapping his nose, I smile because this kid is just the cutest. "Yes. It means he wins third place and a spot on the podium."

"Yay!"

I laugh. "Exactly." Cheering with our hands, we both yell, "Yay!"

Laura can't stand still and looks away from the screen more than she watches. "It's so close."

"I can feel it. Something big. He's going to win."

I shift Cullen to my other hip and take hold of Laura's hand. We share a quick glance and then turn our nervous energy toward the TVs.

The volume is turned up, and the announcers talk about Breckon Rhodes, the other Westcott Racing driver, who took a swipe at Cash two laps ago. "It's a rivalry that's been a long time in the making."

The other announcer says, "Rhodes is not giving way for Ryatt despite the team direction. They're coming up on the final lap and hitting the chicane. Oh—Ryatt's been hit!"

"Is that Daddy?"

The look of horror on Cullen's face has me running to get him away from the devastation. The crew runs out during the snippets of announcements I hear. "Spinning toward the wall . . ." I run to his dressing room with the volume still blaring in the garage. "Fire . . . no sign of him getting out—" And I slam the door shut.

26

Marina

I STAND when Harbor opens the door, expecting to see Cash or even Laura coming to check on us. I moved Cullen on autopilot, but now reality is sinking in.

Cash is not okay.

Wiping my hands down the side of my jeans, I glance from him to Cullen who's playing an online puzzle game on my phone as a reminder to be careful of what he says.

The sounds of the game are loud. I was trying to do anything to divert Cullen's attention from what was happening outside that door. And I lied, telling him his dad was okay.

A million questions cling to the tip of my tongue as I stare at Harbor. I restrain myself from asking a single one in front of Cash's son, but the knots in my stomach tighten, seeing how disheveled Harbor appears. His usually tan face has paled, his brow hanging low. Even his shirt is covered in what looks to be soot. The announcer's yelling comes back in a flash. *"Fire . . . no signs of life . . . Cash Ryatt has crashed."*

Tears fill my eyes, but I still refuse to let them fall. He says, "I need to speak with you."

I nod so carelessly like the fate of my heart isn't on the line. Rubbing the top of Cullen's head, I kneel next to him. I can't look into the eyes that match his dad's and keep lying. So I keep my eyes trained on the game like he is. "I'll be just on the other side of the door. Okay, buddy?"

"Okay," he replies, too engrossed to seemingly care. Maybe this is his way to cope, so I won't force a different response. I start pulling the door closed just enough to give us privacy on the other side of it but hold on to the knob. For my own support? I have no idea how I'm even standing here other than I'm using my best skills to pretend I'm okay.

I'm not. It's not been thirty minutes, but it's felt like torturous hours. I've been dying inside from the moment he crashed. Cullen matters more than I do, though, so I've been holding it together for him, acting like this is normal. I know it's not . . . okay, so it's for me as well, but now I'm faced with the strong possibility that everything won't be fine, and worse.

Through the door's crack, Cullen asks, "Is my daddy okay?"

Looking down, I see one green eye peeking up at me. I open the door enough to kiss his head and say, "He's fine." The lie doesn't convince me, but I tell it anyway and put on the only smile I can force on my face, hoping it passes as genuine.

Cullen returns to the floor and picks up the game again, settling in against the couch. I close the door all the way this time and put on my bravest face for Harbor, wondering if he'll believe it. It's hard to swallow around the lump in my throat, but I manage to and whisper, "Please tell me I didn't lie to his child."

My brother holds on to my arm as if I'll need the support and whispers, "He's been taken to the hospital." My head spins. I'm grabbed by the shoulders. "You need to sit down."

"I need to get to Cash." I glance at the door where Cash's son plays on the other side. "I need to take care of Cullen. Where's Laura, Cash's mom?"

"Loch took her to the hospital."

"That's not good."

"The belt didn't release . . ."

I stare at his eyes, trying to make sense of the words he's saying. *I just can't.* "What does that mean?"

"His left side is burned. We don't know how extensively."

"Burns? He'll survive, right?" I'm finding relief in the details. "We need to go to the hospital."

Harbor stops me. "We need to temper our expectations."

"What are you talking about? He can recover from—"

"They're concerned."

"Who?"

"The medical team. He was airlifted out of here."

Airlifted? "How far is the hospital from here?"

"It's not far, but traffic is an issue." He steps closer and leans, making sure our eyes are connected. "We need to get Cullen to his father as soon as possible. I need you to hold it together for him. We don't want to scare him, but we need to leave now. I have a helicopter—"

"You have a helicopter?"

"We can't waste time. Minutes matter." Stepping back, he looks down and rubs his forehead. "I'm sorry, Marina."

I blink back tears. "Why are you saying sorry?"

His own eyes are glassier. "I'm just sorry."

The first tear falls, and then another. I wipe across my cheeks and hold back the rest. His sorry doesn't mean anything. "Cash is going to be fine. I feel it." It doesn't feel like such a lie when I say it with conviction. He nods, studying my face. When he opens his mouth, I say, "Not another word, Harbor."

Dabbing my shirt to the inside corners of my eyes, I turn, take a quick breath, and go back inside. After explaining that we get to go on a helicopter ride to see his dad and grandma, Cullen holds my hand like the brave boy he is, and we're led through the paddock.

Silence overwhelms the space, though it's filled with people. Cullen skips at my side as they all stare. Harbor pushes through the back door, leading us to the helicopter. Duncan and Noah are already buckled in when we first load Cullen, then I climb up and sit in the middle with him.

Cullen's enthusiasm for being up this high has us all smiling at some point on the short ride. He points out buildings and water, bridges, and clouds. Dread returns when we start landing, devastating to the joy he is bringing.

As soon as we enter the hospital, Laura rushes to pick up Cullen and embrace him so tight that I know he's going to start squirming for his freedom. I stand nearby, unsure of how I fit in—I'm not Cash's family or part of the team. I'm a small partner in the business and his girlfriend. I'm not sure either will give me access to him.

I look down the hall as if I'll find a way to sneak in. He needs his mom and son, but won't he also need me? My heart aches in a way that I've never felt before. I cover it with my hand as if the small gesture can hold it together.

Laura sets Cullen down but keeps a firm hold of his hand and turns to me. "Thank you for caring for Cullen." Her swallow is heavier, the struggle shared. "I knew he was safe with you and that you'd protect him so I could be with my son."

"Yes, of course."

It's quick, but I feel a little squeeze on my wrist. "And I'm glad you came," she says as if I wouldn't. *How could I not?*

Half of my soul is in the other room.

Looking into her eyes, I'm unsure what to say other than, "I'm sorry."

She reaches out and rests her hand on my arm. "I have faith."

I'm not sure in what—God, his recovery, or that things will work out how they should. I don't question her because we all handle tragedies differently, but I want to taste that same faith that makes her eyes shine through the tears she's holding back. "Have you heard anything?" I ask in a whisper, careful not to have Cullen overhear. I'm grasping for any news that will give me the same buoy to hold on to while still finding comfort in her touch.

"He's going to be okay, but they still don't know the extent of the damage since they didn't want to cut the layers of his clothes before reaching the hospital. They're doing that now, separating the fibers from the burns." Cullen wiggles at her side. She turns to me and says, "I'm going to find him a bathroom."

Noah comes over and envelops me in his arms. I didn't know I needed the embrace until I was wrapped in it. A stifled cry chokes me up, and the tears threatening to fall this whole time finally do. I turn into him, hugging my brother. He's always been here for me, and like in the past, he rubs my back and tells me everything will be okay.

He's never lied before.

A doctor comes out and speaks to Duncan, Loch, and Harbor. As much as I want to rush to hear the diagnosis, a part of me wants to see Cash for who he is instead.

Laura joins them, letting Cullen run to me. I turn with

open arms and pick him up to hold. Hugging him gives me the most comfort I've found.

Their bodies sag in relief, and the lightest of laughter is heard. The doctor smiles when he glances over at us. I breathe, not realizing I hadn't been in the moments of their meeting. The pressure on my lungs eases as I take a few sobering breaths.

Noah rubs my shoulders as we continue to watch the others. They look over a few times and then at us. Harbor says, "Laura and Cullen are allowed to go in."

She runs her hand over Cullen's cheek, but her eyes pivot to me. "We have it approved for you to join us if you'd like. I understand if you'd rather see him privately later."

"I want to see him." Cullen's wriggling in my arms to get down before voicing the same request. I hold his hand, and Laura holds his other as we're led down the hall.

"Do we need to worry?" I ask, whispering above Cullen's head.

That smile full of the faith she holds reflects in her eyes. "He's going to be okay. His organs are fine. There might be nerve damage, but we won't know at this stage."

I try my best to digest the information, but I feel at a loss for what I'm walking into. The doctor opens the door, and I follow them inside. The usual hum of machines and heart-beats reach my ears before I can see him in the dimly lit room. The curtains are drawn closed, but a small lamp glows from the bedside.

Cullen runs around to his dad, who's sleeping. I hang back, still uncertain of my place. I love him. That love is bigger than my entire existence, but I'm not his family when it comes to having the right to see him.

I stay at the end of the bed, holding the railing. Laura moves to her son's side and brushes the hair off his forehead. She takes his hand between hers and then glances back at me. "He looks good." Her voice is shaken as if the worry she hid has finally revealed itself.

"He does," I whisper, turning back to him. There's no sign of the accident other than a scrape across his cheek and some bruising on his forehead. It's minor compared to what I expected.

But I know that means the damage is beneath the covers. I admonish my shallow thoughts that worshipped what was superficial—his handsome face, hard body, tanned skin. None of that matters to me now. I know the man, which I didn't know then. I know his heart, and I'd recognize his soul in the dark. God, I love him so much.

Menacing tears return. I won't let them fall, not in front of him. Cash would want me to be strong. So I will, for him.

"Hey, buddy." I barely hear him as he taps the bed for Cullen to hop up.

Laura says, "I think we need to wait on that. He could hurt you, and we don't want that to happen or for him to feel bad."

Cash nods, not seeming to have the energy to argue. Rolling his head forward, he locks his eyes on mine. I don't get the usual smirk or cocky half smile he wears like a statement in life. I also don't get the smile that appears when he looks at me like he's the luckiest man in the world. None of the familiar expressions are here, and I get nervous that I've unknowingly overstepped a boundary of his. He says, "C'mere." His voice is so low that I barely hear him.

I move around to the other side of his mom and son. She pulls Cullen to the window, and they slip behind the curtains to look outside. I appreciate the diversion she's created so I can have this moment alone with Cash. I suddenly feel shy standing at his bedside with him looking at me and not saying anything. I'm struggling because the usual words don't fit in this situation.

When he reaches for me, I cling to him. This is the lifeline I needed, the touch I craved to heal me so I'm strong enough to do the same for him.

I hang my head, and a tear hits the top of his hand.

"I'm okay, babe." His words comfort me. Even his raspy voice puts me at ease despite the circumstances.

I finally swallow down the lump in my throat, the one that kept me from breathing normally. "Next time you need attention, I prefer it to be on the podium, hotshot."

"Me too, but there's always the next race in Canada." He chuckles, but clenches and groans. "I'm thinking laughing is against the doctor's orders."

I'm not surprised he's already thinking of the next race, but it's unlikely he'll be there. I don't know how this will affect his career. At a minimum, there will be a delay . . . at worse—an ending. "You'll be back on the track very soon."

He nods again, the brief smile that was a balm for my soul already gone. He knows nothing is written in stone in sports, whether extreme or recreational.

His hand slips to the bed, and he looks toward the window, his lids hanging lower over his eyes. "Thank you for taking care of Cullen."

"Of course." I already miss his touch, but I won't steal the last of his energy.

"Cullen?" he calls so low that I almost don't hear him.

I move across the room and peek around the curtain. Smiling at him, I whisper, "Your dad wants to see you."

He runs around me and hops at the railing. I move a chair so he can stand, and both can get a better perspective of each other.

Cash lifts his arm, and Cullen falls into it with an

oomph. A groan escapes, but I know Cash will push through for his son. Cash is tired, his lids dipping closed. He glances once more at me and smiles before kissing Cullen's head and whispering against his hair, "I love you."

"Love you, Daddy."

The moment they share is sweet, and Cullen will probably never be the wiser to the pain Cash is in. But I sense something is off, tweaked in his trademark grin just enough not to be caught by most observers. As if this is all for show.

But I am not most.

27

<hr />

Cash

ONE WEEK LATER . . .

THE WHISPERS ARE DRIVING me fucking nuts. "I can hear you. If you want to know something, just ask me."

Marina holds up two tea packets in a bout of challenge. "Does your mother want peppermint with no caffeine or super green to drink?"

I look at my mom sitting at the bar in front of her. "Got it. Not everything is about me." I walk to the terrace, hiding the pain that scorches my side with every step I take.

My mom says, "He's always been a bear of a patient."

I close the door to block out the noise. Ironic since I'm in the middle of the city. It's quieter from the chatter, the how are you doing, the looks of pity, and the constant negotiations of whether I'll get to drive next weekend.

"She flew in on the red-eye to be here," my mom starts, coming outside. She closes the door behind her, then moves to the railing with her attention forward. "Marina leaves tomorrow on a late flight just so she can have as much time with you as she can."

"I appreciate it."

When she directs her gaze to me, worry wrinkles her brow. "You haven't said more than twenty words since she arrived, though. What's going on, Cash?"

Do I tell her?

Do I tell her that the injuries are worse than they know? That the nerve damage alone can keep me from what I spent my whole life training for? No. She's my mom. She doesn't care about my career or a stupid legacy. She only cares about me.

I don't.

I need to do better than my father. I need to leave something of value to take care of my son. I'll give Cullen the only thing I can and what I never had from a father figure. *Security*.

"I'll talk to her."

"I'm not forcing you to do something you don't want. If you've changed your mind about dating her—"

"Stop, Mom." Dropping my head, I let it hang and close my eyes. When I look up, she's not fazed. I'm a moody fucking bastard. She's probably used to it. That still doesn't make my behavior okay. I sit back on the lounger and turn my gaze to the sky. Choosing a more palatable tone to alleviate any signs of an argument that I don't want to have right now, I say, "I'll talk to her."

She glances toward the glass door. "My tea is ready. Do you need anything?"

"No."

After the door slides closed, I think about Marina and her constant effort. But I see it in her eyes, that question suspended in her pupils and the distance her light blues travel to delve into my green waters. If I let her stare too long, she'll see through me and know something is wrong.

That's the problem, right? Scrubbing my hands over my face, I release a heavy breath of stress, though it returns to my chest just as fast as it left.

Like her brother's enjoyed reminding me, she's an owner of the team. One word . . . one slip of concern from her to any of them, and my career could be over.

So is this the choice?

My son and the security I could give him for the rest of his life or my soulmate?

Fuck. I shake my head to get out of the tailspin. I don't need to invent scenarios that aren't in play. I don't need to premeditate a response. I'm fine. We'll all be fine. I'll be back in my seat on the grid next Saturday.

"Do you want to be alone?" I look up to find Marina standing with her back pressed to the door as if she's scared to be left alone with me. I'm a fucker for causing her distress. She says, "I know you have a lot on your mind." She angles to leave without giving me a chance to convince her otherwise.

"Stay." *My heart's reaction.*

She turns back to ask, "Are you sure?"

Am I sure?

Fuck. I've done that to her. I've made her small in this big world like her ex did. My pain is one thing, but I hate myself for causing her any. "I want you to stay, babe. Come sit by me."

Marina's hair is knotted in an elastic on her head, her face free from makeup, and dark circles induced by restless nights, which I'm sure I've caused her. A familiar T-shirt that

I've been missing is draped over her small shoulders with her jeans.

She's fucking gorgeous.

I don't deserve her beauty or her heart. I'll steal her soul, though, because there's no existing for me without it anymore.

Coming to sit on the inside of the other lounge chair, she keeps her feet on the ground. "What can I get you? Are you hungry or need water?"

"I don't need you to dote on me. I have my mother already doing too much."

Her sympathetic smile isn't reassuring. "We're just trying to help."

"I don't need help. I don't need anyone to take care of me. I can do it myself. I've done it my entire fucking life."

Getting up again, she moves to the table and stands on the other side. "Why are you yelling at me, Cash?"

"I'm not yelling."

She touches her fingertips to her chest, slightly leaning forward. "Okay, why are you raising your voice at me?"

"I'm tired, Marina. I'm tired of sitting here 'healing,'" I say, tossing air quotes in there for some stupid reason. "I'm tired of doctor's orders to rest and get some sleep. I'm tired of being treated like a—"

"Patient?" She straightens her back. "You are. You're healing, which is necessary for a full recovery." When she yanks her gaze away, I can see frustration ripple through her body language. Her arms cross over her chest when she finally sets her sights on something in the distance. "It's like you're being difficult just to be difficult." A hard glare lands on me. "What's so hard about recovering when everything in your life is taken care of?"

An idea dawns in her eyes before I can explain. She asks,

"Is this about racing?" Returning to the end of my lounger, she sits and rests her hand on my leg. "It's only a few races, Cash."

"Only?" The word sets me off, her hand jerking back in reaction. "A few races means I'm replaced, Marina. I get that you don't know shit about Principle One Racing and were given ownership as a fucking present for your twenty-fifth birthday, but this is my fucking life. If some eighteen-year-old fills my seat on the track and gets on that damn podium, my career is dead." I try to weather the storm inside me and temper my anger, but my hands shake and my side is fucking killing me, so I fail. "Get it now?"

She stands, her expression void of any emotion other than a fire burning in her eyes. I know it well, and I'm reminded of the first time we met. "I get it."

As if she's the judge and jury, I plead my case. "Why can't you understand I should have never had this chance? And I'm blowing it."

"You're injured. That's not the same thing."

Bolting to my feet, I reach my boiling point. "It is to me. Fuck this." I push the chair out of the way and gave her a wide berth, leaving her standing there. I grab the door and slide it open.

"You're willing to kill yourself for a trophy," she says to my back, "and expect everybody to sit by and be okay with it. I'm not okay with that. I'm not okay that for thirty minutes, I sat in a room with your five-year-old son, isolating him from something horrific. That for thirty minutes, I had to hold myself together for him because I thought you were dead." I turn back to see tears streaming down her face. "So no, I'm not okay with it."

"That's too bad, sweetheart." I stand there in my contempt for the circumstances that have nothing to do with her. I boldly cross my arms over my chest as she stares at me like a stranger. I even move out of the way when she comes toward me.

Only a few inches away, she stops briefly to look me in the eyes. "You're right, babe. That is too bad. Heartbreaking actually." Marina enters the living room.

I watch as she grabs her purse from the counter, her phone from the coffee table, and drags the suitcase that never made it to the bedroom toward the door.

My heart starts thumping in my chest, but my pride is too wounded to say the right thing. "So that's it? The fun's over, so you walk away?" I move inside behind her. "You give me an ultimatum to make yourself feel better? It's all or nothing with you?"

I see her shoulders rise and then fall slowly back into place. She looks back at me with the fire put out, and says, "I never gave you an ultimatum, Cash. That's all in your head, but if it makes you feel better and helps you sleep at night, you can blame me. And then when I'm just a memory, you'll convince yourself that you did the right thing." She grabs the doorknob and pulls the door open. "To help that along, I choose nothing over the *all* I'm being given."

I stand a good ten minutes in my righteous indignation, thinking there's a chance she'll walk back into my life.

She doesn't, though.

When I finally turn around, I don't need the disappointment I see in my mom's eyes to know that I fucked up. I feel the absence of my soul reminding me of what I've done.

I should have never let Marina go.

28

Marina

I RUSH BACK to my trailer, swinging the door wide open, and scramble to find the remote.

Clicking the TV on, I search the channels until I find P1 racing. I have no idea if I've missed Cash qualifying or if he stayed off the track this week like he should have.

"Dumonte. Pace Set. Rogue Automotive." I gasp when I see Westcott on the track. "Who's in the driver's seat? Come on. Come on."

"Had their reserve at the paddock this week . . ." The announcer rambles blah blah . . . "Quite the accident . . . lucky to be alive. Back in the saddle. He was cleared, but we're about to see if he's recovered."

I don't know why my heart sinks other than knowing Cash shouldn't be out there. What are my brothers thinking?

I sit on the couch with my legs tucked under me, clasping my hands together nervously. He was so worried about sitting out a race, but one mistake could cost him his career.

"This is the end," Corbin says, taking a seat on the top step.

"We've been long over." I turn my eyes back to the TV. I don't have the will to fight with him. I think I'd need to care to garner the strength, and I just don't. Not now that I've had a taste of what real love is.

"I meant the movie. One more day of shoots and then it's finally come to an end."

"Thank God."

"I think it's kind of sad." He watches with me as Cash does his qualifying lap. I appreciate the silence. My stomach is already twisted. I've been so worried about Cash and dealing with my own emotions during the breakup.

"I'm going to miss you, Marina."

I've been up since four o'clock and on the set since six. I'm too tired to fight any reactions he's trying to create in me. "Please don't do this. I'm really not in the mood for you today. Or ever after."

Excitement on the TV pulls my attention back. The announcer says, "He's the comeback kid for a reason. Qualifying into fourth puts him in reach of a podium position."

"Yes," I say, jumping up. And then I remember that we're broken up, and the heartbreak sets in again.

Corbin stands and asks, "You're really into this racing thing, huh?"

"No, not racing," I say with such authority that I begin questioning why I haven't been able to respond to any of Cash's text messages.

There were only a handful, and they didn't encompass his understanding of what he did or how he chose to handle the situation. He treated me as the enemy keeping him from his real true love—racing.

Corbin hangs around, though he embodies everything I don't want in my partner. I won't settle again.

I didn't with Cash when I lowered my walls and let him in, but I lost the man I love in that wreck. Until he returns, I can't go back. I'll work on finding my own happiness instead.

"I broke it off with Sherry."

"Who?""Sherry from wardrobe."

I almost laugh. Not that they broke up even though that's laughable. But that I had blocked her out of my head and had been working exclusively with Mindy, Sherry's assistant.

When he stands there staring at me, I'm not sure what he expects me to say. "We're not friends, Corbin."

Acceptance drowns any hope building in his eyes. "Right . . ." He looks out through the door and then takes a few steps down, stopping on the bottom. "I screwed up. I'm sorry."

His apology won't heal deep gashes, but since they never caused the ones my heart's dealing with, I say, "Thanks." Closure isn't something most get, so I appreciate the effort, even if it is months later.

When he turns back to me, he asks, "Do you want to grab lunch sometime?"

I chuckle this time at the irony of the situation. "No. Thank you, though."

When he exits, I reach down to close the door. "Hey, Corbin?" He turns back but keeps walking backward as if he knows this is the last time I'll see him off a red carpet. "Good luck."

"You, too. And congrats on the play."

"Thank you." The article came out in *Variety* two days ago. I've heard from everyone I care about but one. We always agreed to only learn more from each other. Guess he's holding strong unlike our relationship.

I didn't realize how fragile we were when I was in it, but our love was a house of cards teetering on destruction all along. It only took the wind blowing our way to knock us down.

Closing the door, I stop to look around the trailer. Corbin's right about endings. Doesn't matter what good things are ahead. There's a sadness when leaving a part of life to become a memory.

Sometimes we don't get the endings we want. I was fortunate to whisper goodbye to Laura on my way to the door. I didn't get the luxury with Cash. I didn't even get to say goodbye to Cullen or explain why I wouldn't be around any longer since he was at his mother's place. Maybe that's easier for kids, or maybe Cash made something up to tell him. I find it sad either way.

I start packing my stuff, wishing Poppy was here to help with my melancholy. She'd make the task fun at least. But there was no point in her flying to Vancouver, not even to run lines with me. It's an easy week of scenes, and she's busy with a short-term job cooking for a family summering in the Hamptons. I'll get to see her next week back in Beacon.

When my phone rings, I immediately check the caller ID. Lauren always has me debating about whether I want to answer. I do because I always do. "Hello?"

"How are you doing? I just heard the news."

"Which news?" I ask, panic rising that I've missed something significant.

"The breakup news. Why didn't you tell me? I had some plans in play."

"Because I don't want plans on how we're going to serve my breakup to the public. I just want to suffer in silence and eat pints of mint chocolate chip ice cream like any other woman."

"That's the thing, Marina. You're not any other woman. You're famous, and that's not going away anytime soon."

"Maybe it should. I never wanted to be famous. I wanted to act—"

"And you're acting," she barks. "You're actively getting offered scripts and being talked about in high-level casting meetings. What more do you want?"

"So much more than this. You're fired, Lauren. Good day." I hang up, waiting for the anxiety to kick in. I even sit on the edge of the bed, ready to welcome it so I can start working through my fears. But it doesn't come. It never comes because I know I did the right thing.

I'll get another agent, but I won't get a second chance at living life on my own terms unless I take it.

THREE WEEKS LATER ...

ESCAPING to the one place I know I can get away from everything—Manhattan, twelve-hour rehearsal days, and the paparazzi—I lie on the pink float and drift under a blue sky. *And then the splashing begins.*

"Hey. Hey," I say, tapping the float. "Not over here. I don't want to ruin my book. It's made of paper." I haven't managed to read one page of *Never Got Over You* because I've been doing research on my phone while sunbathing. I still shake the paperback for emphasis, but I think most of my nieces and nephews are too little to understand.

Loch's wife, Tuesday, rallies the kids to the opposite corner of the pool at my parents' house. I'm usually the fun aunt, but I let her hold the title today, needing a few more minutes to search Cash Ryatt online.

I caved and broke the rule.

It started when I stopped receiving messages from him. He gave up on me so easily. I was looking for the grand gesture, and he just wanted me to make him feel better by replying.

One article led to another puff piece and then onto a feature spread, and I was deep into the rabbit hole. I've learned a lot. I had no idea his mom lived in the same building as him. He bought her the apartment three years ago to keep her close to him and Cullen. And it's only mentioned in a small indie press, but he also paid off the homes of the two men who paid his karting dues. As an eighteen-year-old who had just signed his first major contract, that's how he chose to spend the payout.

My heart beats a little quicker thinking about Cash.

This is the stuff that's never mentioned. They focus on how he and Terpidy wreaked havoc on his career with the drinking and smoking. I've barely seen him drink a beer, and he must have given up smoking along with that rela-tionship because I've never seen him do it. The bad boy of racing was under a bad influence back then. That's not who he is, but the title stuck. Catchy headlines always do.

Like the heiress and the injured. I'm surprised they don't call me the black widow for destroying so many innocent men's lives. I roll my eyes.

The headlines blew over like I was told they would. My new agent might have had a hand in it. She's out of New

York and a huge advocate for Broadway, so she doesn't play those Hollywood games. I'm so glad to have found someone who asks my opinions and offers guidance instead of falling back on tired tactics.

Once I gave up Hollywood, they came calling. *It's ironic.*

That's the key—*holding the upper hand.*

It's great money, though, so now I'll try to balance a film here and there into my career.

Moving my sunglasses from my head to protect my eyes, I try to embrace the newfound fame of my movie star era to practice for my cover of *Style Magazine* I just booked earlier in the week. I'm bored after one selfie. Leaving my book and phone behind, I jump into the deep end and swim to the other side of the pool.

Tuesday holds one kiddo in a floatie and the other on her hip. Harbor jumps in to play with his wildlings, and Noah's sitting under a canopy on a blanket with Liv and their kids taking a nap. It's been a long day of fun. A nap is tempting.

Leaving my dad to man the barbecue pit, Loch comes to sit on the edge, plucking his baby daughter off Tuesday's hip. Bouncing her on his legs, she giggles. Tuesday says, "So sweet." She then lifts their eldest out of the water to set her next to her dad to take a break and hang out with me. "I've been thinking about you. How's the play going?"

"Well, but I wish we had another week. Our soft opening is next Thursday for critics and bigwigs, and I'm nervous."

"I saw the clip you sent. You were really great. I can't wait to see it. We have tickets for Saturday because Friday sold out too fast."

"I could have left tickets for you at the box office, you know?"

"It's good to support the arts, but even better to support

family." Bending down to smile at her baby, she coos and touches her head gently, pushing her baby-fine hair back from her face. All ten strands of it. But then she turns back to me and asks, "How's your social life?"

"Nonexistent."

"And that's . . .?" she asks, picking up on my tone.

Shrugging, I move to the side of the pool to lean against the edge. "I don't know. It is what it is. I didn't respond, so he stopped trying. What does that say about us?"

"I don't know the details, so I don't think I should weigh in on that part. Only you know the answer to that, Marina." Sidling up next to me, she rests her elbows on the edge and kicks her feet in front of her. "Is there any chance he lost his way? A lot was happening at that moment in time. I'm not saying you should be with him—"

"I've thought about this more than is probably healthy, Tues. I just . . . I can't accept an apology over text. A phone call isn't enough. I need to see the man I fell in love with and hear his voice, see his eyes, feel his heart. I feel crappy sometimes for not accepting the bare minimum. And then I snap out of it, remembering that I don't need to settle. I just need more of something. I need to mean more to him."

Liv uses the steps and wades over to us. "What are we talking about, ladies?"

"Cash," Tuesday replies before I can pretend we're discussing the best romance book we've read lately. I'd rather be stuck in that conversation, quite honestly.

"Ah," Liv replies with a hint of hesitation. "And how is that going?"

"Good. Right, Marina?"

I almost start laughing. I never consider her a trouble-maker, but she's perfect for my uptight brother. If she'll be this open with me, I can imagine she keeps him on his toes. "It's okay."

"Do you mind me giving my two cents?" Liv asks, throwing her hands up in caution. "And you can totally say yes, and I'll zip my lips on the matter."

If I called a car service right now, I might be able to get back to the city before I die under this relentless discussion regarding my love life. I wave her forward. "Might as well hear it."

"My husband aside because he's a romantic," she starts, glancing at Noah sleeping soundly on the blanket while my mom plays with the kids in the grass nearby. "But other than him, I've never seen such a romantic grand gesture play out in real time."

"What do you mean?" I ask, biting right on to that hook.

Tuesday nudges me with her elbow. "None of us can. We're obsessed with what Cash did at the premiere."

My head jerks back, almost tweaking my neck. "Ow!" Rubbing it, I ask, "Obsessed with Cash? My Cash? I'm so confused."

"We know," they say in unison.

Liv says, "That's why we're here. To help unconfuse you. And don't think we didn't note the 'my Cash' part of that sentence."

Tuesday adds, "Noted."

I move to deeper water so I can dunk under if this chat goes sideways more than it already has. They follow. Of course, they do. I laugh, partly amused and partly curious. Might as well get this over with. No one in my family, related by blood or marriage, gives up easily when they've set their mind to something. I'm the something today. It's only fair since I've done the same to all of them over the years. "You get five minutes to say your piece."

Their smiles are ridiculously big. I hope that's a sign of good things. Tuesday says, "The red carpet was called a stunt in the media since they wanted to make it about Corbin and his new fiancée."

"They broke up, by the way." Raising my hands up in surrender, I add, "Sorry. Carry on."

Liv says, "It wasn't a stunt. That was a man on a mission. Cash put it all on the line to be there for you when you felt alone."

"It's not the same having us there for you," Tuesday adds. "You know we always support you, but Cash was there in a different capacity. He was willing to lose his job just to hold your hand through a difficult time.

"It wasn't as difficult as everyone thinks since I was over Corbin a long time ago. It was hard because I was called names when I did nothing wrong." I'm struck with two sets of eyes glaring in my direction. "Okay. Sorry. Sorry. Go on."

With a huff that keeps her back on track, Liv says, "He put you first, above all else."

My heart starts racing, and my chest tightens. Just hearing them describe what I was blinded to at the moment, I sigh. I always knew he was there when I needed him, but he risked everything to save me that night.

"Gah!" Tuesday interjects. "I could watch the replay on a loop. It's so stinkin' romantic."

I grew up with brothers, but it is great to have sisters-in-law in times like these. "I'll be right back."

I chase my float down and grab my phone. Walking toward the pool house, I do what I should have done a month ago.

I text Cash.

29

Cash

"WHAT THE . . .?"

Standing in the middle of the sidewalk, I stare at my phone and the message on the screen. My chest aches where my heart used to be, but I rarely feel it anymore even with adrenaline pumping through me.

"What is it, Daddy?" Cullen whines, "This is boring?" I've heard that a few times over the past two weeks. It was nice to have him for an extended period, but I think he might be sick of his old man.

I shove my phone in my back pocket because I can't reply with my mind going in a million directions and my kid tugging on my hand. I try not to be on my phone as much when I'm with my son, but I can't stop thinking that I'm imagining the message that just popped up.

"It's not boring. We walk to experience life instead of sitting in the back of a vehicle. Look around, Cullen. What do you see?"

While he's busy trying to spot one of a million differences from the last time we walked this route, I can't help but wonder why now? Why would Marina text me out of the blue?

Has the anger dulled?

Her hate for me subsided?

Change of heart?

Decided to return mine?

I want to reply so badly, but I can't think straight.

"Are you listening?"

"I missed that, buddy. Say it again?"

He points. "Mommy."

I look up to see Terpidy standing by a tree we always pass when walking to her place. Something's different, but I can't quite put my finger on it. Maybe her outfit? Not as tight? Her hair is pulled back? How does she usually wear it?

"Hi," she says, bending down to greet Cullen. He runs excitedly into her open arms.

Keeping my pace, I need a few extra seconds to suss out the situation. She never meets us. She barely even opens the door.

With Cullen in her arms, she meets me halfway. I'll never entirely burn this bridge because we share a son, but I'm not letting my guard down.

"Hello," she greets me, her voice breezy as if we haven't been to hell and back at least three times.

"Hey." I hand her Cullen's backpack and shove my hands in my front pockets, still unsure of her motive.

"I was hoping we could talk?" She turns, and we start walking together, but I sense I don't have much choice. Hopefully, we can remain civil for one block.

"All right."

"How are you doing since the accident?"

The question still elicits raw emotion. The surface has healed, but there's nerve damage. It's the organ underneath that was most affected, and that's not something I'm getting into with her. "Almost healed," I lie.

"That's good. You're having a great season." She laughs, setting Cullen down and letting him walk a few feet ahead of her. "Five feet, Cullen. No more."

"I'm almost six," he complains. It's not a busy street, which is why we go this route, but it's interesting to see her parent. It's not something I've witnessed much since we've been apart from the time he was born.

She glances at me with a knowing grin and back to him. "When you're six, you can have six feet. Five feet until then."

"Ugh, fine."

"Sometimes he reminds me of you."

I laugh, watching Cullen in the beginning stages of a meltdown. "Is that a compliment?"

She laughs in response. "It actually is."

I'm starting to think she could fill an hour with small talk, which is not typical for us. As much as I want to get along, I'm not opening the door to hang out like old friends. "What is it that you want to talk about, Terpidy?"

"I used the past two weeks to reevaluate my life and how I want to be more present in Cullen's."

I don't hold her past against her because I was no saint, so I'm not one to lecture, but the part about her reevaluating her relationship with our son has me listening closely. I stop and look for him. He's seven feet. Always pushing boundaries. "Cullen?" Turning back to her, I ask, "Why are you telling me this?"

Not shying away, she holds her head high and says, "I started talking to a therapist."

That is not how I saw this going. "And?" I check on

Cullen, who is spinning around and looking everywhere but at us. Guess we're not interesting enough for him. This is one time I'm glad he's bored.

Having the rest of this conversation in private is probably a good idea. We keep things light for the rest of the walk. And when I give him a hug and kiss his head, I say, "I love you so much."

He leans back and taps me on the nose. "I love *you* so much, Daddy."

We get him inside, and I take a few steps back down. I feel more comfortable keeping space and our lives unentangled outside of our son.

She sits on the top step of the stoop and says, "I've blamed you for so long that I believed the lies I told. I'm sorry, Cash. I'm sorry for what I put you through. I'm sorry for what I put Cullen through as well. But I'm also sorry that I treated myself so awful." She's busy fidgeting with the hem of her shirt but looks back at me. "I didn't feel alive on that photo shoot last month like I used to in my twenties."

Something I can relate to since I lost Marina.

Struggling to hold eye contact, she looks away when she continues, "I wish I would have gotten therapy years ago. I didn't expect it to be so . . ." She laughs. "Therapeutic."

Standing, she brushes the dust off the back of her skirt. "I know you're probably anxious to leave. I won't keep you any longer. I just wanted you to know that I'm getting help." Grabbing the concrete railing, she appears to summon another bout of courage. "I love Cullen more than anything. I would never put him in danger."

"I appreciate you safeguarding our son."

"Yes, always."

She's said in court that Cullen was a priority on many occasions. This is the first time I believe her. I rub the back of my neck, wanting to give credit when it's due, but uncertain what I should say. I can't forget what she's put us through, but she's taking a big leap of faith in telling me. "I think it takes a lot of courage to get help. You wanting to be better for yourself is better for Cullen as well." I smile, and it feels genuine around her, which is foreign more recently. "I also appreciate the apology. It means a lot."

Healthier. Happier. That's what is different about her.

I take a step down onto the sidewalk as she steps up to the platform.

Since this has gone so well, I push my luck. "I've been thinking about Cullen's last name."

Her brow peaks as her smile fades. "What about it?"

"I want to change his name to Warren. I thought Ryatt was about legacy and racing. I'd rather the legacy be tied to me as his dad. That's how I want to be remembered."

I expected her to be mad and flat-out deny me, so I have no idea why she's smiling again. "Have you talked to him about it?"

"No, I wanted to talk to you first."

Resting her hip against the railing, she says, "I appreciate that, but he's already a Warren."

"As the name he lists with Cullen."

"I know what you mean. You're a great dad. I'll never take that away from you, but you're more into the physical activities with him. You should see how he signs his artwork. I don't think you'll get an argument from him." She heads to the door but doesn't open it. "Cullen Bryne Ryatt Warren?" she asks, swapping the last two surnames around.

Feeling like we're turning over a new leaf, I reply, "I was thinking Cullen Bryne Warren if that's okay?"

Her smile grows as she opens the door. Holding her head down, she wipes her eyes. "It's okay with me."

"Thank you, Terpidy."

I'm given a nod before she disappears inside. Just before the door closes, I hear her call to Cullen, "Come over here and give me a hug. I missed you so much."

New leaf and second chances.

As soon as I get to the corner of the block, I pull my phone out again, and read the text Marina sent: *I was mad.*

Fuck it. I stop overthinking and text her back: *And you're not now?*

I will stand here all fucking day if I get the chance to speak to her in any way.

Another message arrives: *I was also hurt.*

Me: *I fucked up. I'm sorry.*

Fifteen. Thirty. Forty. Every second that passes without hearing from her is fucking torture.

Marina: *Don't fuck up again.*

Me: *I won't.*

As desperate as I am to see her, I can't make this about me. The breakup was done selfishly. The makeup must be about righting the wrongs if given the chance.

Ten minutes pass and I hear nothing. Do I text her again? Or let it lie for now? Do I yank the door she cracked open or bide my time? *Fuck.*

Apparently, patience is a virtue.

But I've never been the virtuous type.

Tucking the phone in my back pocket, I start home, chalking the day up to a good one overall.

"Cash?"

I cross the street toward my building and see Harbor standing next to one of his million-dollar custom cars that built his business. One day, he's going to give me one. Until then, I'll just admire his. I walk the perimeter and squat to get a good look at the grill. "Nice."

"Thanks."

But Harbor doesn't make house calls for fun, so I step back on the sidewalk and ask, "What brings you by?"

Dipping inside the car, he grabs something off the seat. "I wanted to give you this."

I take it, turning it over to see what the event is listed on the front. "A ticket?"

"It's a new play opening tomorrow. I'm a donor, so I get extras."

"Are you asking me out?" I can't hold a poker face and start laughing.

He chuckles. "Lark is going with me, but we were given a third. Unfortunately, it's for standing room only."

"Best way to see a play." Marina's words come back like they were yesterday.

"I didn't take you for a fan of Broadway?"

I didn't realize I said that out loud. It's easy to get lost in the memories of her. "It's become a new passion of mine."

Staring at me, I have a feeling he knows why. He doesn't say anything, which is a first. I'll take the win while I'm ahead. "Thanks for the ticket."

"Will we see you there?"

"I'll be there."

"Great. Have a good night, and get some rest. We leave on Sunday."

Taking the ticket, I tap it against my hand a few times, then dash up the nine flights of stairs to my apartment. Out of breath, I shoulder the door open and rush to the gallery display on the side of my fridge. I see it at the bottom. It's not really legible unless you know what you're looking for.

How did I not know? Did Cullen ever signed Ryatt? Or has he always written Warren? He doesn't want a legacy of race car driving or a TV personality. He wants a father.

He's my proudest accomplishment, and I'll happily trade ten world champion titles for the one where I'm called Cullen's Dad.

Good fucking day.

Tomorrow is going to be even better. I've not only been given an olive branch from the Westcott Brothers but the second chance I've been waiting for. It's Marina though, so I know it won't come without an argument.

That's okay. I'll fight for her.

30

Cash

I WAS DAMNED to hell of my own making until I kissed her lips and tasted heaven.

Nothing has changed.

I'm in hell without her. My heaven on the stage before me brings back the same emotions, while hers runs the gamut in three acts. It's when she sings softly that I see a new side I didn't know existed. Her talent extends further than the stage, and I've only scratched the beautiful surface.

"Are you Cash Ryatt?" a fan asks, pulling me from the daydream I had disappeared into with Marina. "I didn't want to ask during the performance."

A man, mid-forties maybe with what looks to be his wife standing behind him, holds out a playbill to sign. "What did you think of the play?"

She says, "Really good. We're here to review it for *Bloomington News* back home in Indiana. Did you like it?"

"Brilliant." I take the pen that's appeared out of nowhere and flip over the playbill. It doesn't feel right to sign the front where the actors' names appear. I sign over an adver-tisement for a local deli and hand it back. "Take care."

I try to slip out during the standing ovation before the masses exit. There's no plan in place. I won't bother her backstage, but I want to see her, so I'll wait as long as it takes in the alley with the other fans.

A few of the actors have caused a stir when they walk out, and the crowd has thinned when the male lead makes a fast getaway.

Two hours is longer than I expected to wait, but the weather's nice, and the crowd is in a jovial mood. I don't blend in, but I've managed to get away with only a few people recognizing me along with one paparazzi. More photos to deal with. I'm not sure if she'll appreciate it, but it's all I got. This one shot.

So I stay, waiting for my turn to see her again.

The door opens, and the stars align, shining in this dingy alley on my soul and universe. Her hair falls over her shoulders, lighter than a few months back, and the heavy stage makeup has been replaced with her natural beauty shining through. But the clarity of her eyes and the happi-ness residing inside have me questioning if she's better off without me.

She works her way into the alley, signing playbills as she moves through the crowd toward an opening at the other end from where I stand. Shifting directions, she keeps her eyes down as she signs everything handed to her. "Thank you for being here tonight."

When she gets closer, I do what comes naturally. I hand her my playbill as well. "Thank you for being—" The words catch in her throat when those bright blue eyes that frequent my dreams lock on me. Her hand stills. A slow exhale. A lingering blink. "Cash." For so long, I've wanted to hear her say it again. I knew it wouldn't be final if I could hear it once more, but this time feels like an ending with no question involved.

She finishes signing and hands it back to me before fixing her expression and the shock she was wearing to smile for the fans. "Thank you," she says, waving and then dashing in the opposite direction.

I'm five steps behind and call, "Marina?"

Just beyond the crowd, she reaches a car with the headlights on, but stops with her hand on the hood as if she needs the support.

Catching up to her, I stop a few feet shy. "Can we talk?"

She turns around, those blues watery and the smile she had for everyone else is gone for me. "In the neighborhood?"

"Nowhere near it, but I thought I'd stop by anyway."

"Why?" Easing into her anger, she crosses her arms over the green dress that looks striking on her. "Aren't you supposed to be somewhere else in the world right now? Isn't there a race next weekend?"

"Yes. I leave on Sunday."

I'm gifted an eye roll, and she looks down at her shoes. I hate when she looks away, but she has the right to the walls that surround her.

Tossing me a bone, she peers up at me under long lashes, and she asks, "What did you think?"

"The most magnificent thing I've ever seen."

Her expression brightens, a small smile even shaping her lips. "You loved the play?"

"That too."

A quiet scoff punctuates her chest, but the grin remains. Thumbing over her shoulder, she says, "I should go. It was good to see . . ." A change of heart pivots her words. "Thank you for coming to the show."

I stare at her, wondering what that text exchange was about if she never wanted to see me again. Frustration sets in as she opens the car door. Still standing in the headlights of the car, I throw my arms out wide. "So that's it, babe?"

With one foot already in the car, she stops and looks at me over the door. "I didn't wage this war, so it's not mine to finish."

"But you're in it." I come closer. "You're in the middle of this battle, so you have to fight it."

Both her feet land back on the street, her lips tightening as the fire is lit inside when she stands. "I don't have to do anything. You didn't just break my phone. You broke my heart, Cash. It's up to you to fix it."

"I'm trying."

"Try harder." She slams the door closed. "You think saying sorry is enough. It's not. I can't forgive you just because you're ready to be back in my life. You shifted the blame to me under fears of . . ." Planting her hands on her hips, she says, "I have no idea. I don't know what happened that day. I just knew I was never going to win, so I cut my losses, realizing I had to save myself."

"Save yourself from what? Me?"

Staring into my eyes, she doesn't blink. "Yes."

"You weren't going to win that day. No one was. Not even me. I lost you because I was afraid to lose my career."

She reaches for the handle again, staring at it like this is the last time we'll do this. "Seems you made the right choice. You're doing better than ever without me."

Just as she pulls the door open again, I rush closer. "I could say the same to protect myself from the pain of seeing how happy you look without me, but I don't want to fight with you." I hold the top of the door, a physical barrier between us, and my heart starts beating for the first time since she left me. "I want to love you through the happy, the sad, successes, and failures. I want to love you through everything, the good and the bad, because no victory will ever replace the feeling of waking up next to you."

I swear the beats of my heart echo against the brick walls caving in on us. She looks past me and into the flashes of the paparazzi cameras. In a sigh of what only appears to be defeat, her shoulders drop, and she gets into the vehicle. Looking up at me, she says, "This isn't over."

"Not by a long shot."

Doubt is written in her eyes so clearly that it pains me to see. And then she says, "Want a ride?"

"Yes." I move to the other side of the car and get in, leaving the crowds and paparazzi outside. The car slowly pulls through as theater attendants shuffle people to the sides of the alley.

It's a few blocks before she says, "I asked him to drop you off at your apartment."

"Thanks." It feels different with her in the confines of the car versus the night air to plead my case. I lower my voice and say, "I'm not driving better because you're out of my life, Marina. I'm placing higher because you were. I now know what true love feels like."

"I thought I knew because you saw me, Cash. You saw the real me and who I wanted to be. You saw me for who I am. Not the daughter of the Westcotts of Beacon. Not my brothers' little sister. Not the girl who failed on Broadway. I was never anything until you saw me and loved me for who I am." A tear slips down her cheek and as tempting as it is to catch it before it rolls off her chin, I don't. That's not my place in our relationship right now. But it kills me to see her cry when I could have prevented it. "And then you ripped it out from under me. You took your love and weaponized it. You gave me no choice but to leave."

I've never felt worse, not in the hospital or the tumultuous Terpidy period of my life. Not when I lost my seat on the grid or even when I realized my father never loved me. The pain I feel is worse because of the pain I've caused her. "I'm sorry—"

She swallows and looks ahead through the windshield. "I know you are." Her eyes find me in the dark of the back seat, and she says, "My trust was broken, but I rose from that and created my own life. On my terms. I should thank you, Cash. You're the one who opened my eyes. I'm not just an actress. I'm a business, an entity, an owner of Westcott Racing. I filled the seat I had left vacant at the table all in the name of chasing the dream. I use my voice and not only give my opinions but also have vote and veto power."

I thought I was broken before. Now I'm shattered.

What have I done?

"You've got it all wrong, babe." I rest my elbow on the door and rub the side of my face. "That stuff doesn't matter." Reaching across the leather seat divide, I cover her hand with mine just as the car pulls to the curb. I glance out the window, knowing this is where we end. With nothing left to lose, I say. "Just remember, I loved you more than anything."

I pop the door open, but she pulls my arm to a stop. When I turn back, she asks, "What did it feel like?"

Holding her gaze, I study her face, memorizing the damage that only makes her more beautiful, the way life has created flaws that she'll never appreciate, and I'll never forget. "When I had you, I had everything."

Her fingers fall from my jacket, her hand to the seat. I wait seconds, but nothing is going to change. I get out and shut the door behind me. There were so many things I wanted to tell her, things that needed to be said. Apologies and regrets.

The car pulls into traffic.

"Fuck."

I scrub my hands over my face, not knowing what to do next.

Go upstairs?

No. *Fuck that.*

I take off running, praying to whatever saint will help me catch up to her. I've done something right because her car hits a red light one block ahead. I push myself harder, really needing to get back into long-distance running. My endurance sucks.

I reach the car, my hands landing hard on the window. I hear a scream from inside, but then the car takes off when the light turns green again.

Are you for fucking real right now?

Thank the heavens for heavier traffic tonight. The window rolls down as I'm running on the sidewalk parallel to the car. Sitting forward, Marina shouts, "What are you doing?"

"I didn't say everything I needed to," I huff, pumping my arms.

The car hits another red light. Thank God. I drop my hands to my knees, gasping for air.

She asks, "What more is there to say?"

"I'm sorry. I'm sorry for betraying your trust. I'm sorry for putting my fears of losing my career on your shoulders to carry. But most of all, I'm sorry for letting you walk out that door. That is the biggest regret I live with every day of my life. I should have fought for you."

The car drives forward.

"Mother *fuck*."

Her eyes never leave me until she's too far to catch up to. I have no idea where she's staying or if she has an apartment in the city now that she's back. I could run another ten blocks and never see that car again.

She's been given every green light in the city to get farther away from me. I should turn back, but I can't.

Call it a second wind, but I feel the need to start running again.

I run, knowing I've lost her but can't give up on us like I stupidly did before.

I run, passing cars and searching every black sedan in hopes it's hers.

I run, my left side burning, the few nerve endings that survived the wreck ache.

I run until it makes no sense to keep going, but still do.

My feet slow as I approach a busy street. A truck passing in front of me, and I imagine if I would have caught up to her, if this night would have played out differently. Cars are streaming while I catch my breath. I have to because I refuse to lose her again. When only cars remain, I stand there staring at the other side.

Caught in the breeze of passing traffic, the face of an angel stares back at me. I stop running.

"Marina?"

The cars stop blocking the passage, so I move to the corner and cut through, rushing to reach her. Her chest rises with the deep breath she takes. I finally reach her and almost pull her into my arms. Almost, but I don't. I ask, "Why are you here?"

"I was in the neighborhood."

I laugh, and then it builds. My exhaustion hits my head, and I burst out chuckling. "Literally."

"Why are you still running, Cash?"

Taking a step closer, I say, "Because I'm so in love with you that I can't fucking think straight. I'm begging for a second chance. You're not just my soul, Marina. You're the part of me that didn't exist before I tasted your kiss. You're the breath that feeds my lungs that I can't survive without. You're more important than my career or any race."

She looks down and takes another heavy breath. "I was so worried when you were in the accident. I thought I would have to live without you, and I didn't think I would survive that." When she looks back up, she says, "Choosing to walk away from you was the hardest thing I've ever had to do. But I've learned to stand on my own two feet." The doubt from her eyes earlier has now disappeared as she takes two steps forward, closing the gap. "So tell me, what would you do differently if you got a second chance?"

"I'd love you every day like it's the last, fully with my entire soul."

Resting her head against my chest, she wraps her arms around me. This is what heaven feels like. I secure mine around her, certain I'm never letting her go again. I will never get enough of how she looks at me like I hung the moon for her. "I trust you with my life, babe, but I also need you to safeguard my heart."

"I will." I kiss her head. "I promise."

When she breaks our embrace, she asks, "How many blocks back to your place?"

"I might have to call a car."

She starts laughing. "I feel like walking, or are you too tired?"

Cupping her face, I lean down and kiss her. I kiss her lips and her cheek, her forehead and the tip of her chin. "I'm never too tired for you."

Her hands cover mine as she looks up at me. "Tell me you're okay."

The concern she has for me, the kindness she showed my son in protecting him on the worst day of my life will never be forgotten. "There's some damage, but I'm healing. Eventually, I'll be good as new."

She kisses me, the pressure firm, her hands holding me to her as she needs the contact, and then she says, "I'm sorry it took so long for me to reply."

I could list off a thousand times I wondered if I would ever hear from her again. It would be petty and take us backward instead of the direction we're heading in now. "The time apart doesn't matter. Only that we make use of the time together."

She lifts to kiss me, then hugs me a little longer. I would stand here all night holding her tight on this street corner if that's what she wants. But then she takes my hand, and we start walking. "I wasn't happier without you," she says.

"No?"

She bumps into me and laughs. "No. I'm just a good actress."

"The best. Now tell me about you taking charge. Does that extend to the bedroom?"

"Guess you're about to find out."

I did three times.

Life is pretty damn perfect.

31

Marina

"Does it hurt?"

The burned area is larger than I remember, the skin raised and still angry, but healing coats the surface. I'm careful to only trace around the edge, not wanting to add to any pain Cash might be experiencing.

His arm tightens around my shoulders, and he kisses the side of my head, making me feel so much like no time has passed. I snuggle in, wanting to be as close as I can. He says, "Not now that you're here again."

I tilt my head up from his chest and lift onto my elbow. "Your side?"

Staring deep into my eyes, he doesn't blink when he replies, "My heart. My soul. My everything is better with you in my life."

My heart feels bigger than it has since I left. It's odd, though. It's as if I didn't have a heart while we were apart. It was steeped in a slumber that makes me realize I was breathing but not living. *Not truly living.* I went on autopilot, drowning myself in work and business, sidetracking my mind with anything that didn't make me think about him, which wasn't much. Grinning, I ask, "Are you feeding me a line or trying to charm me, Mr. Ryatt?"

"Warren." He lifts on his elbows to kiss me and whispers against my lips, "Always Warren with you, babe."

Babe. My heart beats harder in my chest for this man and his nickname for me. I didn't expect him to run the length of Manhattan to be with me again, but I know he would have. He ran half of it. He would have done whatever he could to get to me. I just shortened the journey back to our reunion.

I was always his, like he is to me—*my heart, my soul, my everything.* Nothing exists without him.

I lean down to kiss his shoulder and then a little higher to the crook of his neck. Rubbing shamelessly against his leg, I find the hot and heavy foreplay that landed us in bed has subsided as we start to rediscover each other. One kiss here, a gentle touch there, and ending with us talking. I don't mind slowing down because hearing him whisper, telling me how much he missed me, is an opportunity I'll never pass up.

"I never," I start, almost too choked up. I clear my throat. "Not for a moment did I ever stop loving you. I just . . . I just had to find my own way back." A smile overcomes me as I remember how all my hopes and dreams were wrapped up in those minutes of waiting. "Apparently, standing on the corner of 42nd seemed like a solid plan. I stood there worried you wouldn't come that far for me."

Running his fingertips over my temple, he studies me as if memorizing every newly developed freckle. "I'll travel as far as it takes to reach you." He cups my cheek as he looks into my eyes with a hunger that only I can satisfy. *Intoxi-*

cating. "Never doubt that I'll always come for you. Always." His hand slides to the back of my head, and he encourages me closer. I move down, never wanting to cause his injury to flare, but even more, him to doubt that I'll travel any distance to get to him as well.

I reach his lips again, the urge beginning to drown the patience I thought I had. Before we kiss, he says, "I'm not a perfect man, but I want to be everything you need. I want to make you happy, Marina."

My emotions get the better of me. Reuniting with him is more beautiful and more consuming than I imagined. I dreamed of this since the day I set my hurt feelings aside and saw why I walked away for what it was—one of the worst days for both of us. The turmoil he must have held inside since the accident came out in ways it shouldn't have. I refuse to hold his worst against him when he puts in the effort to show me his best.

We're all flawed people.

After a major failure, I had accepted less than I deserved —personally and professionally. I believed the critics. I believed my ex and an agent who didn't have my best interests at heart. I believed in everyone except myself. So I understand when fear gets the better of you. I understand why Cash acted out of character and so unlike the man I knew so well. "You're not responsible for my happiness," I reply. "You're responsible for yours."

"I hear what you're saying." As he shifts gently under me, his groan is slight but noticed. I readjust to the side, so careful. "I will support you however I can. I'll do it. I'll do anything for you."

We have mountains to climb in our careers, and physical and emotional healing, but being in his arms again means nothing matters more than our lives together. We're two people who have changed in ways that make coming back together so much sweeter. "You showed up for me. That's enough."

"That's the least someone should do for you."

Shrugging, I laugh so softly that I barely even hear it. "I don't need much to make me happy. You and maybe a Tootsie Pop or some chocolate."

His grin extends, carving into his cheeks as his eyes stay steady on mine. "I'm going to give you the world, Marina Westcott. I'll buy you a whole candy shop just to see your smile."

"It's not for me that I want it." *Too subtle?*

A roguish grin takes over, and his hands lower to my hips, pulling me on top of him. He's already hard when he shifts my hips forward and back again over his length. "I'm going to spoil you rotten, my love."

The teasing gets the better of me, and I finally kiss him, briefly losing myself in the headiness of being together again. "Good thing I love to be spoiled." Slipping lower, I take hold of his erection and add, "But I want to go first." I spoil him with every ounce of my being, making love and making him come so hard, first with my mouth and then with my body. I take every inch of him and savor the night until the early hours of the next day.

Morning comes too fast after only a few hours of sleep, shining through a crack in the curtains like it's trying to set the world on fire. I know the feeling. Although I didn't get as much sleep as I'd like, I'm in his arms, so that's all that matters.

Cash is still asleep when I slip out from under the heaviness of his arm and into the shower. The water is warm, like the comfort of the man in bed. I run the body wash scented like him over parts he touched, cognizant of the delicious soreness he evokes.

"Good morning," he says, opening the door. "May I join you?"

He's already stepping in like he did my life, crashing into my world with his full intentions and all in from the get-go. Secretly, I love how he consumes a room with his presence and how he consumes me with his love. "I was hoping you would but didn't want to wake you," I reply, taking my sweet time to appreciate him. Even with the wound covering his left side, the man is a masterpiece. "Is the water too hot?"

"It's just right." A smirk angles his mouth to one side as he steps under the shower, drenching his hair. His eyes close, but as the water runs over his injury, I notice a slight wince strike his face.

I hate how powerless I feel to heal him. I'm gentle when I touch his arm, whispering when I ask, "How can I help you?"

Opening his eyes again, he cradles my sides and runs his hands from my ribs to the swell of my hips, pulling me closer under the spray of the water. "I was hoping to help you. That's what I want."

Maybe he doesn't need to be reminded of the accident. Instead, I should be the reprieve he needs. With his eyes set on mine, one hand slides over my hip again and lowers to caress my inner thigh.

Tamping down my worries for him, I lean against the cold tile, tilting my head to the side, already so at home with him again and feeling more myself than I have in a long while. "Well, since you brought it up," I say, smirking. Covering his hand with mine, I encourage his slick fingers to slide deeper between my thighs and against my lips. "I can't quite reach this one spot. Maybe you could—*Oh!* Yes." My lids flutter closed as I release him and press my palms to the stone. "That's it. Exactly where I needed your attention." His fingers slip through my folds and circle the need he's discovered—*teasing, taunting*, my entire body pulses for this man, wanting him to touch every part of me that he can.

His middle seeks a connection, pinning me to the wall as his lips kiss along the precipice of my willpower and cover my jawline. I wrap my arms around his neck, holding on but pushing for more. That amazing tongue and lips kissing me like he does my mouth after filthy language has come from it. My moan is consumed before it has air to breathe, just as it clears my chest and becomes too much.

Just as my head rests back, he dips to his knees. The teasing ceases as he anchors my leg over his shoulder and takes me with his mouth. My fingers weave into his hair, and I give in to the ecstasy, allowing my mind to still and my body to feel. Close. I'm getting so close that I'm about to lose myself in him all over again, but he stops and stands to kiss my mouth with passion permeating my existence. "Turn around." He whispers the command, leaving no room for any misunderstanding.

I turn, my peaked nipples pressing against the cold wall as my thoughts trace my body along with his fingers, every nerve on fire despite the stone. His erection aligns with the line of my ass while holding my hips. My breathing picks up, my mind going wild with theories of where he's going with this. I'm not stopping him. He can take all of me, devour me whole, and I'd still come back begging for more.

That's what he is to me—love and trust, taking and giving, being and feeling everything with him. We had no slow start, and the finish will be just as dramatic as the race we've begun. I'm madly in love with this man and will happily take what life throws our way because I know we can weather the storm together now.

Kissing my shoulder, the back of my neck, and the top of my head, he lingers there a moment before sliding his hand between my legs and teasing my entrance. "Brace yourself." It's just a whisper, a cool breeze against my heated skin, but it brings me back to the here and now unwillingly.

With Cash, I prefer the dark, the stars, the fireworks between us, the blissful abyss, and being lost in him.

And then the command sinks in.

I raise my hands and hold the wall with my palms flat. When his erection is lowered and the tip replaces his fingers, I become a wildfire of nerve endings.

Alive.

Alert.

Anticipating.

Then nothing . . .

I wiggle just enough to overtake him, but he stills my hips and whispers in my ear, "Patience is a virtue."

"We were never people who honed that trait."

Surrounding my body and entire being, Cash feels so much bigger than the world I'd built. My heart pounds, my breath quickening. His hand covers my breast and then goes higher to rest on the mound of it. *Feeling.* Stealing my heartbeats like he did the rest of me. Kissing my shoulder, he asks, "Do you want me, sweet girl?"

Drunk on him, my words come fast, "I want you so —*Ah!*" I catch myself before my chin hits the tiles. Pressing so deep into me that I feel him in every part of me. He pulls back just as fast but never loses contact.

I brace myself for the onslaught, welcoming it, wanting it, and him so much that I can already taste the delicious completion. "Don't stop." A plea embodies the words.

Covering my hands with his, he pushes back in with no reprieve. The onslaught of thrusts and groans, the sounds of our bodies slapping together under the water, and the steam that surrounds us have me dazed. Closing my eyes, I release any tension I was holding on to and give myself to him.

With his arms wrapped around me, I feel . . . I feel . . . I take, and then I press my hands to the wall and push back, take . . . take . . . I take what I need and give him more than I have until the coil unwinds and springs to life inside me. "Oh God, yes. Yes. Yes."

The sensations are everywhere all at once, dragging me under to where I'll float freely in the aftermath of my orgasm.

Bringing me back, he slides his hand over my collarbone and neck, higher until his fingers reach my mouth. Pressing along my lips, he holds me as he penetrates my body, claiming me as his. I already was, but my soul thrives on the repeated declarations of his heart. One final hard thrust sends me forward, a sharp breath pushed from my chest as his hand blocks my head from hitting the tile.

The heat of his jagged breath coats my shoulder, and his forehead drops. We're lost among the breathless emotions linking us together forever. Doesn't matter how much time we were apart. We were never without each other's hearts. Souls. Entire beings. Nothing feels insurmountable when we're together. The whole universe is ours.

"I missed you," he says, lifting his head and kissing the side of my neck. "Not this." He chuckles, turning me around and caressing my cheek. "Definitely this, but also and more of you. I missed you so fucking much. I knew it, but feeling whole again is a damn good reminder."

My energy has waned, but I reach up to caress his cheek as he is mine. "I love you. I just love you so much, Cash."

His temple cradles mine, and we take in the over-whelming emotions. I smile, but the best part is when I see him smiling with his eyes closed. I kiss his cheek and whisper, "You missed a spot."

He leans back. A wry grin crosses his face, and he arches a brow. "Did I now?"

"You did." I purse my lips to restrain the smile that wants to bloom for this man. I fail. He's opened my eyes, my heart, my life to unadulterated happiness. This kind of joy just can't be contained. "Want me to show you?"

He chuckles again. It's low and growly, and pure sex appeal that speaks right to my core. "I think I know my way around these parts."

I lean my head back with a wide smile as he finds the spot that needs tending.

When I return the favor, we finish showering and then dry off. With a towel wrapped around his midsection, he reaches for an ointment. I tighten my towel around my chest and take the tube. "May I?"

Somehow, with all we've been through, this seems to be what causes his lips to part and another emotion to take over his eyes. Trust shapes his expression, and he nods.

I'm careful, so careful as I start around the edge of his injury, smoothing it over the surface. He's still, watching me with rapt affection. The ripple of his skin, the parts trying to scab over, the burns that will forever leave their mark intimidate me, but I push through, wanting to do anything I can to be a part of his healing as much as his life. "Is this okay?"

"Yes." His answer doesn't come easy, so I pause to look up.

"Are you okay?"

"I've never had anyone care for me like this." He looks

away. "My mom worked a lot. If I was injured at the track, I had to deal with it myself."

I finish the final section and stand straight again, in awe of this incredible man opening up to me. "I'm sorry you had to go through that alone."

He takes a breath, and the smallest of half-hearted grins appears. "It's okay. It got me here and led me to you."

I couldn't have fallen more in love with him, but somehow, I did, all over again and deeper than I ever imagined. "That makes standing on a street corner with a hope and prayer worth the wait." I lift to my toes and kiss him, and then do it again just because I can. "I love you."

32

Marina

Love came fast and from the right as I recall the day I met Cash.

We've been living in the fast lane ever since. *No complaints. No regrets.* I can't even make myself grieve the time we spent apart. That's when I finally came into my own. I stopped living in the shadows of the greatness my brothers had achieved. I stepped out of the failures I had in my past and accepted that I deserved better—personally and professionally.

Being stubborn, mad, or holding a grudge only kept me from living the life I wanted. Now I have the second chance I thought I'd never get. *Full throttle, baby.* Cash might be rubbing off on me.

"Are you awake?" he whispers against his pillow.

I open my eyes, unable to see anything in the dark until

they adjust to the low level of light from the outside. Rolling to my side, I prop my hand under my head and watch Cash come into view. It's an incredible sight to see that I'll never take for granted. I love when he's home.

His smile makes my day so much better, those eyes that never hold less than pure love when I gaze into them, and the fingers that—

"Yes, right there," I breathe after the tips of his fingers slip between my legs. "That feels so good."

Balanced on his arm, he hovers over me and kisses my neck. "You feel so good, babe. I can't wait to be inside you."

I can't either, so I shift, breaking the connection, and push up to straddle him. With him on his back, I rest my palms firmly on his chest. "I need you inside me. So much."

A growl rumbles around his chest as he holds my hips, his palms spreading the width as his fingers dig into the cushion of my ass. "You're so fucking tempting."

"How tempting?"

"Tempting to fuck like there's no love lost between us."

He lifts me so fast, sinking me down on his erection, that I groan in pleasure and shock before I have a chance to reply. My breath is stolen, my body stretched to acclimate. Every time with him feels so much like the first all over again.

When I drop my head, my hair curtains my vision, so I close my eyes and feel instead. "Oh God, yes, Cash."

He can't hide the way he craves me, his need is visceral, his mouth marking my chest. It's all so much, so much at once, that my head spins. My body is a traitor to me and Cash Warren's number one fan. It's easy to feel drunk off this man.

"Ah," I moan, falling into ecstasy just as fast as I did in love with him.

And he falls just as quickly.

"THEY'RE HERE." I scamper from the terrace to answer the door. "Come in. Come in." I bend and give my best buddy a big hug. "How are you?"

"Hungry," Cullen complains, his mom shuffling him inside the apartment.

"Your dad has snacks on the terrace." He drops his backpack against the back of the couch and is gone as soon as I mention food. "He's growing fast. Soon, he'll be taller than me since I'm the shorty around here." I'm not that short, but Cullen will be tall like his dad and model mom.

I turn to Terpidy and smile. "How are you doing?"

There's a shyness, which I understand and relate to. We're not close friends, but we're friendly and in this together. We get along well, but for Cash, boundaries are best kept in place.

Terpidy smiles, and it appears genuine. "I can't stay long."

We stand there together. I rock back on my heels and make small talk. "Any fun plans?"

"I have a date tonight that I'm looking forward to. A great guy I met years ago. He has a daughter a little older than Cullen. They all get along." I can see how much she cares about him by how her whole personality comes to life.

"Sounds really nice."

"The place looks nice. You've really made it home."

I look around seeing a few pieces of mine that I've added over the time I've lived here—a green vase on the island that Cash fills with flowers each week, a small painting I found in the Paris flea market when I traveled with Cash to the race in September, and bright yellow cushions on the couch that don't match at all but somehow soften the harsher darks of the main fabric.

It's not mine, but I love the present I gave Cash for winning his first podium this season in August—a large-framed photo hanging in the dining area that a popular photographer friend of mine, Story Salenger, took of Cullen last summer in Central Park.

"Thank you."

She opens her mouth and then stops, closing it. "I—"

"I—"

We both say at the same time. I say, "You go first."

Nodding, she starts, "I, um. I just wanted to tell you how much Cullen adores you. He talks about you all the time."

Sometimes I wonder if it bothers her that we get along so well, so I'm glad she brought it up, even if it's a little uncomfortable. "I adore him." I feel this is the time to tell her what's really on my mind. "I'll respect you and Cash as his parents."

Reaching over, she touches the top of my hand. "I know. I appreciate it." She glances out the glass doors, watching Cullen and Cash on the terrace, and says, "I used to drink on race days." When her eyes return to mine, her expression falls. "I struggled to let go of the image of the family I imagined I should have."

How does she see this going? I glance back at Cash, silently worrying I'm crossing a line I shouldn't without him. "That can be hard to reconcile."

"Don't worry, it was reconciled a long time ago. Cash and I are oil and water. Things are how they should be." She leans in and whispers, "I'm so glad he found you. You saved his life."

This time I open my mouth, but then close it, thinking

about what she said. I always thought he saved me, like on the red carpet. But when I look back over my shoulder, I think she might be right. Cash didn't care about anything but Cullen and his career.

Now he has a life.

I cross the imaginary line and give her a hug. She hesitates at first, but then she embraces me. I whisper, "Thank you." I don't break down how grateful I am that they were a disaster or how she didn't just make him a father, she helped create Cullen. I have him in my life because of the role she played in his. Tears well in the corners of my eyes.

"I've been so emotional lately." Stepping back, I dab with my knuckles, laughing at myself.

She starts to laugh. "Maybe you're pregnant."

And then dead silence.

It's a few seconds before my mind catches up to the conversation, and I laugh, though even I don't hear the humor in it. "There's no chance. I'm on birth control."

Suddenly, she's backtracking toward the door as we stare at each other. She turns and steps into the hallway, and then says, "So was I. Have a good time."

As soon as the door closes, I grab my phone and text Poppy: *I need all the pregnancy tests you can buy.*

Poppy: *On it.*

No questions asked. Dropping everything to be here for me. And that is why she's my best friend.

I get a glass of cold water and down it. This is not what I expected to bond me to Terpidy, but oh my God!

I refill the glass and set it on the counter. With my hands resting forward, I watch how happy Cash is with his son and hear Cullen's giggles even with the doors closed. He's such a great father.

Stop, Marina.

I'm not pregnant.

I'm just in love. Happiness of this depth and width can't be contained. That's why everything feels big in life.

Critics raved about the play, and we're sold out every night. My family adores Cash, and my brothers have learned to separate the man from the driver, especially at family get-togethers.

And though he's on the road a lot, he's in constant contact. I don't just hear I love you. He shows me every day. The sex is also spectacular. The things he can do . . . he's a dream come true.

Life is so good.

I couldn't ask for more.

NINE MONTHS LATER . . .

"DELTA, PORT, LOCH, HARBOR, NOAH, MARINA." Cash shakes his head. "But why?"

I shrug, looking up at him. "Guess my parents figured they were onto something, so they continued with their own tradition."

"But Noah isn't the name of a body of water."

"Shh." I hold my finger up to my lips so Noah doesn't hear us. He's only a few steps ahead as we make our way backstage to meet the band Faris Wheel who just performed. "He'll hear you. He's a little sensitive about being left out. The Noah's Arc connection is a stretch of the imagination, but it fits, just like Noah fits who he is."

With his arm around my back, his hand holds my waist. I'm pressed against his side, making it hard to maneuver through the throngs of people celebrating after the race. Concerts and fireworks—they do it up big in Texas. He asks, "Is this a tradition you want to continue?"

I shouldn't be sad, but a part of me is that I wasn't pregnant. Just happy. Go figure why that would be disappointing. Maybe I'm ready for that next step. We talk casually, but what if we started planning? "We'll cross that bridge when we come to it," I reply, snaking my arm around him and loving the way he holds me like I'm precious.

Chuckling, he says, "I get it. Bridge over water. The names."

It wasn't even a pun I intended, but I'll take the credit and laugh.

Poppy turns back and asks, "How do I look?"

I glance at her with her blond hair looking freshly brushed, her lips glossy, and makeup not running down her face like mine did. "Beautiful like always."

"For real, Marina. I've been sweating at this track all day. It's like a hundred and ten." She leans against me. "Do I smell?"

"I have this guy making me sweat. I don't need you getting on my other side. You do not stink, Pops. Actually, can I borrow your perfume? Smells good." She hands me a rollerball tube, and I run it over my neck and chest, then dab it on my wrist. "Thanks."

"You're welcome." Keeping up with us, she asks, "What are we doing after this? Going out?"

"What do you think, Cash? Hotel or out afterward?"

All it takes is a look for me to know his answer. "Sorry, Pops."

She rolls her eyes. "You guys are so boring."

We are. *I love it.*

Considering how many days he's gone a year while I'm

working in New York City, I take advantage of every single one I get to spend with him.

We're ushered past security and pass an opening between two heavy-draped black curtains. The lead singer is already gone, but the two other band members welcome us. "Great race, man," one says, slapping his hand into Cash's. "Congrats on third."

"Thanks. It's good to be back on that podium again." Cash adds, "Killer show." Turning to me, he smiles. "This is Marina Westcott."

"Yeah, I know. I, uh, might be a fan."

I laugh. "I appreciate it. I loved your performance."

Some moments feel intimate, a space in time that only two people share that no one else should bear witness. It's theirs alone. That's this moment. I see it as soon as he lays eyes on Poppy, and she sees him.

"Laird Faris," he says, holding out his hand.

When hers connects, it's electric. "Poppy Stanfield. Nice to meet you."

That's our cue to leave.

Pulling Cash by the hand, I slip us back through the curtains and down the steps past security.

Cash says, "Guess she has plans tonight after all."

"So it seems." I grin, my happiness extending to my friend. I've met all her boyfriends, and I never saw her come alive like she did for him.

Smiling all the way back to the hotel, I can't wait for the plane ride back to New York to get all the details. "They looked good together, don't you think?"

Cash chuckles. "Sure," he replies, humoring me. "They make quite the couple."

But that's what we do. We compromise.

We humor.

We support each other.

We love endlessly.

I lean my head on his shoulder, letting myself feel the bigger emotions coming over me lately. I love him and want so much more with him, so I whisper, "I want to get married."

He shuffles, careful not to disturb our positions. With one arm around me, a kiss is placed on my head while his other comes into focus in front of me. More specifically, his hand and the ring he's holding between his fingers. I don't move, not a muscle. I don't even know if I'm breathing as I stare at the sparkling diamonds. "I've been thinking the same thing."

EPILOGUE

Cash

"WE HAVE A . . ." Marina pauses on the other end of the call.

I adjust the phone to my ear, eyeing Duncan who's silently asking me what's wrong. "What do we have, babe?"

"An issue."

Turning my back to her brothers who are adjusting their suits, I whisper, "What kind of issue?"

"Can you come see me?"

"What about tradition?"

"I think we're past all that, don't you?"

She's been a firecracker all week. Reminds me of when we met. That fiery personality of hers is so fucking sexy I can't keep my hands off her. That sugary smile of hers looks all innocent to the outside world, but trust me, all's fair in love because she's just as handsy.

"I'll be right there."

"Don't tell anyone," she snaps, panicking.

She's starting to worry me. I hang up the phone and act

casual as I slip out of my dressing room, trying not to raise any suspicion of my whereabouts.

"Hi," I say, walking through the paddock like it's totally normal for me to be wearing a tuxedo at the track.

"Looking good, Ryatt," Darren catcalls and bursts out laughing with Hansen.

I flip them off just before I take the stairs by two. Heading toward Harbor's office, which is her home base today, I stop when I hear, "Psst."

As soon as I look over, I'm yanked by the arm into an office. "What the—"

"It's me." She's gotten strong. I didn't know Pilates could do that.

The door is closed, and the lights are out. I can't see a fucking thing. "What the hell is going on? I thought you were a psycho fan or something. I almost popped you in the mouth."

"I need your help, Cash."

"Okay, anything, but why are we still in the dark?"

"Because of this," she says, flipping on the lights.

Holy fuck. My heart leaps from my chest at the sight of her. I caress her face and move in, needing to be close to this woman. "You look like an angel, babe." Taking a step back, I hold her arms out. "Look how beautiful you are."

Her cheeks pink, and the corners of her eyes soften. I bring her back to me, earning the loveliest smile I've ever seen. Holding my elbows, she says, "Why do you have to be so sweet to me?"

"You act like it's hard." I kiss her gently and whisper, "You make it so easy." But her eyes fill with tears as she stares into mine. "What's wrong?"

"Nothing," she says, sniffling. "I'm just so happy."

I'm not sure what to do with this. "You said there was an issue?"

"There is . . ." She takes a deep breath and huffs. Turning around, she points over her shoulder at her back. "It doesn't fit anymore."

Bending down, I look at the trillion and one clasps to figure out how to operate this dress. I didn't have a two-hour unclasping session built into our schedule. Checking out the skirt, I don't lose hope for our wedding night. It will lift right over her hips.

"What am I looking at?"

She points her finger like a dagger in the air. "How it doesn't close."

Should I bring up the late-night burrito run last night? *Probably best if I don't.*

"Still lost back here."

A sigh escapes her, and she turns back around. "Maybe this will help." She holds up—*oh shit.*

"Is that a—"

"Yep."

My gaze leaves the stick and darts to her eyes. "You're pregnant?"

She sucks in a staggered breath and nods. When she drops her head forward, I pull her into my arms and rub her back. I'm not sure what to say. This is the happiest day of my life two times over—marrying the woman of my dreams, and now she's having my baby—along with Cullen's birthday, but she's crying. My heart thunders as I constrain my joy to my chest.

I need to be here how she needs me right now. Kissing the top of her halo of hair, I whisper, "I'm sorry."

Her head lifts, and her brows pinch together. "Why are you sorry?"

Shit . . . "*Foooor* impregnating you?" I ask as if I'm approaching a wild tiger.

When her mouth drops open and the match strikes in her eyes, I know I've fucked up. Throwing my hands up in caution, I stammer, "No. No. I'm not sorry."

"You're not sorry now? You're glad you got me pregnant so I can't wear my wedding dress today?"

Tilting my head, I'm getting lost. "Wait, no. Nope." Her eyes narrow further, and I keep blathering, hoping to land on the sweet spot of pleasing her with the right answer. "Did not plan to ruin the dress today. Happy side effect?"

"Oh my God, babe." She face-palms herself and shakes her head. "What are you saying?"

With an arched brow aimed at me and her hands on her hips, I tread carefully, "Truth?"

"Truth."

I let myself smile. "I'm so happy you're having our baby."

She can't hide hers either. Moving in, she fists the front of my jacket and looks up at me. "You are?"

"So happy."

Lifting, she kisses me and stands there, grinning. "I am, too."

"But you were crying. I thought you were upset."

"Happy tears. I'm so happy about the baby. This all just feels so right, marrying you and having this baby." Her smile melts me every time. "How do you feel about Coral or Adriana, which means sea or water?"

Cullen is already karting. Can't wait to have a racing team. "I love them both, but what if it's a boy?"

"Murphy stands for sea warrior."

"I think we're stretching into Noah territory with that one."

"Okay. Okay." She laughs. "I'm still working on that one."

Stepping back again, she turns. "But I'm not sure what to do about this situation."

If we weren't about to be late to our own wedding ceremony, I'd be happy to talk about names with her all night. But I'm ready to cross this finish line and have her as my wife. "I have an idea."

STANDING on the start line of the track, with her back tied up with a purple Westcott Racing shoelace stolen from the shoes I was wearing when I won the Dallas Grand Prix, Marina fights back tears in front of our closest family and friends.

With Cullen as my best little man, I ask for the ring. I tap him on the nose when he hands it to me. "Thanks, buddy. Good job."

Duties done, he runs to sit between my mom and Terpidy.

I slip the diamond stunner onto Marina's ring finger and repeat the vows we'd written. But I add, "There's no start and no end to us, babe. You're the whole damn race and championship. You're worth the effort. You're worth the work. You're worth the fight." Cupping her face, and not waiting for permission from anyone to kiss my wife, I then whisper, "Being married to you will be the honor of my life. I love you so much and I can't wait for this to come."

She stills in my palms, making me realize that maybe I just accidentally shared our incredible news, a secret we agreed not to share until after the honeymoon.

Fuck it. "We're having a baby, and I'm so fucking happy."

I kiss her like her parents and three older brothers aren't

watching. And then I scoop her into my arms among cheers and tears and carry my bride down the aisle.

"You ready for your present, Mrs. Warren?"

"We haven't even reached the end of the aisle?" Her laughter has my heart beating to the beautiful sound. "Okay, tell me. What is it?"

I set her down just inside the paddock and pull the gift from my pocket. She gasps. "You didn't?"

"I did," I say with pride.

Snatching it, she asks, "How did you know grape was my favorite flavor of Tootsie Pops?"

I give her a wink and kiss her again. "Just a wild guess." *Not at all.* I will never forget one thing she shares with me. *Never.* It's worth every effort to see that smile beaming at me.

She's so excited about the lollipop that I add, "Wait until you see the box of chocolates I bought."

Throwing her arms around my neck, she says, "Don't tempt me with a good time."

I wrapped my arms around her, planning onto hold her forever. "I'm tempting all right."

"You sure are, babe."

You met Harbor Westcott in When I Had You. Now you can read a sneak peek of his story by turning the page.

YOU MIGHT ALSO ENJOY

Recommendations - Three books I think you'll enjoy reading after *When I Had You are the Westcott Brothers' books*. All are stand-alones that will grab your heart and have you falling in love along with the characters.

**Turn the page to read a sample of Swear on My Life

Read in Kindle Unlimited and Listen in Audio

Swear on My Life - You met Harbor in When I Had You. Now read the captivating and emotional journey that will break and heal your heart. Free in Kindle Unlimited.
    READ NOW

Never Saw You Coming - You met Loch in When I Had You. Now is the time to jump into this unexpected amnesia journey that will have them discovering who they want to while figuring out the mysteries that surround them. Free in Kindle Unlimited.

READ NOW

Forgot to Say Goodbye - You met Marina's brother Noah in When I Had You. Now you get to follow his journey from playboy to the journey that leads him where he never expected - right into being a dad. *Surprise!* And how the life you thought you needed isn't the one you're destined for. Free in Kindle Unlimited.

READ NOW

SWEAR ON MY LIFE

New York Times Bestselling Author

S.L. SCOTT

ISBN: 979-8-9861994-7-4

*Visit my website for warnings. Please note this page contains spoilers.

You are not a drop in the ocean;
you are the entire ocean in a drop.

~ Rumi

PROLOGUE

Numbness beats the pain I endured, but I realize the next stage is death.

I close my eyes, too tired to hold them open any longer. *So tired . . .* I just need to rest to save my energy. My breath stalls in my throat as darkness takes hold. Despite what you hear, there is no light to guide your soul.

There's music.

My breath returns as a melody calls me back. I open my eyes to a cloud-laden sky and trees that bend to the will of the stronger winds. Roots creep over the edge of the cliff above me while a bird sings from a low-hanging branch.

Broken, I lie there, captivated by the brown-feathered bird and its yellow mask keeping me company. I grin, but the pain that has returned is too much to maintain, so I listen for hours, waiting for my date with destiny.

An ambulance shows up instead.

CHAPTER 1

Harbor Westcott

ROOM 156.

   Row 14.

   Seat 20.

I recognize her the second I see the back of her head. *I should.* I've stared at it enough to memorize every subtle strand of brown and golden blond that weaves through it, even when it's pulled and twisted on top of her head like it is now.

She's a nice reprieve from the memories that haunt me, like sunshine shining through a crack in the blinds and the first warm spring day after a long, dreary winter.

As I walk toward her, this is the first time I've been this close. She's five-three, maybe five-four on a good day, though I would have guessed a little shorter, sizing her up in the auditorium.

Usually, I see her dressed in a pair of faded exercise pants with a baggy T-shirt hanging over her waist. Today, she's looking damn good in the denim cutoffs hanging on the swell of her hips, and the shortened shirt doesn't dare brush against the top of the shorts, leaving the slope of her waist exposed.

Though, I'd always wondered what color her eyes were, I'm now given the privilege as she looks up as if caught in a thought. Green and bright despite the shadows of her dark lashes under the fluorescent lights of the convenience store. Her sneakers have hit the pavement a few times, judging by the scuffs and black asphalt staining the bottoms that leave the slightest of prints on the white linoleum.

I've always thought she might be a runner by how toned her legs are and her chosen wardrobe in the past. I like that they're not sticks and hold strength in muscle.

It's not that I'm *not* a tits man, but I do love a great ass. *Hers has been noted.*

I move down the aisle from her, eyeing the groceries lining the shelves. There's nothing I need here, but her sweet scent and my deep-seated hunger to be near her draws me closer.

What am I doing?

Why am I acting like a fucking idiot?

I see her in class all the time, at least on the days I go. But I've never craved her company, not like I do now. Sure, she caught my eye. Lots of chicks do. She's different though . . . seemingly oblivious to my existence inside—and apparently, outside—the classroom, judging by her lack of awareness of my presence.

My ego isn't fragile.

I like a challenge, but I *love* the taste of victory.

My life's been boring walking a straight line for too long. This woman is just the detour I'm looking for. *At least for a night or two.*

I imagine she has a boyfriend, probably some schmuck

back home, wherever she calls home, who's waiting for her to return after graduation. I'd bet a day's work that doting middle-class parents who saved every penny to send their only daughter to an East Coast university are a part of her story, along with a hand-me-down Subaru with another good fifty-thousand miles before the odometer rolls over for the third time.

Such a charmed life she must lead.

My assumptions don't do her any favors, but I never claimed I wasn't an asshole. I was never good at balancing bad deeds while looking the part of an altar boy. Not like Lucas was. My cousin is probably laughing beyond the grave, watching me act like a nervous pre-teen having a brush with a middle school crush.

He might have laughed, but he'd also know that hitting on girls isn't my usual MO . . . Opportunity usually presents itself and hits on me first. We never had trouble turning the heads of the fairer sex.

My innuendoes aren't subtle. She's either playing hard to get or is wholly consumed by the can of Beans & Franks in her hand. I'll assume the latter and make the effort. "Don't get hurt," I say. Not my best work, but we're in a convenience store, so I'm certain the bar is already pretty fucking low. When I latch my gaze onto the pale-pink hem of her shirt, a flash of skin is given when she moves. But I catch her gaze just in time to see it sliding up my chest until her eyes meet mine.

Tilting her head up, she studies me in silence, making it hard to read her thoughts. *Did I screw up?* Is she going to give me the time of day or a tongue lashing . . . must rid that wicked thought from my mind or start praying she's into that kind of play. I straighten my shoulders, debating if I should grab the requested diet soda and move on.

But then a half-hearted smile graces her lips. "Is that a warning?" She furrows her brow as her eyes narrow in the slightest. "Have we met?"

I shove my hands in my pockets, eyeing the full package. *She's cute. Innocent, like prey that doesn't recognize the danger around her.* Not sure she would stand out in a crowd, but she stood out to me prior, even in an auditorium full of people.

"No."

"Are you sure?"

"I'd remember." I'm too quick with a response. If I'm not careful, I'll show my cards, and I'd rather her reveal her thoughts first.

Her expression eases, soaking in the compliment. "You would, huh?"

"Absolutely. I'd never forget you."

She laughs, the sound ringing in the air. "Very charming." Her gaze slides down my chest and back to the can as if it's much more interesting.

"I try."

Sighing, she does the slightest of eye rolls before I'm on the receiving end of her glare. "I have a feeling you don't have to try at all when it comes to girls."

Not seeming to break through her cooler composure, I finally realize I have no game with this girl.

"It was a warning," I reply with full intention.

"For you?" She holds up the small can with an all-knowing grin and sees right through me. "Or this?"

This girl.

Fuck me.

What was I thinking? I just hit on her in a gas station convenience store in the middle of the day like she'd fall at my feet. *What did I expect, for fuck's sake?*

I'm arrogant enough to believe I'm worthy of her attention, so I keep my eyes on her. "If you're wise."

"What happens if I'm not wise?" Her voice is as steady as her eyes are on me, which are locked in place.

Call me impressed. The girl can stand her ground, but I'm also starting to think she might be into me. "You might get hurt."

Her gaze shifts, lengthening to a back corner of the store before she looks at me again. "Sometimes the pain is worth the risk." Her body fills with attitude, shoulders straightening and chin held high. "Don't you think?"

"Guess it depends on the risk."

Biting her lip, she smiles to herself and looks back down at the can in her hands. "You're probably right, but I'll take my chances."

Rubbing the pad of my thumb across my lower lip, I then say, "Don't say I didn't warn you."

"Don't worry. You won't be held liable for any damage in the aftermath." She starts to leave but turns back a few feet away. "We're talking about the beans, right? Like, this isn't our meet cute?"

This girl. *Fuck.* She's got my full attention and couldn't care less. "I don't know what a meet cute is."

"It's how they meet in the movies."

"Who's *they*?"

"The main characters," she replies like everyone knows what she's talking about.

I'm still staring at her, trying to figure out what the fuck we're going on about when I realize what she means. "You're really into movies, aren't you?"

"I am. It's a nice escape."

"From what?"

"Life."

That has to be one of the most honest answers I've ever been given, and I've never felt more understood before.

With straightforward honesty like that, I'm determined to find out why this fascinating woman needs an escape from life. "I get that." There's a pause as her eyes look into mine, seeming to search for answers to questions she hasn't asked.

The last thing I want to do is pour out my heart under the stench of gas or show that side of myself that I've worked fucking hard to bury. I need to get over it. I need to get on with life.

I say, "Did we ever decide what you wanted to discuss? The frank and beans or how we met?"

"Quite frankly, pun intended," she says, laughing lightly, "I'm not sure." I have a feeling that's the only thing she's ever been uncertain about.

She has me competing with beans, for Christ's sake. I'll do it if it gets me closer to her. "How about we find out? You can eat that alone, or we can discuss the virtuous qualities of canned meat and beans versus our meet cute over something we didn't heat in the microwave. What do you think?"

She takes me in unabashedly, not seeming the least displeased with what she sees, but then says, "I'm good," and walks away.

Damn.

I played this all wrong . . . *I played her all wrong.*

But when she starts back to me like she's on a mission to settle a score, I know I've gotten to her. Guess I played this right, after all. She holds the can up and waggles it in the air. "And who said I'll be eating this alone?" Cocking an eyebrow in challenge, she knows she scored the winning point. The rubber bottoms of her sneakers squeak against the linoleum tiles as she heads to the register.

I cover my wounded heart. Okay, not really, but I fucking hate to lose. Throwing my arms out to the sides, I ask, "So is that a yes?"

Shooting me a glare that buries any chance of redemption I thought I might have, she says, "It's a no."

They say you can't win them all, but my record remained undefeated until now. I look around, glad there are no witnesses.

I grab the soda for Marina, almost forgetting the reason I came in here, and head to the counter.

"Hey, how are ya?" the guy asks my current fixation . . . *Is that what she is?* Am I fixated or fascinated? I might side with fascination more than fixated, which borders on obsession. Though by how I've watched her over the last month in class, obsession might not be far off.

I don't like the way he's staring at her with his smarmy smile after a quick rattle of his fingers across the register keys. He dips down on one elbow and smacks his lips together. "I get off in an hour if you wanna . . ." Clicking his tongue, he continues, "You know. I'll even let you come behind the counter. There's lots of room down here."

What the fuck? I move to her side, staring the fucker in the face. "What'd you say?"

"Mind your own fucking business, kid," he snaps.

Kid? He's what? A few years older than I am? *He's got some fucking nerve.*

As if I'm the one in need of defending, she edges her shoulder in front of mine. "First of all, you must be new here." Can't say I'm not impressed and a lot amused. The girl's got bite.

He replies, "Just started Thursday."

Leaning closer, she says, "Secondly, ever talk to me or any woman like that again, and you'll be looking for work elsewhere. I know TJ doesn't take kindly to creeps working his counter." She slaps her money on the counter. "And for the record, I am his 'fucking business,' and I want my change for the soda and beans." Turning to me, she adds, "You good, babe?"

I chuckle under my breath. "Yeah, all good, sweet cheeks." I lean in for a kiss because I'm a fucker like that, but I'm met with her middle finger pressed to my lips.

Tugging me by the beltloop of my jeans, she pulls me close, our bodies pressed together, and whispers, "Save it for later. When we're alone."

Fuck. I think I'm in love.

The change clangs against the counter, all twenty-three cents of it. She slides it into the palm of her hand, skipping the tip jar, before taking the bean can from the counter and walking to the door.

Just outside, the door closes, and I say, "I take it you're not friends with that guy?"

She bursts out laughing as we clear ourselves away from the entrance. Eyeing me, she grins. "Can't say we are."

I shove my free hand in my pocket and look at her as if I'm seeing someone entirely different than the girl inside the convenience store. "It's too bad you have to deal with shit like that."

"Part of being a girl." She tries to shrug it off like it was nothing. It was something and made me want to punch his fucking face.

Although I have no doubt she can take care of herself, a vulnerability entangled in her strength causes my chest to tighten. "He was out of line," I say, keeping my voice low between us.

"It is what it is." She starts to back away. "Enjoy the soda."

The soda reminds me of Marina, who's sitting in the car waiting on me. I can barely make out her silhouette behind the tinted window, but I'm really hoping she can't make me out at all, or I'll be hearing about this over the dinner table at every major holiday meal and then some.

"Hey," I say just to the beauty in front of me. "I owe you for the soda."

"My treat." Her shoulders pop up and then down before I'm met with her back as she nears the corner of the building.

I don't go after her, but I make a last-ditch effort. "For real, let me give you some money."

Glancing back over her shoulder, she shakes her head. "It's a soda. It's no big deal."

"But . . ."

"Really. It's okay," she replies, stopping under the awning of the sketchy gas station. Even the potent smell of gasoline and oil slicks on the ground don't make her any less pretty.

Stepping out on a limb, I close the gap by half, leaving enough distance for her to make her own decisions. "Okay, no money, but what about dinner sometime?"

The corners of her lips slope just high enough to back her entertainment, but her eyes reveal a gleam of interest in the way they shine for me. My breath gets caught somewhere between telling her she's gorgeous and reminding her to steer clear of the trouble I bring.

"You don't even know my name, and you're asking me out?" There's no offense to her tone or in her stance by how relaxed she appears.

I should probably take the opportunity she's giving me to prove I'm not a total asshole. Holding out my hand, I say, "People who know me call me Harbor. You can do the same."

She comes a little closer, the heat of her proximity reaching me. As she slips her hand against mine, her chest rises as her lips part. "Are we friends now, Harbor?"

Since not one PG image crosses my thoughts, friends aren't what I had in mind. I'm not friends with anyone these days, but she might be worth making an exception. "It depends."

I'm not sure why my directness puts her at ease, but her smile reveals only intrigue. She should probably run, get away from me as fast as she can without giving me a second thought. "Depends on what?"

"What happens next."

She laughs, rocking back on her heels. "I have to go, so I guess we'll leave it to the fates to decide."

While the distance we had just closed widens, I throw my arms out wide. "You're not going to tell me your name?" In a class of almost two-hundred students, her name is one of the few things I've not caught. I was hoping to remedy that.

The afternoon sun shines on her. "Isn't it more fun this way?"

"Fun is subjective." I watch as she turns around, her shoulders rattling with laughter. "But I'll play along." *Helps that I know I'll see her in class.*

Glancing back, she says, "I had no doubt you would."

"Do you ever have doubts?"

"All the time. See you around, Harbor." She gives me a little wave before she disappears around the corner.

I could chase her down and ask for her number, but two rejections from the same girl is enough for one day. I pull my keys from my pocket and spin the ring around my finger. Anyway, she's right. It is more fun this way. Just wait until she sees me on Monday.

I walk to my pride and joy—my Ghibli Modena—and open the car door. I don't have time to get in fully before Marina asks, "What took you so long? I thought I was going to die of thirst while waiting."

"I didn't think you'd notice since your eyes are always glued to that screen."

"Okay, Dad," she says in a deep mocking voice.

Handing over the soda, I look at her, knowing one day, if she hasn't already, she'll face assholes who will treat her like that guy in there. That's not a conversation to have now, but one we need to have soon. "Don't ever go to this station."

She looks up briefly, her eyes looking at the building behind me. "Ew. I wouldn't anyway." *Good.* "I don't even know where we are."

It's true, this isn't my usual store or gas station, but it's close to downtown, so I made the detour. I reach over to ruffle my little sister's hair, but she blocks me. "You're welcome, by the way."

"Thanks," she replies, pushing my hand away. "Long line?"

"Yeah," I lie, knowing firsthand that sixteen-year-old girls can be ruthless when it suits them.

I start the Maserati, acting as casually as I can. We don't even hit the street before she asks, "Did you at least get her number?"

The last thing my sister needs to hear about is how I hit on a woman with great legs, an even better ass, and a mouth I wouldn't mind occupying for a night. *And then got rejected.* "You saw that?"

She's at least polite enough to keep her laughter under wraps . . . *until she can't.*

"Everyone saw it."

"I didn't ask for it." *Not a lie.*

Her phone is now the least interesting thing in the car when she angles toward me. "Why not? It seems a shame to let all that flirting go to waste."

"Eh," I say, "I think I'll leave it to the fates to decide."

"If the fates have their way, you just met your soul mate."

Surprised to hear the seriousness in her tone, I glance over at my sister. "Why do you say that?"

"Because you weren't the only one flirting."

I return my gaze to the drive ahead, but there's no stopping the stupid grin on my face. I'm not sure about anything when it comes to the gorgeous girl I just encountered, but she's got me thinking about her and this main character business.

I may not believe in fate, but I believe in myself. Wonder what it takes to be the hero of her story?

To continue reading *Swear on My Life*, it's available on Amazon, Kindle Unlimited, in audio, paperback, and in special edition hardback and paperback form.

ACKNOWLEDGMENTS

Thank you so much to this incredible team:

Andrea Johnston, Content Editing/Beta Reading
Jenny Sims, Copy Editing, Editing4Indies
Kristen Johnson, Proofreader
Cover Design: RBA Designs
Photographer: Scott Teitler
Back Image: Depositphotos
Audio: Erin Spencer, One Night Stand Studios.
Narrators: Sebastian York & CJ Bloom

Thank you to my amazing Super Stars and my awesome SL Scott Books & my Super Stars Facebook members. To my friends who are not only peers but also friends. I adore you! Adriana, Andrea, and Lynsey.

My husband and sons are everything to me. I adore you so much! Love you always. XOXOX

www.ingramcontent.com/pod-product-compliance
Lightning Source LLC
Chambersburg PA
CBHW020353260626
47156CB00007B/2093